WHAT CAME AFTER

A Novel

Sam Winston

WHAT CAME AFTER

Prelude:

In the Empowerment Zone

"Close your eyes."

But the boy looked. At eight years old, why not? At eight years old, he hadn't seen anything.

And they passed by torchlight, adults and children. Not one of them was old, for nobody out here got old. Nobody got old in the cities either, in New York or Washington or Los Angeles, but it wasn't like this. In the cities people stayed young for years, young for nobody knew how long. It was out here in the Zone that they decayed and died. Died without even aging. Without the dignity of it.

"Seriously, son. You don't have to look."

But he did.

And they passed by torchlight, this parade of the fallen. Walking if they could. On homemade crutches and in wheeled chairs and stretched out on the low beds of wagons.

"We've done our best for them. You know that."

The boy nodded. The boy who couldn't take his eyes away.

"Once they've reached this point, it's just too late."

And they passed by torchlight and by lamplight and by no light at all. Some with extremities intact and senses working and no visible signs of their inward troubles. *Help us,* their presence said, and *See what you've done.* And *You have a duty to make this right.*

"Live and learn," said the man to his son. "You are what you eat."

1

One:

The Polaroid

A howling drew them to the road. The high-pitched wail of air horns dop-plering in the distance, beyond the derelict town and beyond the cultivated fields and beyond the thin margin of trees. One by one and two by two they appeared on the roadside, moving hesitantly but with intent, their heads cocked. Shy of the traffic. Their workday done, they were mud-stained and boneweary and they came from the woods like a vaporous army roused up against its will. Moving toward a yellow car that had come to rest at the edge of the highway.

They'd never seen anything like it. A big SUV slumped on the shoul-der with its engine going and a little exhaust shimmering out of the tail-pipe and the front end collapsed down onto the gravel. Tilted forward like an animal feeding. The SUV was bright yellow, the color of panic, and it drew attention. Trucks careened around it into the left lane, avoiding it and avoiding whoever might be behind the wheel of it. Some dangerous luna-tic, out here unauthorized and probably unbranded. The truckers were old timers on old time CB radios, giving one another the heads-up and won-dering over the air what might be going to happen between that stopped car and those ghostly figures now coming from the treeline. But not stop-ping to find out. It was none of their business and they had schedules to keep.

Only trucks from National Motors used this road. The company owned the highway and they owned the trucks that traveled on it and they owned the security that kept order even though there wasn't much call for security. The trucks were their own security. The need for them that no one would deny or disrupt, not even out here in the no-man's land between New York and Boston, so deep in the Zone that the cell towers and the power lines had long ago been taken down for salvage. Imagine the industry and daring of bringing them low. The muscle and the risk and the sheer courage.

The trucks rolled on. There was nothing to keep these ragged figures from converging on the broken car.

*

People were inside it. A man and a boy watching them come. The man cut the engine and pressed the button to lock the doors but the circuit needed power so he started the engine again and pressed the button again but it turned out the doors were already locked. His mind wasn't working right. The boy beside him taking an old Polaroid camera from the glove box and unhinging it and holding the lens up near the window. Tinted glass blocking a good deal of the light and the man saying, "That's going to flash and wash everything out."

The boy not listening. The boy not caring.

The man saying, "You don't need the flash," and wondering where he got the clarity of mind to say it. To focus on such a small thing while these people were edging toward his car and himself and his son. Advancing like an army of insects or ghouls. Some of them with mismatched limbs and strange sprung gaits and some of them with faces twisted like old burled wood but most of them just worn out. Broken by time and labor. Worn out but coming.

With the engine off, the interior warmed up fast. The yellow sun beating down on that yellow car. He had half a mind to turn the engine on again for the air conditioning but he didn't. The boy kept scrambling around trying to get the right angle on the scene outside and he said to his father, "Gee it's hot in here," and the man said, "Tough it out. Those people never had air conditioning and I don't see them complaining about it."

This is what had become of their adventure. Anderson Carmichael and his son, bound for Boston from New York. Just about the richest man in the world doing it the hard way because he dared to. Any other man of his standing would have teleconferenced or flown, but not Carmichael. Call him eccentric. When you're poor you're odd, but money makes you eccentric. Money buys you better words for things, and he had money. Money for this car, for example. The last of its kind anywhere. A yellow Hummer of all things.

There'd been a day when just about anybody could have owned one, but that day was gone. Before everything collapsed, any working man in America could have bought one at zero percent interest for five or six years. Just sign and drive. Anderson Carmichael's bank had ended up holding the paper on most of those loans by the time they'd all gone south. But that was just paper and this was a car and it was the only Hummer left in the world. Not that it was a particularly good example. It wasn't top of the line or anywhere near it. Just a cheap H3 with a cloth interior, not much of a step up from a Chevrolet if you could get your hands on a Chevrolet that ran, which you couldn't. But nobody else had one. That was the thing. That was the reason they were out here on this adventure to begin with. Out here in what used to be Connecticut. The Northeastern Empowerment Zone. Now if only the damn thing hadn't broken down.

The boy settled on a vantage point and pressed the big button on the Polaroid and sure enough it flashed. The man put his hand over his eyes and said, "That's not going to come out," and the boy ignored him. Watching the big white square feed out of the camera. Blinking his eyes from the bounced light and waiting for the picture to materialize.

*

A burst of light from inside the car.

They drew nearer and surrounded it up close. Exactly enough of them to do that and no more. Waiting for a gap to open in the traffic and moving in, a wall of them, and then bending as if they had one mind. These people who labored side by side every day of their lives, the lame and the sound together, lowering themselves with their backs straight and their knees bent and straining all at once to lift. They picked up the SUV with Carmichael and his son inside it. Ants with the weightless husk of a bumblebee. Two and a half tons of solid steel set moving. They didn't know who was in the car but they knew it was somebody. Somebody important. Ownership. Capital O. They didn't take the car any great distance, just off the shoulder and down into the damp swale at the edge of the woods out of harm's way. One last truck wailing past on the highway with its air horn fading out to nothing and one more flash from inside the car. Just that one burst of light and dim figures moving through smoked glass and then nothing.

They set the car down and backed away. Some of them wiped their hands on their pantlegs and one or two pushed at their lower backs and blew out air and winced. Most of them just stood in a rough circle waiting for a sign. Anything at all. Any sound or movement.

Inside the car they waited as well. Waited for whatever these people meant to do, until it became clear that they meant to do only this. To perform this service. At which Carmichael told his son to stay right where he was, and unlocked his own door, and got out.

At his appearance, they collapsed to their knees.

*

In the end there was nothing to do but go where you were invited and where you were made welcome, no matter how little you liked it. So it was that Carmichael and his son came to witness that long slow passage of the suffering, of those damaged by life in the Empowerment Zone, of those who had eaten the wrong things and suffered consequences beyond the imagining of whatever God had created them.

Beyond the Zone it was different. In the cities Ownership made the decisions and Management looked after the details and there was plenty of credit to go around. Credit to buy food grown out here under PharmAgra licenses and trucked south to PharmAgra factories for irradiation prior to sale. Green beans and asparagus and squash and corn, sealed up airtight and shipped down south to have the poisons burned out, straightening the crooked genes that kept off the bugs and the mold and the disease. Making it all safe for human consumption. A miracle of science.

Out here in the Zone, people got desperate. They didn't always have the money to buy back what they'd grown with their own hands, so they ate untreated food that they had no claim to or else they ran risky experiments of their own. Going back to nature. This was the result. Damage that passed from generation to generation. Father to child.

Carmichael sat on a pile of metal scrap like some reluctant caliph. The president of AmeriBank and the very definition of Ownership if Ownership needed a definition. Nothing but a silvery metallized blanket between him and the world. His son at his side. The two of them eating for supper the things they'd brought with them from New York, delicacies refrigerated in the cooler built into the SUV. Fresh fruits and vegetables from distant blue islands remote as Eden, islands dotted about the Pacific and shielded around by gunships in ring after bristling ring. Preserved meats straight from the fabled stockyards of Chicago where men still butchered cattle fed on real grass in certain sectors of the Midwest, walled sectors where undoctored grass still grew free or at least free enough, provided you had the means to acquire a leasehold.

A man stumbled against the scrap metal pile and the boy jumped. Dropped his fork. The man was blind and he tracked the fall of the fork by the sound it made. He stopped and bent double at the waist and retrieved it, and then he pulled himself upright and held the thing straight out. An offering. Smiling sweetly and saying, "What's your name, child?"

"Peter," said the boy. Reaching toward the upraised silver until his father stopped him.

The man just stood. Arm out and trembling. "Peter," he said. As if he'd learned a secret.

Carmichael spoke to his son. "You tell him he can just hang onto that. It's solid sterling. Not plate. We don't use plate."

"Many thanks, Peter," said the blind man. Rubbing his thumb against the family monogram cut into the handle. "Solid. I could tell." Raising the tines to his pale tongue and licking them clean. "Many thanks to you as well, sir." He bowed his head and moved on.

*

They spent the night in a borrowed farmhouse. More like commandeered. Darkness and dead quiet all around. No trucks on the distant highway and no insects in the tall grass and no creatures scrambling through the underbrush or calling from among the trees. The lack of sound made an unearthly void, although it wasn't so unearthly anymore. A normal night on a poisoned earth.

To the boy it was a source of terror. He had never heard such silence in the city. Not even in the high walled nighttime precincts of Central National Park, where his father had taken him on another of their adventures. It was closed at night and they had it all to themselves. The park preserved such wildlife as had once made New York its home. Coyotes and alley cats and field mice. Cockroaches and crickets. A tiny tattered population of scavenging pigeons that flapped like rags against the wire mesh that over-arched the compound. To the boy's innocent ears, that small wilderness had been a roaring arena where a million blood contests took place at every moment.

This was different. This terrible silence. It made him claustrophobic and self-aware, it filled his head with the sound of his own blood, and he wanted to stopper his ears to keep it out.

He was alone in the bedroom and his father was in the front with some people. The people talking low and his father listening. He'd left the boy alone hours ago, after trying the satellite phone one last time and reminding him that a Black Rose team would be on the way before long. On the way to pull them out. *Extract them,* he'd said, using that military term. They wouldn't just send little bitty choppers either, but those big Hueys and Black Hawks they kept for real emergencies. The ones that no eight-year-old could get enough of. Wasn't that right? Maybe even that twin-rotor Chinook they had down in Washington under glass. What did he think of that? The office would wait twenty-four hours and they'd decide something had gone wrong and they'd send Black Rose after them, guns blazing if necessary. Wouldn't he like to see that? Sure he would. That's what they paid Black Rose that retainer for.

His father had said there were a half-dozen radio tracking devices built into the SUV, as if that yellow paint weren't enough to get their attention. You could practically see it from outer space. "So don't you worry about a thing," he said.

But now his father was gone and the boy was alone. Poking at his throat with one finger, trying to locate the brand that had been implanted there the day he was born. The brand was a transmitter, too. It wasn't long-range, but it might help. If these people cut the Hummer up into a million pieces and Black Rose couldn't find them and he and his father were at the end of their rope, out here in the Empowerment Zone, where anything could happen.

He lowered himself out of the bed and crept to the curtain that hung across the door and listened. His father humoring a handful of locals. The truth was they sounded pretty polite out there in the dim front room. Taking turns. He held his breath and put out one hand and drew the curtain back no more than an inch and looked. A half dozen of them on the floor, squatting or on their knees. His father on a wooden chair. There were five other chairs around the kitchen table but those chairs were empty and everybody else was sitting on the floor so his father would have the highest place.

Kids he knew in the city had a name for the people out here—*Zoners*—but what did they know? They'd only heard about them secondhand. They hadn't seen them right up close the way he was doing. As far as he could tell, at least when they weren't suffering from bad DNA or malnutrition or something else you could see from the outside, they looked like regular people. People who knew their place in the world.

One of them was talking the most. A little man no bigger than a child. No bigger than Peter himself. He was stunted somehow. Down there kneeling on the floor, a little beyond the reach of the candlelight from the table, he almost disappeared. He was broad in the shoulders and sinewy from a lifetime of hard work, and he twitched as he spoke. Animated against his will. Moving from side to side on his knees, and his arms waving. He was talking about a man he knew. A man named Weller. The mechanic, he called him. He said Weller could fix anything and he could fix that SUV if he got the chance. Get them on the road again right away. Call off Black Rose. Save Black Rose for more important things.

Carmichael nodded and said that was fine. No doubt the little man was correct. No doubt this Weller of theirs was a highly skilled individual. All the same, he was extremely fussy about who touched that car of his. It was among his most prized possessions, and that was saying something.

The little man jumped to his feet and caught himself and kneeled back down again and begged Carmichael's pardon. He said he hoped not to offend him or to press too hard, but Henry Weller wasn't just anybody. Henry Weller had a gift. The way he said the word made it sound religious.

"I'm sure you're right," Carmichael said. "And I'll consider your recommmendation very carefully." Anybody could have heard the finality in his voice. He tilted his head down in the lamplight and set his voice lower and told the little man that he ought to put Black Rose out of his mind if that was what had him so keyed up. Whispering to him like you'd whisper to a baby. Saying he hadn't meant anything when he'd mentioned Black Rose. Not anything that he and these other nice people needed to worry about. They should think of Black Rose as they'd think of the fire department, rescuing somebody from a little trouble they'd gotten themselves into. That's all. As simple as that. He said the words *fire department* as if these people had ever had a fire department. As if these old houses of theirs wouldn't burn straight to the ground in a heartbeat with nobody prepared to do a single thing about it.

The boy let the curtain close and went back to bed but didn't go to sleep. When his father came in later he asked him about what he'd heard. About the man who could fix the car. His father shook his head. "Don't pay them any attention," he said. "These people believe all kinds of stuff. Plus they'll say anything."

The boy asked him why.

"To get a little bit of what we have," he said. "Something to make them more like us."

"You'd pay him, though. The mechanic. If he fixed the car."

"Of course I would. But I know these people. He can't fix the car. I don't want him fixing the car. I don't even want him touching it." He put his hand on the boy's shoulder and told him to go back to sleep. "Don't listen to them, son. That mechanic of theirs. The miracles they say he can do. It's just an old wive's tale. You'll learn for yourself soon enough. People who are afraid will believe anything."

*

Carmichael awoke to the sound of a hammer. A high ringing, steady and insistent, metal on metal. The blows had a machine regularity to them except for the way they stopped and started and stopped again. Coming and going through the trees from off in the direction of the highway on a fine light breeze from the south that pushed the window shade back an inch and set it bumping. He sat up and shook himself and groaned. Groaned and stretched and realized. There was only the faintest gray light coming through the window. Hardly anything at all. People out here didn't begin working until the sun was up. They couldn't.

It was that mechanic. Damn him.

He let Peter sleep and went out, following the sound toward the woods. Hearing people rising inside other houses and smelling the smells of cooking and listening to the sounds of talk. He kept going past where the houses gave out and walked across a cultivated field with his shoes sucking mud and entered the little woods. The hammering got louder but still had that little thoughtful pause now and then, and he went through the woods and came close to the far edge of it and the hammering stopped and he stopped too. Saw the car propped up in the mud on a jack with boards under it. Saw a man drawing himself out from underneath the car, wet mud from the wet ground streaking his back. Weller, the mechanic. In one hand he held the hammer and a bent iron bar with a hole in each end. With the other hand he was slipping something into his pocket. He stood looking at the car. The car and the ground it was sinking into. Rapt and greaseblack and concentrating hard. He slung the hammer into a loop on his coveralls and held the bar out against the horizon. Running his thumb along the top to gauge the bend in it. Cocking his head.

"Get away from my car," said Carmichael.

Weller gave him a slow look, letting his eyes adjust to the distance. He wore a thick pair of horn-rimmed glasses, third or fourth or fifth hand, things that had passed more than once through some Lions' Club donation box back when there'd been a Lion's Club. Back when there'd been lions. He gave him a slow look that was adjustment and appraisal at the same time and after a minute he nodded once and stepped backwards. Slow. Like it had been his idea. Nothing to it. He was just leaving anyhow. He had work to do.

*

The boy was gone when Carmichael got back. He wasn't in the kitchen, and he wasn't in the bedroom, and he wasn't anywhere. His father felt the bed and it was warm. He tried the outhouse but the outhouse was empty. The boy was gone and it wouldn't be long before Black Rose lifted off from New York and how would they know him from anybody else. A little kid like that who could be anybody. Goddamn it. The town couldn't be that big. He'd find him.

*

Peter had woken up alone and explored the house and gotten hungry. There were familiar cans on the kitchen shelves but no way to get them open that he could find. Boxes and bags with familiar labels but no way to reconstitute what was inside them. No way that he trusted. He'd been brought up suspicious and it served him well. Looking at the faucet and picturing drinking the water from it raw and imagining the kinds of things that would happen next. Horrible things. Things he'd seen by torchlight the night before. Worse things if worse things were possible.

There was still food in the cooler in the back of the SUV, but he wasn't sure which direction the highway was. He was disoriented because they'd come to the house in the dark, and he didn't want to get lost. So he set out straight down the street that fronted the house, figuring he'd come to the end of it and then decide what next. Be methodical. Ask somebody if somebody showed up. Or else he could just keep turning the same direction at every corner he came to, as if he were in that maze he'd read about with the torches burning and the thing that was half-man and half-bull chasing after you in the dark. That maze in the story. You couldn't get lost if you kept turning the same way. You could only get out.

The town was bigger than he'd thought. Maybe more than a town. The street he was on didn't seem to end, running on and on through cross street after cross street, the houses along it taking on variations he hadn't expected. Brokenbacked lean-tos and rusted sheetmetal sheds and tumbledown duplexes leaning into each other, half against half. A couple of tall brick buildings that looked like apartments but were empty. Commercial buildings too. Vacant storefronts. Blackfronted offices with the windows knocked out, and the terrifying mouths of underground parking garages. He kept going. People were waking up in the houses and cooking and talking to one another in a hundred different voices. Men were coming out front doors and coming out shed doors and coming out underneath moldy sheets of blue plastic nailed up over holes in plywood walls, entering into the day. Looking at him the same way they'd look at any boy.

He walked on. Up a long hill with a grassy yard gone to dirt along one side of it and a big mansion sitting up on the hill past the yard, stranded there like it was beached. Rotting down to a cage of bone. He kept walking until he saw the gray rooftops of a ruined city in the distance, and then he stopped and turned back. Whatever fields and woodlands stood along the highway weren't in this direction. He went all the way back to the house where he'd started and past it. Keeping pace with more men walking. Men coming out of houses and gathering in little groups to pause and talk and smoke and walk on together. The farms must be this way. He was learning.

He walked past a corner lot with an old service station set back in it and sounds of work coming from inside. He drifted across the broken pavement. Drew near. Looked in through the one raised overhead door with the words *Mechanic On Duty!* painted across the lintel and saw a man at work. A welding helmet on his head and a leather apron going from his shoulders to his knees. Greasy coveralls underneath that, workboots scarred and cut raw, and big ruddy leather gloves insulated against anything. The man was hunched over a Franklin stove salvaged from someplace. It glowed around its edges with a red light and it gleamed blue inside. He had one of the double doors open and he was pushing something inside of it around on a grate over the blue flame. Tapping at it. Turning it and studying it through the welding helmet and lifting it out with tongs. Kicking the door shut and hollering at somebody behind him in the shadows to stay clear and aligning the hot thing he'd taken from the Franklin stove on the flat top of a big iron block. He hammered at it with a kind of brutal delicacy, the blows ringing and the metal sending off sparks that flew out the door and either vanished into the air or slipped into the cracks in the broken concrete. Running into those cracks and down along them like water and dying.

The boy was enchanted. He watched as the man sized the metal he'd been hammering and grunted some sort of rough satisfaction toward it. Watched as he snapped his head backward to raise the helmet's big pitted visor on its hinges and kept watching as he plunged the worked metal into a bath of water that boiled and steamed and sighed and finally grew quiet. Wondering how much heat the metal might hold even now. Wondering when you could touch it again if you ever could.

The man's thick glasses were fogged over and he didn't see the boy and he didn't see the boy's father when he came. Careening around the corner and spying the boy and launching himself across the lot to embrace his son and squeeze him tight for protection or punishment or both. Probably not making any distinction between the two. Carmichael looked up from his knees and saw the man with the iron bar raised up for appraisal and the raising of it could have been a threat, some territorial maneuver not quite comprehensible from this side of those fogged glasses, but it didn't seem that way.

"Tell you what," said the mechanic to no one but himself. "I think we've just about got it licked."

"Got what licked?"

The sound of Carmichael's voice surprised the mechanic, and he slid his glasses down to see. One fingertip of his glove leaving a crooked black trail along the bridge of his nose. He set down the bar and saw Carmichael kneeling there on the pavement and looked at him the same way he'd look at anybody. Unsurprised. "That little problem you've been having."

"With the car?"

"With the car." The way you'd say it to a well-meaning idiot. Like what other problem was there.

The bar was still smoking and the water bath was still steaming and the Franklin stove was still glowing, blue inside and red outside. Carmichael studied it. "That's not a wood fire you've got going in there," he said. Not a question. He wasn't accustomed to asking questions. He knew everything.

"No sir, it's not. It's natural gas all the way."

"I'll be." Carmichael shook his head. "Where would somebody get natural gas out here?"

"I don't know where somebody else might get it," he said. "Me, I get it from the dump. I pipe it in."

"The dump."

"The dump. The garbage dump. Anaerobic decomposition. If you wait long enough, all kinds of things will turn into gas." He reached behind the stove and turned a valve and the flame died.

"I'd forgotten that," said Carmichael, as if he'd ever known. Rising to his feet to reassert his position.

"I'm not surprised you've forgotten," said Weller. "People have forgotten a whole lot of things."

*

Behind the shop was the house and behind the house was a leaky quonset hut full of machines. A ruined wonderland brought back to something near life. Old tools restored and new tools invented. A dozen pumps and engines in various stages of restoration. A handbuilt gasburning generator piped into the same cobbled line as the Franklin stove, making electricity to run an air compressor and drive a handful of scavenged power tools and heat water for the house. A water tank on the roof to pressurize the plumbing.

Like everyone else in the cities, Carmichael had heard stories about the wonders and oddities to be found out here in the Zone. Wonders and oddities and terrors too. But he'd never heard the first suggestion of anything like this. Nobody'd heard of anything like this. Gas power and hot water and rudimentary sanitation. All of it, old technology and new, made to rise up and walk by one man.

What looked like a boarded-up greenhouse was attached to one end of the quonset hut, with pipes from the rooftop water tank going down into it. Rusted now and disused. The greenhouse glass painted over. There was an actual Volkswagen in the far corner, a dull red Beetle with a convertible top, underneath a plastic tarp to keep off the rain. Judging by the tire tracks coming in from the dirt yard, Weller had had it running. Imagine that. Where he'd gotten gasoline was a mystery of its own. MobilGo still had plenty of gas, but most of it was tied up in National Motors contracts. Once upon a time the federal government had investigated those deals, and there'd been hearings and lawsuits and at the end of it MobilGo had had to keep its stations open and sell gasoline to private citizens. But that was fifteen years ago now, back when there'd been a federal government. Here they were, not halfway into the century yet, and so much had changed.

Carmichael rushed to the Beetle and lifted a corner of the tarp. Weller barked at him to leave that alone and Carmichael did as he was told. Laughing at being given orders, thinking this mechanic might deserve a chance at fixing the Hummer after all. So he played along, smiling and raising his hands before him like a person up against a bandit. Saying that's some car, is all. It really and truly is.

He asked Weller where he'd gotten the gasoline to run it, and Weller said that was the problem. You could scavenge the dump for what might be left in old plastic gas cans and the tanks of lawnmowers and what have you, but it never added up to much. A dribble at a time. And what you got hardly sparked. He said he couldn't imagine filling the tank of something like that Hummer and just driving. Never mind getting access to a National Motors highway. A real highway going somewhere and you on it.

Carmichael had to admit that he was a lucky man.

Weller showed him around the rest of the place. He gave most of the tour with a little girl riding on his shoulders. His daughter. She was five years old, but compared to Carmichael's son she was tiny. Not skin and bones tiny, but tiny in the way of something magical. Exactly as large as she needed to be and no larger. Skin like milk. Dirty blonde hair cut by her mother on the run, looking like a raggedy cloud in a high wind.

Mainly, though, she was all eyes. Wide eyes blue and deep and spring-fed. Eyes hungry for something not yet seen.

Her name was Penny. Penelope. It was a lot of name for a girl that small, and no one used all of it. From up on her father's shoulders she looked down at the boy with a patient wonder that soon revealed its true self. She was going blind. It was plain from the way she turned her head and studied him. Studied him as they made their way through the quonset hut, pausing here and there and the light shifting so she could make him out better and then worse and then better again. She studied the boy so as to put him together from pieces she could gather up one by one.

Gather up and keep, because even at her age she knew that she had to collect these treasures or lose them.

Weller brought them back through the house and into the kitchen to meet his wife, Elizabeth. Liz. He stooped and put Penny down on the countertop where she sat content, running a toy truck over her knees. Peter looking at her up there, wishing her down on his level or below it.

"Liz," said Weller, "these are the folks whose car broke down."

Carmichael put out his hand and said his name. Syllables to conjure with all the world over, but not here. Not in this house. He introduced his son to better effect. The woman bent and put her hands on her knees to study him closer, and after a moment she decided he looked hungry.

He certainly was, but he didn't say. He just turned to his father, who looked at the thinly stocked shelves and glanced toward the vegetable bin and saw the familiar PharmAgra label. PharmAgra that had engineered the treacherous genetics inside just about everything that grew anymore. PharmAgra whose wheat-stalk logo meant reassurance.

"If you're offering to make us some breakfast," Carmichael said, "we'll be happy to accept."

The boy stiffened. He cast a look at Penny sitting up on the counter, Penny running her fingertips over the truck to know it better.

One bite. God knows. That might be all it took.

Carmichael leaned and took his son by the collar and got up close to him. "Go wash your hands now," he said. And then, softly and rapidly enough that only the boy could hear, "It's OK. We'll get ourselves scanned in Boston first thing. Just in case."

They sat. All of them together around the table and all of them at the same level. Weller on one end and his daughter on the other. The boy held his breath to see such disrespect unfold, and he waited to follow his father's lead, but his father didn't complain because what would have been the point. Weller was a man who'd achieved something. Carmichael could understand that. Let this be a lesson.

Weller saw to it that his wife and daughter got served first and then his guests and then himself. He blew across his coffee cup and said he'd only need a few minutes to put that sway bar back into the SUV now that he'd straightened it out and tempered it properly and reamed the holes at each end back into round. Said he'd had to remove a pair of bolts to get it clear in the first place and neither one of them had been in any hurry to come loose, but he'd soaked them in penetrating oil and cleaned them up good and now they'd go right back on no sweat. Everything would be good as new. Carmichael and his son could be on their way as if nothing had ever happened.

Carmichael said he guessed Weller had earned the right to finish the job after all.

Weller nodded. He hated to see a beautiful piece of machinery like that out of service for no reason.

Carmichael said he owed him a debt. Said he'd never thought he'd say it, but there it was. He owed him a debt.

Penny sat at her end of the table all by herself, not eating much, her occluded vision lending her wandering gaze a kind of grandeur. There was enchantment in her eyes, as if she were seeing a world that no one else could see and not seeing the regular one. Her mother indicated her and looked at Carmichael and said, "Just don't get the idea that my husband never makes mistakes."

Carmichael wasn't stupid. That abandoned greenhouse. Of course. Leave it to Weller to try restoring that technology too. No wonder it was painted over and boarded up and rusting to pieces. No wonder the girl's father himself sat unmoving now at his own end of the table, a bite of toast cold in his mouth, looking and looking out the window through those inscrutable glasses. As if he'd lost something.

*

They went down the street and through a couple of empty lots and across a field toward the trees and the highway. Like it was an outing. Liz choosing a path through the high grass and the little girl on her father's shoulders carrying her toy truck in both hands. Peter balancing the black iron bar over his shoulder with the authority of a duelist. Carmichael bringing up the rear and Weller waving his arms and gesticulating with every step he took, talking as if he meant to describe the operation of every last thing in the universe to anyone who would listen. Every last thing, from the stars on down.

In the roadside swale he took tools from his pockets and asked Peter for the bar and dove under headfirst. Asking if anybody wanted to join him for a look around but nobody did. Nobody wanted a lesson in automobile repair. Nobody trusted that jack. He didn't stay under for long. The work went fast. He kept talking most of the time, naming parts and criticizing their manufacture and calling out ideas for improvement that he could have seen with his eyes shut. He said it was a wonder the suspension had lasted this long. That antique Volkswagen of his would beat it in a fair fight any day of the week. He asked what the world had come to, and nobody had an answer.

He slid out and lowered the car and opened the driver's door to let Carmichael in. Closed it after him and stood right up close watching. Watching him press the clutch pedal. Watching him put the key in the ignition and turn it and listening to the engine come to life. Taking satisfaction in the whole operation. "Go on, put it into gear now," he said, loud through the shut window. "Everybody step back. Get away from those tires. There's going to be mud everywhere."

Carmichael let the clutch out hard and the SUV lurched forward once and died shuddering. He looked at Weller through the window, sheepish. Pressed a button and put it down. "Go easy," Weller said. "Try feathering that a little more. You burn out your clutch between here and Boston, you'll be out of luck." Carmichael took the criticism all right. It was the truth. Weller stepped away and he started the engine again and revved it and worked the clutch with a little more patience this time. The SUV started forward and he turned the wheel and it went on up the little hill and onto the shoulder of the road, the way it was supposed to. Like it could go anywhere. Peter clapped his hands with relief and little Penny clapped her hands with delight and Weller hollered up the hill, "You treat that properly now, and it'll last you forever." Heading on up in the tracks of the SUV. Everybody else following.

Carmichael had climbed out when he got to the shoulder, alongside the car and as happy as anyone had ever seen him. Standing there in the wind from a passing truck with Peter's old Polaroid camera in his hand as if he'd won a prize. "We'd better commemorate this occasion," he said. Handing the camera to Liz and showing her where to look into it and which button to press and then going around to the front of the car. Weller took Penny by the hand and followed, keeping himself between his daughter and the highway. Carmichael took up a stance with one hand on the high garish yellow hood and his son at his side, in the pose of a great hunter or somebody in a formal portrait. Seeing him there like that, the mechanic sat down on the bumper with Penny on his knee. Properly respectful for once. For the record at least.

Liz snapped a picture and jumped when it rolled out of the Polaroid. It dropped to the ground and she picked it up and watched the image begin to materialize. Taking a half step toward Carmichael. He raised a finger to her and said, "One more. One more for you people who've treated us so kindly." Bending at the knees and shifting into a sitting position alongside Weller. Lifting his own child to his own knee, because you couldn't set a bad precedent with somebody you'd never see again.

Everybody smiled. Liz pressed the shutter and handed him the picture and he held it out at arm's length to let it develop. So everyone could watch. A weirdly satisfying miracle in slow motion. At a certain point the image on it had resolved just enough to look the way the whole world looked to Penny, but no one could say exactly when. Only her father and mother even wondered.

When the picture was done Carmichael signed it. Signed it big like it was something they'd want to tack up on the wall. Thought again and felt generous and wrote "IOU" on it in big letters while he was at it. Right up in the blue sky. He gave the picture to Weller and shook his hand and told him he could take that to the bank if he could find a bank. Ha ha. His signature was as good as cash money. Better than that. As good as that famous red white and blue AmeriBank scrip. Weller put the photograph in the pocket of his coveralls and then it was over. Father and son climbing in and slamming the doors and neither of them waving or at least not visibly through that smoked glass. Just Carmichael hitting the gas and opening the sunroof wide and Peter keeping an eye out for those helicopters that ought to be on their way any time now. Ready to wave them off. Victory snatched from defeat. *We did it, son.*

Two:

The Shelter

The picture wouldn't stop eating at him. The picture and the memory of that SUV roaring up the interstate into a world he would never see. The only signifier of it this flimsy little square that Carmichael had left behind. Testimony to his escape. Weller tacked it up after all. He tacked it up on the pegboard over his workbench where he could keep an eye on it. Where it could serve as inspiration to question everything in sight. The junk that people brought in to be repaired and the junk that people brought in to sell and the work he did turning one into the other. Ashes to ashes. Junk to junk. He had the rearview mirror from the red Volkswagen hanging from a hook on the same pegboard, and he hated that mirror in particular. For what it reflected. His own stasis.

Everybody in the photograph was looking into the camera except his daughter.

That was the worst thing.

She wasn't looking anywhere. Her eyes were vague and she wasn't looking anywhere. Sitting there on his knee with her bright and freckled face held to the sun and no idea that she ought to be looking in the direction of her mother and the camera.

He let the picture eat at him for two or three weeks, his mood disintegrating and his anxiety growing and an idea taking shape in his mind. Summer wasn't going to last forever. Fall would come to the Zone and everything would lock down for the cold and the snow. The moment for travel was still with him and if he had any sense he would take advantage of it.

He wondered exactly how far was it from here to New York. Nobody went, so nobody knew. He would be a pioneer, like the old overland travelers who'd first made their way from Plymouth Rock to the Isle of the Manhattoes. Two or three days on foot from this point maybe. Three or four. Then again there might be a ride to be hitched along the way. Some kindhearted Management trucker not made entirely of stone.

The girl would be a help to him there. She'd slow him down as to foot travel, but when the time came to hitch a ride she would prove herself an asset. Who could resist that child? Who could be afraid of her father? On balance, she might shave a day or more off the trip. Cut their need for food and supplies. Not that he would dare go light on that account. And not that he would have gone without her anyway, even if she required a steamer trunk full of equipment and him to shoulder it. She was the whole reason.

Carmichael had said he owed him a favor, and Weller had decided to take him up on it. Get his daughter to New York and get her in front of a doctor. A specialist.

Get her eyes fixed if it was the last thing he did.

*

Liz didn't approve, and the weeks he'd spent wrestling with himself had left him adamant, and as a result they fought. They fought although they usually didn't disagree about much. But they fought over this. About Penny and her fate. About whether there even was such a thing as fate and whether or not it could be thwarted. About the odds and the risks. The odds and the risks of merely making the effort, never mind the dangerous procedure that might come afterwards if everything went according to plan and Carmichael was agreeable and some doctor was up to the task. They fought quietly and they fought cruelly, because they had no secrets from each other. Because they possessed a wide range of the subtlest weapons that time and love can provide. They fought for days, each of them privately fearing that they would never recover. That they had gone too far. That the only way to mend the damage that they were doing was to have it over and done one way or another. For him to bring the girl back healed. Or else not to come back at all.

And so they quit fighting. Reconciled themselves to what would be. Packed supplies and blankets and the tarp from over the Volkswagen into a couple of salvaged backpacks with a week's worth of food. Half of what money they had folded in his pocket along with some other things. That Polaroid photograph. His pack was the size of a footlocker and hers was more like an underfed hatbox. Not even that big. His was made of threadbare canvas and hers was made of stiff plastic falling apart at the corners. Bright red and acid yellow, printed on the back with an outsized drawing of a white cat wearing a purple bow on one of its ears. To see her trudging around the house with that cat on her back made him think of a moth he'd seen pictured in an old magazine, a bug with the huge and startling eyes of some predatory bird etched on its wings to ward off predators.

*

They set out before dawn, everybody in tears.

Rain had come overnight and passed on over but the highway was still wet and the trucks kicked up water. He took off his Red Sox cap and cinched it as tight as it would go and put it on Penny's head, but it was soaked through to begin with so it didn't help much. He asked her what she thought they could do. Did they have anything they could use for a raincoat. Thinking of the tarp. He was a little bit reluctant to cut a hole in it for their heads to poke out but what could you do. You had to make sacrifices.

She thought and thought. The two of them walking along getting wet. Ruminating. Finally she turned that face up and looked at him from underneath the brim of his ball cap and said, "Maybe we should just get away from these trucks." Pointing off into the fields. A gray access road cutting in among the green. Why not.

The fields came right up to the highway here and right up to the edges of the access road too. Cultivated fields fenced in high, sixteen feet of chain link and barbed wire, with PharmAgra tags clipped onto them every so often. Fields of green beans and sweet corn mainly, but here and there tobacco as well. Tobacco the state's oldest crop, from back before there'd even been a state of Connecticut, and persisting now that the state existed mainly in memory. The way things of the world will persist.

He hadn't wanted to take these access roads for fear of meeting his neighbors on their way to the fields and having to explain himself. This ridiculous dream of getting Penny in front of a doctor. A specialist no less. The chances they were taking, and the waste of time if nothing else, in a world where every productive minute mattered. It was absurd. Liz had been right. Anybody they might meet would see that and say it. But they'd gotten such an early start that the roads were empty. Empty and quiet and damp from the rain so the dust hadn't risen yet. They walked side by side. Dirt roads covered this part of the state in a rough grid. Old pavement here and there where it endured somehow, but mostly plain dirt. They'd walk west a few hours he figured, and then turn south and that way they wouldn't lose too much time. Cut into Ninety-Five just a hair later than if they'd stuck to Ninety-One. That was where the truck traffic would be anyhow. The real truck traffic. Loads heading all the way to the Mason-Dixon in a straight line except for that boomerang around New York where the two of them could bail out and see what their future held. If they managed to get a ride to begin with. As long as his breath held out, they'd walk. Then they'd keep on walking.

Penny marched along like a trooper. That little white cat bouncing up and down and looking backwards but the girl herself looking everywhere all at once or trying to. Craning her neck to capture the whole vague world any way she could. The westbound road and the fencelines along it and her own stretched shadow marching ahead. A landscape that rose and fell after they'd turned south onto a track where the sounds of the nearby highway died out and they were back in the cultivated wilderness.

Men emerged from high gates into the fields, tools over their shoulders and a weariness to their gait. A line of long shacks stood on a rise parallel to the road, low buildings painted red a long long time ago but gone to gray now. With strips of vertical siding that wasn't just siding but opened itself up to the wind and the weather here and there. Long hanging slats, hinged at the top and free at the bottom. Banging in the breeze. She tilted her face toward the sound to study the buildings with the sun shining down on them at a pretty good angle right now and asked what it was that people kept in them. Being at that age where your father still knows everything.

"Tobacco," he said. "Or they did in the old days." These were tobacco barns. Drying sheds. Nobody used them anymore. The tobacco that grew around here got processed down along the Mason Dixon, so these barns were empty. Not even worth tearing down. He picked her up on his shoulders and she used his big backpack for a seat and they walked on. "Once upon a time," he said, "there would have been barns everywhere on land like this. All kinds of barns. All over. Filled up with hay and corn and horses and cows. Filled up with machinery like I keep in the quonset hut, but even better."

"Even better?"

"Even better." And more of it, he said. Tractors and cultivators and harvesters. Machines with blades and harrows and cutters that did the work of a hundred men and never got tired. "Machines almost as big as our house."

She laughed to imagine it. She said she thought he was kidding.

"I'm not. Farming wasn't always hand labor. People had equipment exactly that big and even bigger. Machines with rubber tires taller than a man. I've seen those tires in the dump. Sometimes they catch fire, and when they do they burn for days. On and on. That black smoke you see sometimes, that's what it is."

If the machines did the work of a hundred men, she wondered, then where did all the food go when they got finished growing it? There must have been too much. A hundred times too much.

Her father laughed. He described the world his own father had known first-hand. Told her there were more people then, but once everything got automated not that many of them had to be farmers. Not actual farmers. Not farmers who got their hands dirty. Just businessmen running factory farms from a distance. Agribusiness.

She asked if he meant like PharmAgra. She was one smart girl.

He said that was right. That was it exactly. PharmAgra was the only agribusiness left these days, though. They owned it all. She knew that because she saw their labels everywhere. She knew who her friends' fathers worked for. What she didn't know was that PharmAgra was the last of a breed that had once thrived everywhere. The last one standing, the sole relic of a system that had started small and gotten big and then gotten so big that it had to get small again. The small taking care of the big just the way things always went in the end. Farmers on their hands and knees pulling poisoned carrots they couldn't even eat.

They stopped to rest by the side of the road and watched a line of men carrying hoes slip into a fenced-in field and space themselves along a planted row at regular intervals and fall to working. Industrious as bugs. He put the backpack down in the dirt and opened it up and fished around for a canteen of water and some homemade granola in a paper sack. Homemade out of oats from eastern Pennsylvania and raisins and nuts from what used to be California, stuck together with something factory-made that tasted like honey but wasn't, since you couldn't have honey without bees and the last of the bees had passed on a long time ago. Not entirely unmourned, but that was then. All of the ingredients hauled in trucks and processed in factories and hauled in trucks again, but the granola homemade nonetheless. That's what you called it.

In the sack was a folded-over note from Liz addressed to both of them, but he didn't read it out loud. He didn't even mention it. He just saw it and drew it out between his fingers and tucked it away.

She sat on her backpack and drank a little water and picked at the granola in her palm. Leaving the nuts. Letting ground-up bits of them slide back into the sack every time she went for another handful and thinking he wouldn't notice.

"Eat those, you skinny thing," he said, when he couldn't let her keep it up any longer. "You need the protein."

She did. Licked her palm clean and made a face.

"Good girl. We've got a ways to go yet. Have some more." He told her about a time when kids her age ate everything in sight and just about couldn't stop eating. Couldn't help themselves since food was everywhere in those days and it cost next to nothing. This was before his time, but his parents had lived through it. Blame those big factory farms, pumping out more food than people needed and finding ways to make them want it anyway. Poisoning it with sugar. It was as if somebody had thrown a switch and the whole business forgot how to stop or even slow down, so it just kept going.

Things were different now. Supply and demand. Hardly enough of anything to go around. But boy did it cost.

*

The fenced-in fields gave out after a while and they walked on among low rolling hills. Trails of broken blacktop going off in all directions and lines of concrete split by tall grass and crumbled cinderblock ruins set one after another. Here and there a metal pole angling up out of the ground with a frame for a sign on top but the sign dangling or just plain gone. He told her they'd called this a subdivision and she didn't ask a subdivision of what. It was just a word.

"Are we getting close to New York?"

"No."

"How much closer are we now than when we started?"

"As far as we've walked."

"Daddy."

"A few miles. I don't know."

"Carry me."

He did.

*

Miles went by with him walking and her on his shoulders. Heading south and a little west with the face of the white cat for warding off trouble. Stopping every half hour or so to rest. As they went along one subdivision bled into another like it was all the same thing, although there had been a day when it was divided up and parceled out. When there were townships out here and school districts and high schools with longstanding rivalries on the football field. When different things belonged to different people. None of this belonged to anybody now. PharmAgra owned the fields and National Motors owned the highways and AmeriBank carried the paper that kept it all straight. But out here in the Zone the idea of ownership had gone back to the way it was before any white man had set foot here. When the Indians possessed it all and didn't even know they possessed it because they didn't want to possess anything.

There wasn't even a means for staking a claim. But some still did. Even right here. Exactly here. The dark low noise of a tarpaulin flapping signaled it. The day was fading and the sun was dying and they heard that batwing rustle from off to one side of the road. Up along a half-circle of blacktop with a big wrecked building at the far end. The blacktop surrounding a patch of broken dirt and in the middle of the dirt a steel pole jutting up. A chain hanging loose from the top of the pole, clanging in the little breeze. The low rustling sound rose from somewhere back in the direction of the building. They weren't ignorant and superstitious like city people about what kind of terrors might be out here, but the girl was only five years old and no bigger than a breath and the sounds were darkly suggestive. The ghost ship clanging of the chain and the liquid rustle of something furtive rising up as the sun went down.

She leaned into her father like a bareback rider and nudged her knees into his shoulders and whispered "Go," and he went. Running or at least jogging, his breath coming harder. Going not away from anything, he told himself, but toward something. Some better place to string a rope between a pair of trees and hang their tarp from it. Some secluded place. All alone he'd have slept anywhere, but not tonight. Not with her. He'd have slept by the roadside with trucks screaming past or under a ragged outcropping with bats fidgeting over his head. He'd have slept in a newdug grave if he'd found one. But not now. He thought he'd pictured this trip pretty well but he hadn't pictured this part. Their exposure in that makeshift tent. Her exposure.

The fear constricted his throat and made his breath come harder, and he jogged on as long as he could but not long. The dirt road was washboarded and riddled with potholes and he told himself he didn't want to break a leg in the early dark. Where would they be then. He looked back and saw his footprints in the dirt and didn't like seeing them. Standing there panting. What if somebody. What if. Don't think. He set the girl down and didn't let go of her hand and she wouldn't have let him anyway. "Let's keep going," he said.

"Where," she said.

"Just a little farther."

"I'm hungry."

"Me too."

They slowed so he could find an apple in her backpack and they shared it bite by bite. The PharmAgra label got caught in his teeth and he spat most of it out. She was still hungry and so was he, but neither of them said it. They'd eaten the apple down to the seeds and the stem and they were starving but who wouldn't be.

She said, "We could plant these seeds if we wanted."

"Sure," he said. "Grow ourselves an apple tree. But that'd take a few years." Working at the rest of that sticker with a fingernail. "We're better off eating what we packed, don't you think? That's quicker."

She sighed and gave a theatrical shrug. "I meant *when we get home.*" Like wouldn't he ever understand anything.

They marched on. They came to a ruined intersection with lamp posts and sign posts and a traffic signal still hanging overhead on wires. Little gabled roofs over the stacked holes where the colored lights used to be. All of it hanging dark up there against the rising moon. He pointed it out and described what of it she couldn't see. He said it sort of looked like a big birdhouse. She asked him what kind of birds lived there and he said they probably didn't have birds here anymore. Just like they didn't have them at home. Which he guessed wasn't much of an answer, so he said maybe robins. Robins like in the book she had. Robin redbreasts. But they're all sleeping now. It's bedtime for everybody.

They turned there and went up a little distance to where some trees grew. Settled in among them and chose two and hung the rope from one to the other and draped the tarpaulin over the rope like a pup tent. Got supper out. Ate it cold rather than risk a fire, even a low one, even here surrounded by close-set trees and undergrowth dense with the last of summer.

*

Whoever woke them up had a flashlight. Over the years Weller had found plenty of flashlights in the dump and he had devised theories about how they worked, but he'd never seen one lit up. This one was shining into his eyes at close range and the man holding it was drawing back to kick him in the kidneys a second time, so he didn't have the opportunity to think about it any. He just recoiled. Recoiled and half sat up and put himself between whoever this was and his daughter.

"Hands behind your head."

Weller reached to retrieve his glasses.

"Behind your head or off it comes." A clicking sound in the dark. "And then who'll look after your baby girl?"

Weller put his hands behind his head.

"That's better."

The voice belonged to an old man. A powerful old man by how he kicked and a cunning old man by where he kicked, but an old man just the same. An old man who'd lived on cigarettes and solitude by the sound of his voice.

Weller shifted to block Penny better but the old man told him not to get smart. Keep his ass right where it was if he didn't feel like getting shot. Although if he felt like getting shot he'd come to the right place and the old man would be happy to oblige. It would make things easier. He coughed and spit and said, "A dead fellow don't complain so much when you take his brand." Keeping the gun on him and making a rapid cutting motion across his own neck with the flashlight. The beam jumping around in the trees and then settling back on Weller and his child.

Penny peering around from behind her father. Light bouncing off her eyes.

27

"Come on now. Get up. We got places to go."

They got up.

"Load those bags full." He stood clear of the pushed-back tarp, among the trees, pointing with the beam. "Don't leave anything behind. That's right. That's right. The blanket and all."

Weller jammed and shoved, but everything that had fit the day before didn't fit now.

"You fold up that tarp and take it. I'll carry the rope. Nobody's coming back for any of this, so don't get ideas."

Weller didn't have ideas.

"Now come on."

They went back the way they came. Weller with Penny on his back and the old man behind with the gun and the flashlight. The flashlight burning like it would burn forever. They went down to the intersection with the birdhouse hanging overhead and they turned and retraced their steps from before.

"That's a nice kitty cat you got there, sweetheart."

No answer.

"You like kitty cats?"

No answer. She just wrapped her arms tighter around her father's neck. Making his breath come harder. He stopped and the old man hollered at him to go on and he went on.

"Turn here." The place where they'd heard that flapping sound. No sound now. Not that low rustle and not the beating of that chain. No air moving and no sound. They kept to the half-circle of blacktop. The way was uphill and they'd been hurrying and Weller slowed from the slope and Penny's weight and his desperation all combined. The man came close and pressed something into his side. The barrel of the gun or the flashlight, who could tell. "March," he said. Giving Weller a shove that set him stumbling. Turning off the light. Sunrise.

It was an old elementary school. Childish drawings still hanging in what few windows were still glassed, faded-out drawings that manifested themselves one by one in the rising dawn. The rest of the windows gaping. They went around to the side. Down a little alleyway cut out of the building like where they'd keep the trash cans. A concrete curb along one side surrounding an opening covered over with a blue plastic tarp gray in the pale light. "Pull that back and go on down." Stairs below it into darkness. "Go on. Nothing down there's going to bite."

It was make a stand now or don't make one ever. Weller kicked at the tarp and said he had to put the girl down or else he'd lose his balance.

The old man said just don't get smart.

Weller put her down. She went backwards a half step and no more. Toward the mouth of the alleyway. Weller looked toward the old man and said, "I don't know what you've got in mind but you don't need us. Just take whatever we've got. Take whatever you want."

The old man pointed the gun at the child and said rest assured he would do exactly that.

*

Alongside a doorway at the bottom, three yellow triangles set inside a black circle. Black paint and yellow paint on a metal sign that was dented and buckled and rusted through in places but unmistakable. The words *Fallout Shelter*. There were no more children in this old school building, but there was still a place for children to go when the worst happened.

"Welcome to HQ," said the old man. He threw a switch and a generator somewhere started up and a half-dozen lightbulbs strained to life. Clear glass bulbs hanging from wires strung around a big shadowy storeroom with pallets stacked along three walls and a long bare table in the middle. A couple of folding chairs. A single cot and an upturned shipping crate with a few things arranged on it. A heavy ashtray and cigarettes and an antique Zippo lighter. A water glass and some old magazines.

"Have a seat. Both of you." Pointing with the gun.

Weller took the girl by her shoulder and directed her. They sat side by side at the table waiting for they didn't know what. For whatever came next.

"Hands on the table," said the old man. "Up where I can see them."

Penny had to reach.

The old man drifted toward the upended crate and picked up a cigarette and lit it. Took the ashtray and put it on the long table. Didn't sit down but looked like he'd considered it. "I'm in the collections business," he said.

"Collecting what?"

"I think you know." Tendons standing out in his neck and a vein pulsing in his forehead in the scratchy lightbulb light. Drawing on his cigarette and blowing smoke and coughing and the smoke making Penny cough too. "I think you know what I'm after," he said.

"I don't. I don't know."

Chewing at his lip for a minute and then laughing in one small burst. "I'm after whatever pays the freight," he said. "A little flexibility never hurt an old soldier like me."

He meant it. *An old soldier.* It was in his bearing and in his quickness and in his ease with the gun.

Weller took in the room more closely. A bunker, steeped in the cold closeness of anything underground, jammed with enough supplies to last a school full of children a month or a single man the rest of his life. Everything packed solid, as if the contents themselves were meant as reinforcement. Pallet after pallet of canned and boxed food arranged floor to ceiling. Water in barrels. Cases labeled *Survival Crackers,* which he guessed meant hardtack. All of that plus piled up medical kits and tightly folded blankets and cardboard cartons printed with mysterious letters and numbers by some government office. Everything neat and square and sharp, policed as if someone important might be coming to inspect at any moment. Including the handful of personal belongings on the upended crate. *Personal belongings.* They stood out, like this was a prison cell or a barracks.

He looked steadily at the old man and asked him straight. "Are you with Black Rose, or what?"

The old man stiffened. Prideful in spite of himself. "You could say that." He smiled just a quarter of an inch. Disappearing behind Weller's back to hide it.

"I didn't know they were out here anymore."

"They're not. But once you're Black Rose, you're always Black Rose." Opening a locker or a cabinet back there. Fussing with something.

"That's what I've heard." Half turning, as if maybe they'd found something to talk about and he could use it to his advantage.

"Don't get any ideas."

"I won't."

"The girl either."

"She won't." She was sitting up against her father rockstill. Frozen like some prey animal intent on making itself invisible. Her hands still folded and her eyes bigger than they had ever been in all her short life. Weller wanted to put his hand on her shoulder or give her some other small comfort but he didn't quite dare, and then he did it anyway.

The old man left off what he was doing and came back around. He stood opposite them at the table and kept his cigarette between his teeth and poked one thick finger deep into the ashtray. Dug around. Separating things. Ash and butts from some other heavier objects that had sunken to the bottom. Little metallic pieces that made scraping noises against the glass. "I probably ought to keep these in a jar or something," he said. "If I had a jar." Pushing the ashtray forward so that Weller could see. A dozen or so little metal lozenges and cubes and bulbs, none of them more than a quarter of an inch long, most of them shiny and gleaming in spite of the ash but some brushed down to a matte finish and some not entirely metal but made partly of plastic or rubber with one or two little knobs or protrusions jutting out. Six or eight different configurations altogether. "These are where the money is," he said. Tapping his ashy finger on the tabletop. An old prospector done with his panning. "I don't mean these particular ones. They've been scanned off clean. Once they've been scanned off they've got no value except as souvenirs."

"Souvenirs."

"Like how the Indians used to take your scalp. Counting coup."

"Those are brands, then."

"Yes sir." The old man picked out a rectangular slab with a narrow black stripe. "This one's AmeriBank," he said. Alongside it was a tiny one not much larger than a ball bearing, perfectly round. "Mutual Electric." A glistening square with a metal prongs like antennas mounted in rubber on either side. "Black Rose." He tapped at the side of his own throat. "Extremely rare."

"I'll bet it is."

"Extremely hard to come by." He tapped ashes over the little metal bits. Drew on the cigarette one last time and stabbed it out and stabbed it out again just to be sure and began circling the table. "What happens is people come around. People with different ideas about how a man might make a dollar. As a rule they're Management types like you, slumming in the Zone. Got some deal they're running when they ought to be minding their company's business."

"I'm not Management."

The old man winked. "Sure. Sure. None of the other fellows are, either. Just so you know."

"I'm not Management. Honest."

"Time will tell," he said. "Anyway, you know what I'm talking about. Black markets. Gray markets. Every kind of market there is." He kept walking around the table. Behind Weller now. The sound of that locker opening again. "Contraband and so forth. Situations develop where the companies that pay for my services just aren't getting their fair share of certain transactions."

Weller turned to see what the man was up to in the locker. He was opening a brown bottle and he was soaking a rag with what was in it, and the air was choked all of a sudden with the high smell of a chemical solvent, and before Weller could move the old man was on him and he had the wet rag tight over his mouth with that solvent smell intolerably strong and he was out. He didn't even hear his own daughter scream.

*

He awoke on the cold floor with adhesive tape around his wrists and a sick feeling in his stomach and a slit in his throat that wouldn't quit bleeding. Crumpled on the floor in the corner, picking at the sticky tape and wanting to vomit but not knowing where. Feeling blood run down his neck. A little warm trickle of it dripping slow with his heartbeat behind it.

He came up to his elbows and saw the old man bent over the table. The back of him, working at something. Holding his breath and letting it out and drawing it in again hard, and then letting it out with a curse on it. The girl's blond hair spilling.

He got to his feet and nearly toppled but didn't. He tried to go noiselessly but his feet went any way they wanted. He reached the table and picked up the big glass ashtray and the old man looked up at him without really looking, and he raised the ashtray and swung it but missed. Miscalculated. Threw himself off balance and the ash tray smashed on the concrete floor. Ash and glass and old brands everywhere. The old man ducking and a scalpel in his hand snagging Weller's forearm, drawing more blood. The girl on the table wasn't taped down like her father had been. She was just lying there limp. A narrow cut in her throat gaping a little, and blood smeared around it, and the old man's index finger red to the first knuckle.

"Go easy there," said the old man. Dropping the scalpel. Raising up his hands and stepping back to let Weller reach his daughter, who was even then coming around. "No harm done."

Weller gathered himself over his daughter and held her close and wanted to stay there with his arms around her forever. Just putting himself between her and the world. He bent there breathing hard and sick with the girl waking up and beginning to get sick herself a couple of minutes behind him. The girl gasping and turning her head to the side and her father helping her turn it and the sickness coming unstoppable and her father thinking it served the old man right. Let her finish. Let her purge herself of the old man's poison. Let her give it all back to him. Wiping her mouth with his shirt when she finished and picking her up and holding her close. Wishing he could kill the old man but still too dizzy to step clear of the table where he leaned and fearful of putting his daughter down anyway. Fearful of leaving her unprotected.

The old man sat on the cot, smoking a cigarette and watching them. Looking exhausted the way an old man will, an old man who's been through something miserable and come out the other side. Even something of his own making. The stoppered brown bottle stood on the crate with the water glass and a different clear bottle stood with it. The gun on the pile of magazines. The cigarette in a fist in between his knees, the white of it stained red. "There's rubbing alcohol if you want to clean up those cuts," he said. "I'd recommend it. Never know what you might catch." He raised the cigarette and pulled in smoke through the residue of their bleeding. "It's your call, though."

Weller kept himself between Penny and the old man. Letting his mind clear. Looking at him over his shoulder. His child just breathing, which was enough. "You didn't find anything," he said.

"No sir, I did not."

"I told you."

"They all tell me. They all lie." He blew smoke at the glass bottle. "Alcohol's right here if you want it. Cotton balls and so forth. Bandaids in the locker."

Weller imagined the sting of the alcohol and turned away and drew Penny tighter if that were possible. Thinking of what he'd have to do. How it would hurt his child again and how he had to do it. "Soon," he said. Bouncing her a little. "Soon." And then looking back at the old man. "I've got a little money if you didn't take it already."

"I don't want your money."

"It'll make up for what you didn't get."

"I don't want it. I start doing a cash business, where does that end? What kind of people have I got to deal with then? I'll stick to credits, if you don't mind."

"Then let us be on our way."

"On your way." He said it like it was a joke. "On your way to where, is what I can't figure."

"That's my problem, isn't it?"

"There's nothing out there. Just more of what you came from."

"Let us go, then."

"Absolutely," said the old man. "Go on and good riddance. I won't stand in your way."

"All right."

"You've wasted enough of my time as it is. You're a total loss already."

The girl had begun to cry. Great deep sobs. Weller looked at the old man and the gun on the crate. He said he was going to gather up their things.

"Fine by me. I'd use that alcohol pretty soon, though. Just from a medical point of view."

Weller didn't want to put her down. Keeping an eye on the old man and the gun he went to where they'd dropped their packs and kneeled and picked them both up with one hand. Coming back to a standing position. Drawing breath. "We're going now."

"Bye bye."

The girl sobbed.

Her father carried her through the doorway out of the cold bunker and into the bluelit stairwell. The girl risking a look back over his shoulder.

"You take good care of that kitty cat, now."

Weller had never climbed faster. The girl howling all of a sudden and both of them bleeding still and his clothes stinking of her sickness. Up the concrete steps and through the blue tarpaulin and into the heat and the sun as if the heat and the sun were cures for everything. The alleyway cut into the school building was bright and the space beyond it was brighter still. Hot as noon. A playground off to one side partly wrecked but mostly just abandoned. A splintered see-saw weathered back into a plank. He sat Penny on the long end of it and she didn't want to let go of him so he picked her up and held onto her longer. Tried again and this time it took. He asked her if she knew what this plank was, knowing she didn't. He told her to watch. He put down the packs and he stepped away and she called him back and then he stepped away again and this time she let him. Went to the other end of the plank and pushed it down and took her for a little ride. Just lifted her up a foot or two into the air. Into a kind of heaven.

She laughed.

It was a lever, a thing with which a person could move the world, and in different circumstances he would have described that possibility but he didn't do that now. He just let her down slowly and lifted her up again a few more times and then he said honey we'll do lots more of this in a minute. Just you wait. I forgot something we need. He backed away and she let him. Sitting on the end of the plank certain he'd come back to lift her up again. The sun working on her and brightening things and helping bring her back.

He entered the little alley and pulled open the tarp and went back down the stairs.

Found the old man sitting right where he'd been. Looking disgusted and weary but not entirely unsurprised. Tipping his head toward the bottle of alcohol and saying, "I knew you'd come for it."

Weller asked about the locker with the bandaids and he told him where it was. Helped himself to all there were and a spool of adhesive tape too and some gauze pads and a little tube of antibiotic ointment. Loaded his pockets with these rarities. Things that were only rumors out in the Zone. He noticed the flashlight and pocketed that as well. He left the locker and came to where the old man was sitting and took the alcohol. Cotton balls and a rag that was there too.

The old man said, "You can have the rag or the cotton but you can't have both." A cigarette between his lips. Picking up the lighter and flicking the top open with is thumb.

"Don't," Weller said. "Wait on that a little."

The old man saying why not. It's a free country. Just choose one and go. Don't try telling me what to do. The old man acting ornery and tired and maybe a little sick of what he'd done. Saying go on clean up that little girl of yours.

Weller put down the rag and that seemed to satisfy the old man, who turned away and studied the table and the mess on the floor with a look in his eyes that said he regretted that he'd have to clean it up sometime soon. Weller took the rag again while he wasn't looking and put down the bottle and took up the other bottle, the brown bottle full of ether. He opened it and doused the rag in one motion and he fell upon the old man. Knocking him backwards and pressing the rag to his face. Saying don't smoke around this stuff unless you want us both getting killed. But the old man was already out.

He had a brand in his neck all right, that little square with two metal prongs mounted in rubber. Once Black Rose, always Black Rose. Weller took the lighter and worked the bottom part of it open and put the brand inside, in with the soaked cotton wadding. Pushing it deep, burying it there for safekeeping. The lighter fluid cleaning the blood from his fingers. He draped the rag over the old man's face and dribbled some more ether onto it and capped the bottle, not knowing what the end of that would be and not caring. How much ether could a person breathe before it killed him. Then he slid the lighter into his pocket and went out to the bluelit stairs and back to the playground.

Almost running.

Lifted up.

Three:

The Tigris and the Euphrates

Children on the broken road. Eight or ten of them in a cloud, all ages, raising dust as they went. A little army moving between green fields, half of its motion forward and the other half a busy side to side tussling.

Penny's face brightened when her father pointed to them from the top of a rise. The swarm of them down below, moving along the valley floor. She caught their movement and their long shadow and heard the sound of their voices, a song filtering up, and she took her father's hand and they walked a little faster. Aiming to meet them at a fenced-in crossroads. The fences were tagged with the PharmAgra wheat stalk and her father was certainly aware of trespassing on this road, but how much trouble can you get into when eight or ten little children are doing the same. No tire tracks on the gravel whatsoever. It had been forever since this road was last traveled by anyone but the likes of these.

They came near, and the children shied. Penny and her father at the center of the crossroads and the children hanging back a few yards, milling, as if they'd met some invisible resistance. Weller raised his hand and called out to them. The sun so low that at this distance he stood practically in their shadow. His own stretching a mile behind him. They didn't answer. They just shied, their eyes like horses.

Penny broke the spell, dropping her father's hand and running forward. The children swarmed around her. Enfolding.

They were brown children, and they made Weller think of Indians. They were creatures of the outdoors and they looked it, even though they'd

37

been on their way home from school. Chattering like birds now that they'd been let out. Imagine that. A school out here. One room, they said. It must have been like in the old days, before education turned into an industry and then into an industry that failed. Just a little antique falling-down one room schoolhouse, as if there was something to learn and some reason to learn it. Something up ahead to get ready for.

He and Penny followed them home. Down the broken blacktop and through a hole in a chain link fence and up rows of tall corn. The children invisible beneath the plants this late in the summer and Weller almost invisible too. They said there were other ways. Other ways for other seasons and other cover. They passed through a wirecut fence again into a different field and down into a mansized culvert running slow with mud. They passed a couple of men coming the other way with backpacks and exchanged not a word. Came up in a tobacco field.

*

There were fences all around, but they were different. Tall fences tagged PharmAgra but poorly kept. Rusted in spots and painted over and rusting through again. Weller guessed the pieces had been dragged here from some great distance. Salvaged elsewhere and brought here for camouflage. To make this place look ordinary. He thought of how much work that must have been. Work and stealth combined.

And all because there was something different about the tobacco here. The leaves were too small, the plants too weak and spindly. It was nowhere near as dense and vigorous and large-scale profitable as the big engineered plants growing everywhere else. It wasn't PharmAgra. Weller didn't know much about agriculture, but he knew this. He thought of those men with the backpacks, going out. Pictured them with their payloads of old-growth plants or disengineered plants or whatever it was they were growing here. Risking a run-in with some bounty hunter like that old Black Rose. The amount of trouble that men doing a job like that would face. And the rewards.

"Children." A voice came from behind him, soft. "They trust everybody."

Weller turned.

"Grownups like us, not so much." The woman speaking was small and intense, her dark hair shot through with gray. She watched the children pick up some game they'd left off before school. Penny included. Lines and squares scratched into the dirt. Pebbles tossed into the grid and shouts raised. She smiled as she stood there watching, but her eyes were rueful. An afterimage of something in them, burned there.

Weller said, "This will do my daughter a world of good."

The woman nodded.

"Which of them are yours?"

"None." Not looking at him. "None of these. I did have two. A boy and a girl. My husband kept them behind."

"Whereabouts?"

"Bangalore."

Weller was silent.

"His parents. Tradition. The plan was that I would fly back once a month." Toeing the dirt. "I did it for the longest time. These days, Bangalore may as well be on the moon."

"I'm sorry."

"Me too. They're grown up now, I would hope."

"I'm sure they're doing fine."

The woman was silent.

In between the rows it was Penny's turn to throw, and her stone happened to land somewhere close to the right place and a cheer went up.

"Take good care of her," the woman said.

"I'm trying."

"It's a shame about her eyes," she said.

"Yes. Yes it is."

"Was it—"

"Yes."

"I thought so. It's a twisted world we live in."

"No question."

"You grow something in God's earth with your own two hands and you can't even eat it." She looked at Weller and he didn't look back. Studied the vertical slit alongside his windpipe. Freshly crusted over. Better to talk about that. "Tell me how you went generic," she asked.

"I didn't."

"I don't think you cut yourself shaving." Narrowing her eyes toward Penny, Penny standing on her toes and clapping her hands together. "*She* certainly didn't."

"She's second-generation. Me, I'm one of those that the Zone just kind of came up around. I still live in the house where I grew up. I still run my father's old workshop."

"Tradition." She nodded. She knew all about tradition.

He touched the cut.

"So what about that?" she said.

"That? That was basically a misunderstanding." He told her about the old man in the bunker. A corporate mercenary gone freelance.

She said knew all about him. Said he'd never managed to find his way to the fields that they kept under cultivation but then again he'd never needed to. All he had to do was haunt the edges, stay near the spots where the gravel roads met the highway and close by the big culverts where men with packs and duffel bags might hide themselves and their merchandise—where they might meet other men with credits in their brands and black market scanners and ideas about the redistribution of wealth—and a bounty hunter like him didn't need to bother locating the actual source. The reward money was more consistent if he didn't. That old scavenger. It hadn't been much more than a day since Weller had left him, and there were reports already that he wasn't in any of his usual hiding places. That he might be out of commission. Apparently they owed Weller a debt.

He said some food and fresh water would do if they had any to spare. He'd left that bunker in kind of a hurry.

*

The people here buried themselves alive underneath the ground, because even though planes didn't come over very often what if they did. They dug wide, deep holes in self-defense. Six of them altogether shared by a dozen families in a clearing that wasn't quite a clearing. Dirt hauled out and heaped up into little low quarter-domes like somebody had buried a gigantic sphere and left part of it poking up by accident. Propped up inside with barn timbers. A doorway cut in and covered over with fencing material with a ramp beneath it leading down, a hole in the middle of the roof for ventilation, and tobacco plants growing everywhere as if these were just humped-up places in the ground. As if in the absence of plows and cultivators the earth had begun retaking its old unknowable shape.

The sun sank low and food appeared and tables materialized. Long tables where they all ate together. The children at one end. The woman at the other, running things. Directing. Not quite the oldest but surely the most revered. Her name was Patel. She was a doctor, but not the medical kind. A laboratory scientist. *"A fish out of water* doesn't begin to describe it," she said. And yet she persevered. She had equipment, although it wasn't anything like the tools she'd had in Bangalore, back when she'd been working for NutraMax. She'd done tobacco there, too. Tobacco was what NutraMax did best. It was the reason PharmAgra had bought them, and the reason they'd shut them down once they'd transferred the technology and commercialized the plant stock. She'd done the transfer and she'd helped with the commercialization. And then the bottom had fallen out and the federal government had quit paying its bills and international relations had gone all to hell. She'd found herself stranded here jobless and hopeless and surrounded by poisons she'd engineered herself. Her two little children back in Bangalore, growing up without her.

She told herself things were better in India. Probably not as good as they were in China, but better than they were here. A mother bereft of her children could take some comfort in that. In the technology and manpower and investment capital that were concentrated where her children were these days. Concentrated to such an extent that India and China didn't need the western hemisphere at all anymore. North America wasn't worth thinking about as a market or even as a source of cheap labor, the transportation costs were so high.

It had taken twenty years and more, but little by little Patel had recovered these tobacco plants. Torn the doctored ones apart cell by cell and reassembled them into something close to the original. The thing she'd started with. Real tobacco, nothing poisonous about it except in the ordinary old-fashioned way, and if you insisted on smoking it then you got what you deserved. Some of that danger had been bred out of the commercial strains when the proprietary code had gone in, and wonder of wonders here it was again. You can drive out nature with a pitchfork, but it keeps on coming back. Nonetheless, people who sought the real thing and had the means to buy it and the health insurance to cover the consequences wanted it just the way it was, cancer and all. They thrilled to the risk.

These last couple of years she'd been working mainly on wheat. Just imagine, she said. Tobacco was profitable, tobacco kept their little village going on this tiny patch of land, but with wheat you could expand. You could reclaim the world. Anyone could grow wheat, practically anywhere. Civilization would spread out again from this very spot. It would seek the most remote of places and recover them by means of its own generative power. The Connecticut River and the Long Island Sound would be the new Tigris and Euphrates. Where it all began.

She looked Weller in the eye. Saying just think how the generations to come will remember us.

Stars began to show and candles burned on the table. The children down at the other end raising up their laughter in the dark, and one tall young man riding herd on them. Their teacher from the schoolhouse. Now and then he turned his head and looked over at Patel in the way he might look upon a saint. Only just daring to permit himself.

Twenty years and more was a long time, she said. Things broke. Things wore out. She studied Weller and said he'd mentioned running his father's old workshop. She wondered exactly what that might mean. What kind of a workshop it was. She hated to be forward but if he could help she needed to know.

Machinery, he said. All kinds.

Oh thank God. The Cradle of Civilization wouldn't wait.

*

Over breakfast in the flat light of sunrise he watched her swallow, trying to spot an incision in her neck. Her own stigma to match his. But there was none, and he asked was she still branded after all.

Hardly, she said. She'd never been branded at all, and it was the only kindness ever done her by PharmAgra. An accidental kindness at that. They had shown her the door just as they were showing others the knife. She recalled seeing her old labmates at the gas station and the grocery store during those first few weeks, when the surgeons were at their busiest. Seeing them marked. Their necks bandaged white. Each of them proud of having been singled out, and each of them reluctant to meet her eyes.

She remembered paying with plastic in those days, showing identification and signing here, while the others kept their heads high and presented their necks to the scanners that appeared everywhere. Assuming that haughty stance. She remembered watching them and paying with plastic and then paying with cash and then not being able to pay at all. Using food stamps until food stamps gave out. And finally this. This experimental station built of refuse and earth. Out here in the Zone.

*

They went to the dump. Just the two of them. "No limits," Weller said. "I want you to imagine how anything here might help, and then we'll work toward it." There were treasures everywhere. Washers and dryers. Stoves and microwaves. Dish antennas and aluminum siding and fleets of rusted bicycles all tangled up. She settled on a gas range and a chest freezer, fire and ice, refusing to hold with any particular convention as to how the world might end. The freezer was going to need electricity and the gas range was going to need gas, but Weller had promised. He located some old generating equipment and some welding gear with a tank still half full and he brought men to haul it all back. He paced off the distance between the tobacco field and the landfill and drew up plans for a gas installation like the one he'd built at home and set people to work gleaning iron pipe for it from the fencing they'd stockpiled. Had them sorting it by length and fitting it together and digging a trench to bury it in. Sank collection columns and gave welding lessons because he couldn't stay forever.

Penny went to school and she loved it. It occupied her entirely, her mind and her heart and her imagination. She was a natural. Only at night did she miss her mother, only at night in the lamplit underground where she kept her father company, watching him work and helping him where she could. Holding a light maybe. That flashlight from the bunker. It was cold until he got the generator working again and hooked it up to a space heater that hadn't run before and the temperature finally began to rise. Things starting to dry out.

They slept side by side on a pallet, beneath a low ceiling with roots reaching down. Clusters and strings of shallow roots and runners entwining themselves with the salvaged barn timbers, all of it combining into one unmovable thing.

Patel herself slept behind a curtain. She had made do this way for all these years. She needed nothing, or at least nothing that she could obtain here. As Weller drifted toward sleep he whispered to his daughter, and his daughter whispered back, and behind her curtain Patel couldn't help but overhear. She hadn't slept right since Bangalore.

An hour before dawn he came awake and lay listening to Penny breathe. Wanting to be up making things happen and wanting to be on his way to New York and wanting to stay right here with her in this moment of darkness and hope. Calculating how long he might delay getting her seen by a doctor in return for helping build a world where mutations like hers might never rise up again. Imagining the other children to be saved. The potential children. But unable to put them over his own daughter for long.

*

He was on his knees in a ditch, checking welds on a length of pipe, when footsteps startled him. Two men with oversized backpacks and weary postures and steady gaits, coming through the high grass. Two men worn out with traveling. He hailed them and asked where they were bound as if he had the right to ask, and they looked at him the very same way. Suspicious men in a suspicious world. He could be anybody. They asked what was he doing here.

He scooped sweat from inside his thick lenses with a dirty finger and looked up at them and said in case they hadn't noticed he was installing a gas line and they said oh is that what that is. They'd thought it was just junk lying in a ditch. Ha ha ha. The two of them adjusting their shoulder straps and moving on. Saying good luck with that. The undiluted arrogance of the man of the world, the man connected to nothing.

He climbed out of the ditch and followed them back to the compound. In spite of their weariness, they moved along with the steady rhythm of machinery. Into the culvert and through the long darkness and up again into the sunlight. Mud on their feet and mud on Weller's feet. In the tobacco field no one paid them the least bit of attention. People bent over plants or tending low fires or working looms. People grinding vegetable compounds into paste between stones in support of Patel's work. People cutting iron pipe in support of his. One by one they looked up at the travelers and looked away. Weller followed anyhow, along the rows and down the ramp into Patel's lab. They knew exactly where they were going.

She greeted them and they laid out the contents of their backpacks on her worktable. Money first, of course. Cash. A sheaf of tattered old U.S. greenbacks and AmeriBank scrip mixed together. The colony's cut. She laid a hand on it and said they'd come just in time. She had to get a supply run under way and back before the fall closed in. They'd have trouble making it through the winter otherwise. The two men nodded their understanding. The filthy pair of them standing there like heroes, smiling through grime.

She riffled the bills and cocked her head and said were they sure this was all of it. She said it seemed low.

They said no, that was all.

She said don't make me count it. I don't have all day.

One of them smiled at the other one and then at her saying he thought maybe they could part with another hundred just to show how much they cared.

She said make it two. Two hundred.

The second one said one-fifty but only because we love you. Teasing her and teasing out the money like this was some game. Weller watching from the bottom of the ramp and hating them for working her over and wasting her time.

She leaned on the table and said all right, before we settle on a number let's see how much you love me to begin with. And then she counted the money. Not just once. Twice. Making them wait while she did it and making Weller wait if he cared to see how this turned out. Maybe doing it for his benefit. He didn't know. Putting the dollars in one pile and the scrip in another and scribbling out a calculation based on the exchange rate between the two. Last thing she knew scrip was going for almost double what the old currency was worth.

When she finished she said to hell with that one-fifty they had said would make up the difference. Unless they'd given her tobacco away, they owed her another five hundred and that was being generous on her part. Even if they *had* given it away. She didn't want U.S. dollars either. She wanted another five hundred in good solid AmeriBank scrip. They weren't the only runners in the world.

They said four and she said five. They could find another source if they wanted.

They said all right five. Five just because they loved her.

She said she knew they did. She had known it all along.

*

The rest of what they'd spread out on the table was a varied lot. Tools. Knives and a file and some wirecutters. A tin of multipurpose oil and a couple of empty flasks bound up in rags. What looked like medicine, tablets of some kind in a plastic bag and dark red fluid in a bottle with an eyedropper in it. Patel went over these and counted them off on her fingers against some mental list and asked about a few things that were missing. Things she needed. The men didn't have them but they had plenty of excuses instead. Places they hadn't been able to get to and people they hadn't been able to see. Short supplies and bounty hunters. She said never mind. She'd go to some other source. They didn't argue. She counted out a little money and said there would have been twice that much if they'd gotten everything she needed and they didn't seem to feel any regret over it. They just shrugged, as if to say let somebody else take care of the details. They had troubles enough of their own.

At the far end of the table they had left some burlap sacks and bundles, rough fabric tied up roughly. When Patel was finished with everything else she turned her attention to these. Took a scalpel and slit the packages open one after another. Vegetable material packed solid inside each one of them. Weller was no expert. It was all just leaves to him. Leaves and pods and fibrous stalks in various stages of drying or decay. Everything labeled on little paper cards half rotted themselves. Smaller bundles inside the bigger bundles with seeds and seedlings separated out, clumps of delicate thread-like roots wrapped in some kind of moss and kept damp. The way Patel looked at them, Weller could see that the rest of the world had fallen away from her. She was beyond happiness or astonishment or delight or any other ordinary reaction. Picking up the labels and holding them out at arm's length where she could read them and putting them back down again. Fingers flying from one sample to the next and lingering there for no more than a few seconds before passing on. Ideas forming in her mind. He could see them coming together. She raised her head and noticed that the runners were still there and she dismissed them. The only word for it. Dismissed them like subordinates who'd been waiting upon her word. They left. Weller stayed.

She took a bundle of glassine envelopes from a drawer and began parceling out some of the samples into them. Writing on the envelopes with the nub of a crayon. Rapid little flicks. Weller looking over her shoulder and after a few minutes hazarding a question. "So it's not only wheat, then?"

No. It wasn't only wheat. And this little compound in the tobacco fields wasn't unique, either. There were others elsewhere. The Midwest. The West. The South. Hidden places like this one set back from the roads, and even more deeply hidden places where there were no roads at all. Isolated outposts where research and development went on night and day, season after season, research and development whose goal was to recover the world as it had once been. To reverse time and bring back the dead.

"These runners, then. They're all right."

"I suppose. They're only in it for the money. They don't care what they carry. It *is* risky, though. These samples are worth a whole lot more to my old employer than every single leaf of tobacco we'll harvest this year. They're world-changers. Fortunately, there isn't a market for them. If one of those fellows got caught, though, or turned them over to PharmAgra, it wouldn't be pretty."

"There wouldn't be a reward?" Thinking of the bounty hunter.

She laughed. It struck him that he'd never heard her laugh before. "They'd take him to pieces," she said. "They'd move heaven and earth to find out where he'd gotten this stuff. Waterboarding, the whole works. And once he confessed, they'd kill him. I know these people."

"Cheney all over again."

"Nobody forgets the good old days, do they." She was holding up a glassine envelope to the light that came streaming down the ramp. Everything else having fallen away.

"You do all of the lab work right there?"

"Most of it." The envelope held a damp tangle of sprouted seeds. "Soy beans from Pennsylvania," she said, tapping on the glassine with a finger. "They're getting close. Not close enough, but close." She put down the envelope and sighed. "I guess you know about close."

Weller sighed too.

He went out and saw the two runners sitting on a dirt berm with a couple of other men he knew. Loading up their packs with bricks of tobacco and filling water bottles and getting ready to go. It made him long for the road himself. For the road and for what lay at the end of it. Penny healed and the both of them home. Liz.

*

He dug in and persevered for as long as he could. Another week of breaking his back and passing on what he knew and getting the trickiest parts of everything nailed down. Drawing plans for others to follow. When he was satisfied enough but not entirely satisfied he knew the time had come to leave. He stocked up for the trip to New York. Food and water and clean clothes for both Penny and himself, washed by somebody else. Somebody else doing their part.

Half of him wished that he could go home for Liz right then and bring her back and dig themselves a hole and settle in. In a place like this where people worked together toward something. But no. Not with Penny the way she was.

At the end Patel slipped him a bundle of cured tobacco leaves pressed flat and wrapped in aluminum foil against the weather. She tucked the bundle into his pack and said, "This is worth more to other people than it is to you. Don't spend it all in one place."

He followed Penny out. He let her lead, because she knew the path from going to the schoolhouse and she was proud to be able to show it to him. They said their goodbyes and lifted their packs and went across the tobacco field toward the culvert. Heading toward no-man's land but some distance to go yet. The sun just coming up. Penny chirped at him and something buzzed in his ear and he slapped at it and pulled back his hand disbelieving. He told her to stop for a minute. Knelt down beside her and said, "Look here, honey. Have you ever seen the likes of this? What's next? Birds, maybe? Give it time."

Four:

The Driver

They left the farms and the rolling hills and the distant emptied-out suburbs, creeping down mile by mile into a denser world of broken concrete.
Not all at once but little by little. Moving into it as it moved into them. It
was a hollow place devoid of people and empty of their recent signs.
Commerce and residence tightly packed together and no more of either
one remaining. Weller held tightly to his daughter's hand as they walked,
helping her when she stumbled over cracks and curbs and heaved-up places
where the annual cycle of freezing and thawing had rippled the streets of
the old densely settled towns and commercial strips and industrial parks.
Heaps and valleys of blacktop, like little mountain ranges thrown up.

It was areas like this, thickly populated stretches along the outskirts of
the cities, that had died the slowest. The old mythical megalopolis that ran
from Washington to Boston, the tightly packed suburbs of Chicago, and
the freeform sprawls of southern California. In the beginning, people had
come here to be close to the cities, to partake of what the cities offered
them in the way of work and riches and culture, but when the economy
fractured fully and the cities turned their backs they had nowhere to go. No
jobs and no savings and no hope.

Some stayed put, and when the price of food soared beyond reach they
cultivated their own little yards and windowboxes with seeds that they'd
saved and dried and pinned their hopes upon. Knowing what they knew
about genetically altered PharmAgra stock but hopeful nonetheless. Others
moved outward, fleeing to the countryside for the plainer life it promised.

In either event the results were the same. You never knew what treacherous homegrown unprocessed food might be lurking in plain sight, either in your own kitchen garden or on some farm stand table. Take and eat and die uninsured, or risk watching your children die the same in a few years. Soon the hospitals were overwhelmed and soon after that they were shuttered, because there is only so much charity in the world.

By and by the farthest suburbs and country towns closed ranks, shunning outsiders who arrived without the skills that they had come to prize. Mechanical aptitude. Physical strength. Plain endurance. People sold off what land they owned to PharmAgra and signed PharmAgra contracts and turned their full attention to the soil again, with the kind of focus that comes only from desperation. Sharecroppers raising poisoned plants and selling them under contract and buying them back again sterilized. Which left outsiders, those who had once believed in their own potential to rise up and those who now believed no more, to suffer and weaken and perish. The time of the Great Dying. At least here in the North some survived, for there were cities to supply. The South was different. The South took it harder and the South died faster. Ruined not by aggression but by neglect.

Weller and Penny walked on. Over collapsed highways and around treacherous sinkholes and across wide intersections dotted with cars and trucks that had been left where they stood when the last of the gas in their tanks had run out. Rusted hulks propped on bare axles in little shining pools of shattered glass. They walked down railroad tracks and through switching yards jammed with railcars of every description, most of them lived-in at one time or another but all of them empty now. Weller telling his child that once upon a time people and goods had ridden these rails to pretty much everywhere. Children have big imaginations, but she couldn't imagine that.

They heard Ninety-Five before they saw it. The familiar roar of trucks, echoing down these empty canyons. The land was flat here, flatter than back home, and the road was elevated. They saw it first from between rows of buildings that might have been either commercial or industrial, it was hard to say. There was no indication other than a number of scarred places high up on certain walls where signage had been taken down a long time ago. Salvaged for glass and metal and plastics. Plastics that had become as precious as gemstones for a little while, back when the factories that made them were closed for good.

*

Every National Motors highway had a checkpoint every fifty miles. More regular than the old rest stops had been and existing for a different reason. There was nothing about them of rest or convenience. Just a McDonald's counter and restrooms with one or two shower stalls smelling of bleach. A single diesel pump out front. Otherwise it was all company business. Scanners and cameras and men with guns. Building these checkpoints out here on this regular plan had been trivial once the suburbs were empty. Zoning. There wasn't any zoning. Not in the Zone.

They drew near to the highway not far past a checkpoint and walked along on the southbound side for a little, hearing the trucks rumble overhead, watching for a place where they might find access. A grassy berm leading up. Everything was fenced. National Motors fences with that big red star logo. Weller found an accessible place just far enough from the checkpoint but not too far, and he scrambled up with Penny right behind him. He knelt by the fence to open his bag for the wirecutters. One eye on the road. The spot was narrow and Penny stood beside him and a truck appeared in the distance and they dropped down flat in the tall grass. Invisible enough, since the truck didn't slow or stop or sound its air horn. He got to his knees and put out his hand to steady himself on the chain link and as he touched it voltage ran through his body. Not enough to kill anybody but enough to discourage an ordinary man. He sat dazed. Shook himself. Told Penny to go back down into the swale. Wait there. Don't touch anything. Then he cut strips from the blue plastic tarp for insulation and doubled them over and doubled them over again and used them to grip the wirecutters. There was still current coming through, but not so much. A buzzing. He made a line of cuts and turned to look at Penny looking back at him. Trying to. He was certainly just a blur against the sun. Her own father just a blur. He turned back and made more cuts and pushed the fencing back and called her up and had her hug herself and put her through. The needle's eye.

The very first truck to come along stopped to pick them up. Weller holding his daughter in the crook of his elbow and sticking out a thumb the old way. That big white cat showing on the back of her pack. The truck was barreling south toward the Mason-Dixon line, loaded up and sealed tight. A National Motors truck on a National Motors highway. The driver threw open the passenger door and called down, "Jump in quick, buddy. I'm on a schedule, in case you ain't heard."

His name was Joe and he'd aspired to this job all his life and he loved to talk, which is why he picked them up in the first place. Risking it. Born into a Management family in Queens. His father a doorman in a Manhattan apartment building and his mother a housekeeper and he and his brother both aspiring to hit the road at the first opportunity. Get out. He checked his watch and compared it against a readout on the dashboard and did a quick calculation on his fingers. Stepped on the gas. Watched the speedometer rise, the arrow pointing a few notches past one marker that was bigger than the rest and flagged in bright red. He squinted into the distance and asked Penny if she saw any trucks ahead of them and she smiled and shrugged. Shy and half blind. Weller answered for her. Said no. Nothing as far as he could see and he could see a long way from up here in the cab.

The driver said fine. That was all right by him. He didn't want to be gaining on somebody who was sticking to the rules. Fifty miles an hour come hell or high water, if they'd excuse his French.

Weller tilted his head and looked over at the speedometer. Sixty-five. He said it felt like they were flying. Flying up here in this high cab at this high speed. Flying at *any* speed, come to that.

The driver laughed and said aww, you'll get used to it. He kept it pegged right where it was and checked his watch again and looked at some readouts on the dash. Drove with his tongue between his teeth, concentrating. Counting down after a while and then easing off the pedal and letting the truck slow back down to fifty on its own. Tapping the brakes just once when it got close. Checking everything one last time.

"How about that," he said. "Looks like we'll hit Stamford right on the button. When the time comes I'll give you two the word and you can climb back into the bunk and nobody'll be the wiser." Grinning like he'd gotten away with something, which he had.

He said they used to do this with GPS but the satellites were down half the time now, so that was the end of that. Sunspots or whatever. Maybe they were just wearing out. Did things wear out in space? It didn't seem possible. It wasn't like there was weather up there or anything to bump into. As he understood it, there wasn't even any air. It was a vacuum, like the vacuum inside a can. A vacuum preserved things, didn't it? A week from now this load right here would be divided up into a million vacuum cans and it would last forever.

Like he said, he loved to talk.

Anyway, security just timed you now that they couldn't trust the satellites. Fifty miles in between checkpoints at fifty miles an hour and you'd best be there on the dot. Show up late without a flat tire or something else on that order to show for it, and there'd be hell to pay. Excuse his French.

Weller asked about the truck. A great sleek red Peterbilt as big as a mountain and moving. More than moving. Lapping up the miles. The driver said it was a 387 and it had come off the line in oh-eight, which made it barely broken in, considering. Compared against the other rolling stock out here. Junk on wheels. Antiques held together with bailing twine and chewing gum. This baby had a sleeper in the back and a Cummins engine under the hood with 450 horses pulling. Eighteen forward speeds.

He'd been assigned to her for a long time. It was all about seniority. You minded your business and you rose up through the ranks and your working conditions improved. This truck right here for example. This interior. They called it Prestige Gray. How about that. Some of these young guys out there starting now, he didn't know how they'd ever make it. How they'd stand the conditions day after day and how they'd earn their minimums given the amount of time they spent broken down by the side of the road. Waiting for a tow or whatever.

Penny said her father could help. Her father could fix anything.

The driver said sure. Gave her a pat on the head. Said man oh man I pity the younger generation. Said you two ought to count yourselves lucky for getting a ride with me. Asked where were they going, anyhow?

"New York," said Weller.

The driver shook his head. "I don't get it," he said. "Everybody wants to see New York. Like I said, I grew up around there. Believe me, it ain't worth the trouble."

"In our case, I think it is." Not sure how much he wanted to say.

The driver glanced from the road to Weller. "By the looks of it, you been chased out of nicer places already." Pointing at his own neck to indicate the cut in Weller's. "It ain't none of my business," he said, "but without ID, you won't get very far."

"I've never had ID. Born and raised in the Zone."

If the driver was surprised he didn't show it. He didn't recoil the way some might have. He just drove on. "Worse luck for you," he said after a minute. "If I had time to slow down again between here and Stamford I'd let you off. Send you back home before you get yourself shot or something."

Penny's eyes got big.

"Not shot. I didn't mean shot. That's a figure of speech." He put out a hand and Penny retreated into her father's arms. "You know what a figure of speech is, honey?"

Nothing.

"All I mean is it's a tough town. Tough on strangers. Tough on generics."

Weller opened his pack and dug around. Located the Polaroid picture and showed it. He said they weren't entirely strangers. Not to everybody in New York.

"Jesus," said the trucker. "That was you?"

"Yes sir, it was."

"Honest? Holy shit. I mean *holy shit*. That was all over the news."

"Really."

"Everywhere. The TV news. That was a close call, buddy."

"It wasn't such a big deal. A bent sway bar. A couple of loose bolts."

"Not for them. I mean a close call for *you*. They'd scrambled Black Rose, for Christ's sake. They were in the air."

"I guess."

"Oh, yeah. They were on their way, and those old boys don't leave much behind when they're finished, if you get my drift." Tilting his head toward Penny. Emphasizing what he wasn't saying.

"So I've heard."

"Man oh man. You're one lucky guy."

"Let's hope it holds." Looking at the Polaroid one more time and then sliding it into his pocket. "Carmichael said he owes me one."

"He said that, did he?"

"He did."

"Well."

"I mean to call in the favor. Get her some help with her eyes." Penny on his lap, settling back.

The driver nodded, noncommittal. "That'd sure be nice," he said. "Those boys do have all the good doctors sewn up. In a manner of speaking." Fingering his neck. "Did you know they keep all their records on board these days? Right here? It's the latest thing. Myself, I've just got the regular financial chip. Company issued. ID, banking and like that. I've been saving for an upgrade, but you know how that goes."

"I guess I do."

"Money's always tight."

"If you've got any at all."

"Them what has, gets."

"Don't I know it." Bouncing Penny a little. "That's why we're going to see that Mr. Carmichael, isn't it, honey? Because he's the one who can help if anybody can. And he made us a promise."

The driver studied the road. "One thing you learn growing up Management," he said after a little.

"What's that?"

"Ownership's got a real short memory."

They rode along quietly for a while. The driver lighting up a cigarette and opening the window. The occasional crackle of a voice over the CB radio until he turned it off. Weller taking Penny's head softly between his hands and turning it to point out landmarks along the highway. That's the mouth of a river emptying into the sound. That used to be a railroad bridge. Those big towers marching along one after another used to carry electricity. Electricity in cables strung from one to the next like a cat's cradle.

They drew near a bridge with a double row of red lights blinking overhead as if somebody had won a jackpot. The driver nodded toward it, his face reflecting the red lights. "Security breach," he said. "They know you're in here. Not you exactly. But they know somebody's in here who shouldn't be." Nodding like it gave him satisfaction. Like he took a little pride in it. The truck passing under the bridge now and the lights gone.

Weller tightened his grip on Penny. "So what's next." Thinking how he'd cut that electrical fence. That was it. That was how they knew.

"Next? Nothing. Nothing's next. People keep an eye out is all." Looking straight ahead. Driving. Checking his mirrors with the lights fading behind. "You'll be on your own after the GWB," he said after a while. "I go west and you go east."

"The GWB."

"The bridge. The George Washington Bridge. They closed all the tunnels down a few years back and there's just the two bridges anymore. Brooklyn and the GWB. I'll drop you on the Jersey side, and after that you're on your own."

"We'll take our chances."

"I guess you will," he said. And then, as if he'd just woken up to it, "Next stop, Stamford. Everybody into the back."

*

There was a narrow closet alongside the bunk and they barely fit into it. Shoved their packs into a compartment overhead and squeezed themselves into the little closet at an angle, Weller first and Penny after. Penny acting like it was a game but a serious one. Weller realizing as he pulled the door shut that whatever happened next was going to be up to the driver and the driver alone. Wondering what he'd gotten himself into.

The truck went over some kind of grating and just about shook itself to pieces. The driver turned on the CB radio again and they heard a few stuttering bursts of a voice they couldn't make out. Just barking. They passed over some more grates and then slowed to a stop and then everything was quiet for the longest time. Only the engine idling and some kind of regular beeping noise coming muffled through the window. Now and then the idle rising and the truck bumping forward and stopping again. Air brakes.

They moved a little and the engine noise got louder without getting faster and Weller figured they'd gone under some kind of portico. Everything sounded closer. He could hear something from under the hood knocking in a metallic way he hadn't heard before, as if the sound were bouncing off a wall and being clarified. Bouncing off concrete or tile or something else hard. Penny turned and started talking in his ear and he hushed her. Wait. This is where things happen. Bad things maybe if we're not quiet. The sound of the engine getting louder yet as the driver opened his window and then a short conversation made entirely of shouting. Pleasantries if you could shout pleasantries. Two professionals going back and forth and then they were done and the window went up and the sound died back and the driver began working the gears.

Weller didn't open the closet door until they were back up to speed. Penny squeezed out and threw herself down on the unmade bed and made angels in the sheets. Weller had her get up. Took her bag down and pushed it through and sent her after it and came himself. Saying it had occurred to him at the last minute that they might get weighed and what then. With these trailers sealed up the way they were somebody must know every load down to the ounce and they could calculate the weight of the diesel fuel and the consumption rate of it and that would mean his own weight would show up. What then. What then, with those flashing red lights and all.

The driver laughed and put the radio back on low. He said there was a time when they used to weigh everything, but not now. Half the scales were broken and the other half didn't work. It didn't matter anyway. These trailers were sealed up so tight that you couldn't get anything in or out if you tried, and as he'd seen they kept the drivers on a short rope. Punching that clock. You'd have to work pretty hard to try anything funny, and there'd have to be a pretty big payoff. Rubbing his fingers together indicating cash money, even though Management didn't have any legal use for it these days. Everything went onto your brand. That old data stream. Some things died hard, though, and rubbing your fingers together still said money.

Weller had U.S. cash in his pocket from when he'd left home and he sat there now thinking how useless it was here on this road. Pretty much foreign currency anywhere but in the Zone. Not even that. He had half of everything he owned in the whole world folded up right here, and it wasn't enough to reward this driver for giving them a lift. For keeping his mouth shut instead of handing them over to security back at the Stamford checkpoint. He bet there'd have been a reward in that. Those flashing lights and all. People keeping their eyes open. There'd been a reward and the truck driver had foregone it out of kindness. It was a debt that he could never repay, and he said so.

The driver said oh, don't worry about that. The reward wasn't all that much anyhow. Plus it was his pleasure to break the rules every now and then, as long as it was for a good cause. That old cowboy ethic that lived on in the hearts of truck drivers everywhere. He lit up another cigarette and cracked the window. Why, it was practically a tradition.

Weller watched him smoke and got an idea. The tobacco. He dug in his pack and located the bundle and worked it open. Peeled the top couple of leaves free. *Don't spend it all in one place,* she'd said. Good advice. He pulled those two fragile leaves out and sealed the bundle back up again and closed his pack down tight over it. Caught the driver's eye with the flash of the aluminum foil but hadn't meant to. He lifted the tobacco up into the light. "Hey," he said. "I brought you a little present."

Even if the driver was a man who'd seen it all, he hadn't seen this. Not by the look on his face. Shock and fear and greed all mingled together. He shook his head. "I thought it was all about the girl," he said. "I thought you were doing it for her."

"I am. Just like I said."

"Then what's with this?"

"It was a gift."

"A gift."

"That's right. And now I'm giving it to you."

"Nobody gives that stuff away."

"I'm giving it to you."

The driver checked his mirrors as if somebody might be gaining on him. Reached over and switched off the radio as if somebody might be listening in. "I can't take it," he said. "I appreciate it, but I can't."

"Can't or won't."

"Won't."

"They tell me it's first-rate." Running the leaves between his thumb and his forefinger. "I wouldn't know anything about it myself, but that's what they tell me."

"I'm sure it is."

"The real thing. Disengineered. It's worth a fortune."

"You're not kidding about that." The driver tilted his head to the right. The backpack. "How much you got in there?"

"Some. I didn't ask. A couple of pounds maybe." Smoothing the leaves on his knee. "They just gave it to me."

"How come? How come they gave it to you? How come *who* gave it to you?"

"Some people. Some people I did a little bit of work for." Thinking maybe he ought to leave it at that.

"Look here," the driver said. Poking at the red National Motors star on his blue overalls. "If I didn't work for who I work for, I might think about it. God knows I could use the dough. But they look at us awful close. Blood samples. Urine samples. Those full-body scanners from the airports? Guess who bought them when the FAA shut down."

Weller was already opening his pack, starting to put the tobacco away. "I'm sorry," he said.

"I'm telling you. My uniform comes in with so much as *smoke* from that stuff on it, the guys in the laundry'll turn me in. I've seen it happen."

"I had no idea," Weller said.

"National Motors does a whole lot of business with PharmAgra. And one thing PharmAgra hates is competition."

"I didn't mean any harm. I've made a mistake."

"You sure have." His breath coming hard.

"I'm sorry."

"Forget it. Just close that up now and forget it. We'll be all right."

Weller finished putting the tobacco away and strapped the pack shut again, and the driver took his eyes off the road for a long time to watch it go.

*

Manhattan, the eternal city. As great an astonishment to Weller as it was to his child. Greater, because the details of it were visible. The commercial and residential buildings of Washington Heights finer than anything he had imagined, packed tight against one another and merging together in some places and grander than the grandest of palaces, surely home to a race of kings. The riverside expanse of Highbridge Park, its flood of lush unstoppable green creeping outward and encroaching on entire neighborhoods and consuming them. Highway ramps and overpasses demolished one after another at some point in human memory, their concrete pulverized and their iron beams crumpled, as if some vast power had blockaded the city in preparation for laying siege to it.

And in the distance, off to the south, wonders even greater. The towers of midtown, appearing through low clouds shot through with sun and vanishing again veiled.

Ninety-Five became the George Washington Bridge and leapt skyward, soaring over the Hudson River toward the high wall of the Palisades. Leaving New York without ever penetrating it. The driver said sorry folks, but there was only one way into the city from here and you had to go through Jersey whether you liked it or not. It was a disgrace but there it was.

The traffic picked up. A sign overhead directing it all through a security checkpoint.

Weller pointed. "I thought they were every fifty miles."

"Every now and then they'll make an exception. It's the big city. What do you expect."

Weller stood up and took their packs and angled Penny through the passageway. Saying, "How far until we get off?"

"Not far. Just as soon as we're in the clear." The driver braked and signaled and merged right. Flashing lights hanging down from steel beams and signs saying *Be Prepared to Stop.* "There's a footpath leads down to a sidewalk under the bridge. People take it over. People who work out here. Hell of a view, they say, if you can stand looking."

Air horns and air brakes and the shuddering of engines throttling down. They slipped into the narrow closet. It wouldn't be far now. Not even a mile.

The driver put the radio on, the regular radio since there were still a couple of stations broadcasting in New York. One news station and one oldies. The oldies weren't old enough to suit him, so he switched over to the news. RealNews, reporting live from their headquarters at the stock exchange. AmeriBank owned RealNews and AmeriBank held Manhattan like an occupying army, from the Hudson to the East River, from Spuyten Duyvil to Battery Park. Right down to the stock exchange proper, barricaded on all sides like the island itself. Ramparts within ramparts.

The smell of diesel exhaust found its way into the cab and penetrated the closet, and the truck slowed to a stop. The wait stretched on and on. Weller didn't know how many lanes they had, but there weren't enough. He coughed in the dark and Penny put her little hands over his mouth. He held her closer. Thinking if they started feeling sleepy it would be the exhaust, and wondering which way to die would be the worse of the two. Carbon monoxide or security. He decided security. Getting caught would be worse than just going to sleep. Going to sleep right here just the two of them nice and easy, even though they were this close to the end. Even though they'd come this far. *With your shield or on it,* the way he'd left home against Liz's will. He thought of her bereft and he told himself that he was being morose and he pushed the image out of his mind. Picturing New York instead. Picturing everything that lay before them. The walk back across the Hudson and the descent into the city streets and the search for Carmichael. Focusing his attention where it needed to be. He let Liz back in again later, but not in the same way. Imagining all three of them at home this time, at home just like before but better. All three of them restored and forgiven.

He heard the driver curse this damned traffic and switch on the CB radio and talk with someone. He felt the truck begin to move. Slow straining motions that skewed both side to side and forward, as if they were leaving this lane for another. Air horns. Then he felt the engine rev and the transmission found a different gear and the truck began pulling steadily forward. He whispered to Penny here we go. This is it.

The familiar sequence of sounds from before. Air brakes. Trucks starting and stopping. Hard echoes of the engine under a portico, and the window going down, and men shouting back and forth. Then a change. Different sounds coming rapidly, one after another. The engine shutting down with a noise like chains falling. A door swinging open on hinges that needed oil. The low voices of men rising up and the scrambling of boots on perforated steel and the abrupt striking of metal on metal. Bodies colliding.

Two rapid bangs at the closet door ended it. Bangs harder than the knocking of any fist and more insistent. Beyond denial and past resistance. A voice saying come out. Hands up and come out. Weller shouldered the door open and would have raised his hands but he had Penny, so she raised hers for both of them. Emerging through the little closet door. Lifted up in the shield of her father's arms.

*

They already had the driver on the ground. Face down on the pavement with a boot on his neck. National Motors security in dull black serge and shiny black leather, blacks the color of oil and fresh macadam and night. Gleaming helmets with visors that dropped down over their eyes rendering them inscrutable. They stood in a rough circle, with handguns drawn and other guns drawn too and a taser that one of them was making use of. The driver jumping. One of the security men was asking him questions he couldn't answer but that didn't stop the one with the taser. The one asking the questions said knock it off and he did and the driver quit jumping but not right away.

Weller kept Penny's face pressed to his shoulder. Walking past the circle of men. Not exactly walking but shoved. Shoved up against the wall and made to wait and hearing the one who was asking the driver questions ask about exactly where he had picked up the two of them. Which mile marker and how near to that cut in the fence. Saying of course he'd seen it, hadn't he. Hadn't he. That hole. He knew all about that hole, didn't he. Asking about why he'd concealed the man and the girl in Stamford only to turn them in here and asking about how long he'd been in the habit of carrying contraband. Carrying smugglers carrying contraband. Smugglers with children for Christ's sake. Asking questions for which there was no answer except greed. Saying all right go on hit him with that taser again if you're so handy with it. Do you both some good.

Weller stood holding Penny tight. Thinking they wanted him to witness this.

The line of trucks kept on passing. Not one of the drivers even looked.

One of the security men lifted his visor and took Penny's chin in a gloved hand and tilted her face away from her father's chest and told her not to worry about a thing. She was going to take a trip to the big city. See the sights. Penny howled, snatched her face away and buried it again, and not one of the men who were gathered around the driver so much as turned to see what the trouble was. Not one of them even flinched at the howling of that child. It was their training. Some of them were old Black Rose and some of them were from other private military outfits, outfits that had specialized in work that Black Rose had found unprofitable. Either way they were all cashed-out with their immunity intact, immunity from prosecution that went all the way back to the Iraq war when things had gotten simpler. When you could run an army like a business for a change. Immunity was a retirement benefit that didn't cost anybody anything. Not like a pension. A pension cost money. And who needed a pension anyhow, when you could always find work.

Weller turned away from the hard man. Just a few degrees. Still almost flat against the wall but keeping himself between the man and his daughter as best he could or at least suggesting that that was his intent. Drawing a line. The man gave him that inch or two and then he leaned over and whispered in his ear. Saying, "That sonofabitch driver works for the same company I do. And you see how much he's worth."

Two of the men raised the driver to his feet. He hung between them, defeated and limp. Not even looking up. They sat him on a curb and one of them knelt beside him and drew a knife from a holster at his ankle. Raised it to the driver's neck. The other not even holding him down. Not restraining him in any way. Not having to. Just standing with his arms crossed, watching. The one with the knife raised it to the driver's neck and held it there and the tiny pressure of the point of it was enough to keep the driver settled as he felt around the flesh of his neck with two fingers of his other hand. He decided on a spot. Took hold. Pushed the tip of the blade against the driver's windpipe and turned it a quarter turn. levering it. Blood and gristle popping out and behind that something silver. His one hand was busy holding the driver's neck and his other hand was busy with the knife so he jerked his head to lift his visor and bent forward and took the brand in his teeth. Leaned back and grinned around it for his buddy and let the driver go. The driver slumped over and he rose up. Sucked the little piece of silver metal clean and spat it into his free hand.

He wiped both sides of the knife blade on the driver's overalls and checked the knife all over and wiped one side again and put it away. Fastidious. "This'll do," he said. Checking the brand. Shaking his head disgusted. "You're free to go."

It didn't even register with the driver. The loss of everything. The loss of himself.

The man at Weller's shoulder said, "Be glad you're not one of ours. Be glad PharmAgra's got that bounty on runners. All of a sudden you're worth something."

FIVE:

One Police Plaza

They plunged down into the city as into a canyon. Weller and Penny in the back seat behind thick glass scratched opaque. Holes drilled through it for ventilation. They could hear the men talking up front and bolts of radio traffic like electricity made audible. One man wondering what caused that sonofabitch to change his mind anyhow. To come all the way from Connecticut and just about get through the toughest checkpoint there is and change his mind at the last minute. Give up this runner and his load of tobacco and have the nerve to ask for the reward. The chutzpah. The other one saying maybe they'd had a fight. There's no honor among thieves is there. More bolts of radio noise coming and going. The first one saying it'll serve that sonofabitch right anyhow. That's the last time he'll ferry a runner. Those radio noises again, hurting Penny's ears.

The car bounded down the devastated street. Deep potholes in Washington Heights and Harlem and the suspension shot a long time ago. An armored Crown Vic, two tons of reinforced steel and bulletproof glass and hard-muscled men lurching toward Central National Park.

"Look," said Weller. Above the engine roar and the complaint of the springs and the hard noise from the radio. Pointing out the window. "Look up."

She did.

A high framework of rusted steel draped with wire mesh netting. Above the trees. Above everything. The ghost of some circus big top with birds fluttering against it. "Pigeons," he said. They looked like gray scraps of newspaper torn and rainsoaked and dried out again by such sun as could

64

reach this deep. Floating skyward on wind. Weller asked himself how long it would take before they quit trying. How long it had been and how long it would take. Generations. Forever, maybe. Not just one bird but the whole species.

Penny just marveled, twisting in her seat and craning her neck. What it looked like to her he didn't know. Just shapes moving. Just shapes moving in the sky. That alone was miracle enough.

They kept going south and the neighborhoods got better and the street smoothed out. Brownstones fronting the park. Management doormen standing on sidewalks in the dappled sun and cars coming and going, small cars and large cars and great long legendary limousines piloted by Management drivers in snap-brim hats. Now and then an old bus of the same vintage, hard used, roaring away from the curb blowing diesel smoke and coughing. It went on for block after block after block with the park opposite, sealed off tight behind wire fences and steel beams and iron bars upright in a line. Razor wire in coils stretched out.

There was a gate near the southernmost end, with a big brushed steel circle suspended over it. So big that Penny pointed it out and said, "O. Does that mean Open?" The car waiting at a light.

Her father hadn't even seen it as a letter. Just a huge circle of steel. Some kind of municipal sculpture. There were people passing beneath it, though, a thin line of people moving through a tall marble archway carved with the likenesses of wild animals in high relief. Bears and beavers and moose. Salmon leaping from cascades of water. There must have been a scanner concealed among the carvings, because each person in the line assumed a certain head-up stance as he drew near. Almost unconscious but not quite. A cheerful man dressed in camouflage greeted them as they came, welcoming them to the park, handing out printed maps. The black pistol at his hip conspicuous but untouched. No need for it. The park was Ownership only, and everybody knew it.

"*O is for Open*," said one of the men in the front seat. "That's a good one."

"Goddamn generics," said the other. The one driving. "You never know what you'll hear." The light changed and a cloud of messengers on bicycles ran it from the right and he hit the gas.

*

One Police Plaza was still One Police Plaza even though the police were long gone. It had become a kind of neutral ground for competing security forces. The place where exchanges got made and information got shared if it got shared at all. Shared or sold or bartered, depending.

The building itself was a great brutal square of raw concrete jutting up near the foot of the Brooklyn Bridge. As complex and varied within as it was plain without. A claustrophobic tangle of hallways and offices and conference rooms. Laboratories and closets and narrow chambers whose uses remained unknown or at least unstated. Long rooms doubled by one-way glass and secret rooms kept dark.

Black Rose had the first five floors and they ran the parking garage and the helipad and the security all around. Nobody came or went without their approval. AmeriBank security had the top floor and the one below that, New York being their city. PharmAgra had the better part of a floor all to themselves, and National Motors shared one with Family Health Partnership if you could call it sharing. A wall of concrete and glass block dividing the two, and scanners mounted on either side. Not even using the same scanner. Not even that much trust between them.

Weller and his daughter sat in a locked room. One table three feet on a side bolted to the floor and a chair bolted down on each side of it. Weller sitting in one chair and Penny sitting on his lap. The afternoon draining away.

She said, "Will that bad man come here?"

"What bad man is that?"

"The man from the school."

"No. He won't come here."

"I didn't like him."

"Neither did I. But he's not coming here. There'll be some other men we probably won't like much either, but he won't be one of them."

She said, "Are those other two coming back?"

"Probably. Maybe."

"What do they want?"

"I was carrying something I shouldn't have been carrying."

"Tobacco," she nodded.

"Right."

"Tobacco is bad for you." Still nodding.

"I know. They think I was smuggling it. Do you know what that means?"

"I do. But you were only carrying it."

"They don't see the difference as plainly as you do, I'm afraid."

"Tell them."

"I will."

"Tell them why we're here."

"I will."

"Tell them why we left home."

"I'll do my best. I promise."

"I know."

They waited. Lights burned yellow in the hallway, visible through steel mesh embedded in a square glass window. They heard footsteps come and go but they didn't see anyone.

After a while the two men came back and a third man with them. The third one was older and impatient. Broad-shouldered in spite of his age and narrow at the waist and disdainful of them all. Not just of Weller and Penny but of the other men too. He was taller than either of them by a head and his uniform was different. The same design but not made in the same way. It was custom and it fit him like the skin of a horse fits a horse and he looked as if he had been born for the purpose of wearing it.

The one who'd done the driving lifted Penny from her father's lap while the other one bound Weller's hands behind his back. As if he might try something right here in One Police Plaza of all places. The tall man shook his head at the idiocy of bothering. Told them to come.

Down the hall and down other halls. Through checkpoints and turn-stiles and tight clusters of armed men. The tall man led the way and he said just the bare minimum to anyone they met if he spoke at all. At the end of one hallway he unlocked a steel door and threw it open to a set of concrete stairs going down and they passed through one at a time. First the tall man and then Penny and then the one who'd done the driving and then Weller. The first three passed all right but a klaxon sounded when Weller's turn came. Not on Penny's turn. The scanner was mounted at neck height and she undershot it, and if there was a scale in the floor she was too small to register. As if she were a mail cart or something. But a klaxon sounded when her father came through and red lights they hadn't even noticed high on the walls began strobing like it was the end of the world. Like every-body had better get out while the getting was good.

The tall man snarled at the driver and backed up. Pushed Weller aside and got in front of the scanner and waited there showing himself to it until the pattern of the alarm slowed and the flashing of the lights slowed and a little metallic square mounted alongside the door began to glow green. His presence calming the circuitry. He put his thumb on the little green square and held it there until the lights quit flashing and the alarm died, and then he kept it there while Weller and the other man went through. Looking like he wanted to push both of them down the stairs or raise his pistol and shoot them dead and let them fall because it would require less effort,.

The door at the bottom of the stairs was painted with the wheat-stalk logo. The stylized suggestion of amber waves. Behind it was a figure in full camouflage, a patch of that PharmAgra brown and green visible through a reinforced glass window. The well-known brown and green that drew a snicker from the man behind Weller. Like what kind of bumpkin wore an outfit like that. And even when the door swung open and the man behind it turned out to be bigger than any two ordinary men and armed with sufficient firepower to level One Police Plaza and the camouflage he was wearing wasn't a regular uniform at all but a hazmat suit with dual air tanks on the back and a helmet like a diving bell, the last man kept that amused look on his face. Like he was born to it the way the tall man was born to wear his uniform.

They handed them over. The one man removing Weller's handcuffs as roughly as he possibly could. Making a show of it. The tall man taking a manila envelope from the man in the hazmat suit and unsealing it and signing three copies of something. Keeping two and handing one over. Then they went back up the stairs toward the locked door. The door with the big red National Motors star on it. The tall man unlocked it and another one drew it open and they all passed on through.

*

The man in the hazmat suit didn't say a word from inside his diving bell. He probably couldn't have made himself heard if he'd tried, but they were at the end of a long corridor and the door was sealed behind them so there was only one way to go. They went. Warnings on the walls about contamination and a red stripe down the middle of the floor and that individual in the hazmat suit breathing air that hissed in and out.

They came to a double sliding glass door with another double sliding glass door behind it and a space in between. A clean and shining space paved all over with stainless steel. The first set of doors opened and they went in and the doors closed again leaving the man in the hazmat suit be-hind. A rushing of air in the little stainless steel chamber. Weller's ears popped. Penny put her hands up to hers and her father said swallow, swal-low hard, and she did but it didn't help. The other doors opened up and they stepped through into a brightly lit room all white porcelain and smoked glass. A steel table in the center with their packs on it sealed inside transparent green plastic. The doors hissed shut behind them and they sat down because what else was there to do. Plus the air in here felt thin and Weller couldn't quite get enough of it. He felt a little dizzy. He was glad to see the packs anyway. It was a positive step.

Penny laughed, pointing to the big white cat encased in green plastic. "Poor kitty," she said. Weller didn't laugh because he felt a little bit light-headed. He thought he felt pretty much like that suffocating white cat in this airless room. Penny wasn't much troubled, but he was.

A screen that occupied the better part of one wall buzzed to life. That low piercing hum that intrudes into a room once and then disappears. The image bloomed and became a person moving. Just from the shoulders up. A woman looking downward and handling something out of sight. Adjust-ing papers maybe. She was half again as big as life, and Penny sat trans-fixed. As if she were looking through a window into some bigger world. Some world lived in by giants. The woman was dressed in camouflage and she wore the PharmAgra wheat-stalk logo on her collar. Her brown hair was pulled back tight. She looked up from her papers as if she were as sur-prised to see Weller and his daughter as they were to see her. Surprised and angry about it. She jerked her head to the side and looked out of the frame and opened her mouth and the image died.

"That's a television," Weller said.

"I know."

"A working one."

"I know."

"The one we have might work, I think, but there's nothing to watch."

"Could she see us?"

"I think so. I think she could. That's not like regular television, though. Regular television was just for watching. Like watching a puppet show or something."

Penny leaned forward in her chair and kept her eyes fixed on the screen, waiting. Her hands reaching out unconsciously to the green plastic film covering her backpack. Touching it and her fingernails seeking out edges and wrinkled places as if she would tear it off if she could without even thinking. Recover what they'd taken from her.

Her father put out a hand and said she'd better not do that just yet. Leave it alone until we know what's next. What these folks have in mind.

The television woke up again and this time the woman wasn't adjusting her papers anymore. She was done with all that and focused on what she had to say. She was looking straight at them and she didn't look happy. At them or at anybody. She didn't look like the kind of person who was ever happy.

She said welcome to PharmAgra.

Neither Weller nor Penny made any answer. They just sat. A person who would say such a ridiculous thing might say anything at all and they needed to be on the lookout. Even a child could tell that.

She said she could see them perfectly well on her monitor and asked if they could see her on theirs, and Penny said yes. The woman on the screen said that was good. That was fine. They could proceed, then. She tilted her head just a little to one side and asked if they knew why they were here. Speaking to them as if they were both children. Something below children. Lowering herself to do it.

Weller said look, it was all a mistake.

She said one thing at a time please. The way she might say it to a child. She asked again if they knew why they were here.

"Because I had a little tobacco in my bag," Weller said.

She corrected him. There was something of the schoolmarm about her. *"Disengineered* tobacco," she said.

"Disengineered tobacco," he said.

"This is all going on the record," she said.

"So I would imagine," he said. "But I can explain."

"I'm sure you can."

He reached out to Penny and half expected the woman on the screen to tell him not to do it, but she didn't object. He rested his hand on his daughter's shoulder and she leaned forward on the table, looking at the picture of the white cat. Bored with the screen already or at least done with the woman on it. "I can explain why I had it with me," he said.

"I don't care why you had it with you."

"I can explain how I got it."

"I don't care how you got it."

He'd begun to perspire. His breath coming harder. Looking at his daughter and seeing her yawning with her head on the table and then looking up at the woman on the screen. "I can tell you who gave it to me," he said. Thinking he'd turn in that old Black Rose renegade. He had the scar in his neck to prove they'd gotten into it. He could say they'd had a falling out. That whatever agreement there'd been between them was spent.

"You'd tell me the name of your supplier, would you?"

"I would."

"No sale." She shook her head. "If he were on the books, we'd know from his accounts that something was irregular and we'd be onto him already. But we're not, which means he's a generic like you. Do you know what I mean when I say that? When I say 'generic'?"

"I do."

"You people are a goddamn enforcement nightmare."

"I'm sorry."

"When you tell me you'll give up your supplier," she said, "what you mean is you'll give me a name I can't possibly use." Not talking to him like a child anymore. "Will it be a real name? Maybe. Who cares, as long as I can't find the person it belongs to."

Weller looked down. "It's all I've got," he said. "I'd hoped maybe—"

"You can hope all you want, but don't hope for a second that you're smarter than I am."

The screen cut out.

They sat. They sat for an hour or more and nothing changed. There was a rest room off to one side, with the same porcelain and smoked glass as everywhere else, and each of them used it. Then they kept waiting. It got hard to judge the passing of time.

The screen came on again.

The woman on it said in case they were wondering, she wasn't in any hurry.

The screen cut out again.

Penny said she was hungry. Her father said he wasn't surprised. He was, too. He was hungry and exhausted and short of breath but he didn't say all that. She said there was food in his pack unless someone had taken it out. She said please.

He tore open the seal and pulled his pack out of its green plastic film. The film was light as air and it slid off the table and fluttered toward a vent in the wall and climbed up to it as if by magic. Or something feigning magic. Fishline. It crawled up the wall and found the vent and stuck there. Penny ran to it but stopped running about halfway and walked the rest. Listless in the thin air. Her father searched the packs. Nothing was where he'd left it although everything was intact, everything except the foil package of tobacco. He looked up to watch Penny taking the green film in her fists and walking back a few feet with it and letting it fly. He said will you look at that. Understanding why it was hard to breathe.

He let Penny play with the green film for a few minutes and then he asked her if he could give something a try. She was tired anyhow so she let him. He took the film and went to the vent and flattened the film against it. Covering the whole thing. The air in the room didn't get any better but it quit getting any worse. They ate and they drank some water from the sink in the rest room and they waited until the screen cut back in.

The woman said once more did they know why they were here.

Weller said that tobacco.

She said use your head. She said remember what happened to that truck driver. She asked why did Weller think the same thing hadn't happened to him.

Because he was generic already, he said. You couldn't get any lower.

"Don't bet on it," she said.

Weller thought the screen might cut out again but it didn't.

She said the problem was that those drivers never knew a damned thing. There was no way they could. National Motors put the screws to them twenty-four hours a day. If they got mixed up in smuggling, all it amounted to was picking up some stranger on the highway and giving him a lift. She said what she needed to know was what Weller knew and the driver didn't. Exactly *where* he'd gotten the tobacco. Not names, because names didn't matter. What mattered was the lay of the land. Secret places he knew that nobody else did. And all he'd have to do was lead some people out there.

Weller didn't say anything. He couldn't very well lead anybody to that old elementary school with the fallout shelter underneath it. That was a dead end.

She said he was a lucky man because if he played his cards right, his daughter would make it home alive. He might not, she had to be honest about that. There might be something different in store for him. But his daughter would be all right. That made him a lucky man.

Weller said wait.

She smiled hard.

Weller put his hands on the table and folded them. He drew breath.

She kept smiling but it changed a little. Like she hadn't expected it to go this easily and now here it was. Like now she'd be able to get off work on time. It was an easy smile with some humanity behind it, and Weller saw the difference.

He said, "My daughter has to come first."

She said, "I know that."

He said, "I'm only here on account of her."

She said, "Don't bullshit me." Her smile going away.

"Honest. I didn't mean to get mixed up in that business. I didn't. I didn't think."

"You didn't think you'd get caught."

"I didn't think period." Unfolding his hands and reaching into his pocket for the picture. Taking it out and holding it in his cupped hand. He and Carmichael in the middle of the scene, on the bumper of that yellow Hummer, side by side like equals. "I'm here to see Mr. Anderson Carmichael is all. He's going to help my daughter."

The woman gave a look like now she'd heard everything. Like she'd been waiting her whole life to hear everything and now she had. Now she could die happy. She looked away and reached off-screen and looked back. A low noise beginning to rumble beneath the floor.

"He said he owed me a favor," Weller said, "and I'm here to take him up on it."

The green film against the vent began to stir like it was alive. Like it was alive but dying. Holes appearing in it where the grates were sharp and bits of it coming away and getting sucked in. Weller's breath came harder. Penny put a hand to her throat. Just like that. That quickly.

"You people," the woman said. "We keep the air pressure low in there so contamination won't filter out. Stray genetic material from whatever you're carrying. It's a safety precaution."

Weller tried to breathe but couldn't.

"It's also good for other things," she said.

Penny lay her head down on the table and yawned and closed her eyes.

Weller didn't speak. He lifted up the photograph and held it with one hand but one hand wasn't enough to keep it up. A single square of paper that heavy. He set it on top of his daughter's backpack and brought up the other hand and steadied it. Both hands shaking. The air from this sealed room bubbling out of an iron pipe in a rock wall somewhere beneath the East River. Everything he had bubbling out with it. Everything he was.

"Come in closer on that," the woman said. But not to him.

*

Up on the big screen, Anderson Carmichael was wearing a tuxedo. He looked frustrated. The image was wobbly. He was standing in a wide hallway somewhere with brocade curtains and flocked wallpaper. Soft lights high overhead casting long shadows and showering down trails of light like coins falling. Chandeliers. They flickered past every now and then when the camera moved and Carmichael jerked out of the frame and something else took his place. Chandeliers and carpet and people moving. A red sign lit up reading EXIT.

Weller had just about come around.

Music was playing, a big sound filtered down tight through some little microphone and coming out all scratchy in this hard room of glass and tile.

Penny was standing over by the vent picking up and dropping the green plastic film to no avail, now that the vent was off. She asked her father if he was done with his nap and he said he was. She asked what happened to the lady on the television and he said he didn't know.

On the screen Carmichael disappeared and everything went black, but the sounds kept up. The music a little bit muffled and something rubbing like fabric now and metallic sounds as well. Carmichael's voice saying excuse me excuse me excuse me. Then the picture coming back and everything pinwheeling around all at once. Creamy tile and red marble black as blood. Harsher light. Carmichael in the frame against white tile steadying what must have been his phone against a wall or a door. His voice echoing. *"You have no idea,"* he said.

Weller didn't know whether to be thrilled or alarmed.

"It seems you're being auctioned off," Carmichael said. Staring right through Weller. "Somebody thought I might be interested."

"I'm glad to hear you were," said Weller. Hardly believing but believing anyhow. A dream come true.

"I didn't say that. I didn't say I was interested." Sounds echoing from his end of the connection. Men coughing and water running. "Honestly," he said. "You people."

"But."

"You people have no idea. *Rigoletto* starts in five minutes and I get this call and I take it because somebody's assistant tells my assistant it's important."

Weller opened his mouth.

"They tell me a friend of mine has run up against PharmAgra security. PharmAgra wants to talk to me about money and I say hell no, patch me through to my friend, and this is what I get. You. Unbelievable."

Weller said, "You remember me, though."

"I don't mind saying I feel badly used."

Weller opened his mouth.

"Badly used. *Rigoletto* in five minutes—four minutes—and why somebody thinks I'd want to bail you out is beyond me. You deserve whatever you get."

Weller said the call wasn't his idea.

Carmichael kept on. Saying Weller deserved worse than that. Worse than whatever he'd get. Picking up speed because the music was coming up louder and the lights had already flashed once and he was torn between finding his seat and getting this out of his system. Too angry to hang up and knowing it and angry at himself for that and that making it worse. What in the world got into these people.

Weller said making the call wasn't his idea, and neither was whatever anyone had said. He'd just shown them the picture was all. The picture that Liz had taken. He raised it up again like a talisman. Penny coming over and standing alongside him, that green film trailing from her fist. Weller saying whatever call they'd made and whatever they'd said was their doing and not his. He was sorry, but it wasn't his doing.

Carmichael said oh for Christ sake you brought the kid. Is that what smugglers do now? Three minutes to *Rigoletto* and I'm talking to an idiot who's smuggling tobacco with an innocent little kid along to learn the trade. Saying he'd had a higher opinion of Weller than that but he guessed he'd been wrong.

Weller said he wasn't smuggling anything. Honest. He'd come to cash in his IOU. Holding the picture up again, as if it had value independent of what the man on the screen might decide it had. Any value beyond Carmichael's merest momentary caprice.

Carmichael checked his watch. He looked back at the screen, studying it and looking absent at the same time. He might have looked at Penny standing there with her deep blue eyes and her fistful of pale green plastic.

He might have thought of his own son and that Polaroid. Who knows. *Rigoletto* in two minutes and he said all right. Consider that IOU cashed in. I'll bail you out. But not until intermission, so you can just cool your heels.

Weller said that wasn't what he'd had in mind by way of that IOU. What he'd had in mind was getting his daughter's sight back. It was hopeless in the Zone. Carmichael knew that. Hopeless. She'd be completely blind before long and blind forever after that.

The sound of water running. Across the screen a single electric jolt of interference from somewhere.

"Please," Weller said. "You said you owe me one. You did. You said it."

A muscle in Carmichael's jaw bunched.

"That's why I brought her all this way."

*

What was the word for a person like that? A useful idiot. That's what they called a person like Weller, and they were right on both counts. He was an idiot by any measure, and he could be useful if you knew how to use him.

Carmichael sat half watching the opera and thinking. He never quit thinking. That was what had gotten him where he was. What had gotten him everything he wanted in the world or almost everything he wanted, and what would get him the rest of it someday.

He was thinking about Weller and thinking about the girl and thinking about cars. That yellow Hummer he'd driven down here from the apartment on the Upper East Side only to have a delivery truck just about clip it in the front passenger side. As if the driver hadn't seen it for Christ's sake. As if a blind man couldn't have seen it. Carmichael had boxed the truck in and gotten out of the car to chastise the driver even though his wife hadn't wanted him to and she'd been right. There was no satisfaction to be had. The man hadn't even spoken English. He was Management, with a National Motors permit and everything, and he hadn't even spoken English. What was the world coming to?

Carmichael tried concentrating on the opera. It was in Italian and he didn't know Italian.

The surgery would cost peanuts. That was a given. So the thing that Weller wanted wasn't the important thing. The important thing was that he was asking at all. His nerve in asking. His audacity.

It was the audacity had gotten Carmichael's attention.

He thought about that yellow Hummer. Ever since the Boston trip he'd been making up his mind that he couldn't trust it anymore. It was a Chevrolet under the skin. He should have thought of that when he'd paid good money for it. So what if it were the last of its kind. That was just proof that the rest of them had died. Good riddance.

His wife was watching the opera and glancing down at a libretto now and then. A libretto in her lap printed in both English and Italian. Carmichael listened to the singing for a minute and looked over at the two languages running side by side on the page and his mind went right back to the driver. *No English* he'd said, so apparently he'd had a little. Enough to deny it.

Give a person an inch back there in the Zone, and this is what happened.

His wife put down her lorgnette and people applauded and he applauded too. Wondering if it was the start of the intermission, but no.

Weller. Weller had poor judgment and he didn't know his place, but he had nerve and he had a dream. Nerve and motivation could make him useful. Never mind what the surgery would cost. The real cost was elsewhere. The real question was what it would cost to acknowledge Weller's request. What it would cost to stoop. And what he could gain from stooping.

There was a car, actually. The idea of a car. The possibility of one.

God, he loved cars. He'd always wished he owned one of those big old Cadillacs with the fins like they still drove in Cuba. How they kept them going was a mystery right up there with the resurrection of the dead. Those gigantic broad-shouldered road-eating monstrosities. Grilles like gritted teeth and fins to soar with. Here in the states they'd thrown out all of that midcentury American iron when gas first got expensive. They'd traded it for the lightweight stuff from China and Japan, or at least the lightweight stuff from those countries was what lasted. What remained, now that nobody was making cars anymore. Cuba had the right idea. Cuba had a sense of history.

Cuba might as well be Mars, even for Anderson Carmichael.

He looked at the opera for a minute, but his mind kept slipping.

There was this one car. He'd seen pictures of it. He owned the full run of *Road & Track* on paper and he kept the copies under glass and he'd seen pictures of it. There hadn't been many made in the first place and there weren't any left now that he knew of. None at all. It was a German car. A German car made here. The badge may have said Bavarian Motor Works, but it was put together in the southern Appalachians back in the time before the balance of trade went down the toilet and parts got scarce and the unions went under and people like Carmichael started to think Cuba had had the right idea all along. Those Castro brothers. You had to hand it to them. Extremely good health care down there and everybody qualified if you could believe it. Fidel was still kicking even now, if what you heard was true. Back on his feet and looking younger than he ever did. Younger than he did when Kennedy was alive and the Bay of Pigs blew up. A walking miracle, that Castro. According to the pictures that got out, the color had even come back into his beard.

But he'd just now realized how he could go Castro one better. A brand new BMW X9, fresh off the line in Spartanburg. Black if possible but he'd take any color. There had to be one or two left down there someplace, one or two parked on a lot gone halfway back to wilderness, one or two that they hadn't been sold when they shut down the machinery and turned off the lights and locked the doors.

If anybody could get it for him, it was Weller. Make the trip and finish up whatever needed finishing on it. If anybody had the motivation it was Weller too. That was for sure. That little girl of his.

Christ, though, it was supposed to be a no-man's land down there. The stories you heard.

Never mind that. Not his problem.

The cost wasn't even worth thinking about. One trifling operation. Strictly speaking he wouldn't even have to go through with it if Weller didn't make it back, but he was hoping he would. What the hell.

The music rose up loud and died away and the audience began to applaud again. His wife putting down her lorgnette and the lights coming up. Before she could say a word he stood and went back to the men's room and made the call.

Six:

Some People Wait Forever

They met upstairs in the middle of the night. On the top floor of One Police Plaza. Weller boneweary but hopeful and Carmichael with his necktie unfastened and Penny stretched out on a long low couch underneath a wide black window, sound asleep. Beyond the window was a panorama of breathtaking beauty and haunting strangeness. The city awash in windowlight and streetlight and the moving light of traffic. The river empty and gleaming, and beyond it the grayblack tenements of Brooklyn Heights rising up and lit with flame. The famous trashlit Promenade. Oil drums burning garbage, with clots of people gathered around. There was candlelight in some windows and lamplight in other windows but most of the windows were black and dead. Not even windows at all from this distance and in this light or this light's absence.

Traffic moved on the far side of the river too, but not much of it. Buses. Long buses gliding through dim remote intersections like eels, appearing and disappearing, their segmented sides gleaming. The graveyard shift in a Management town. Commuters.

Carmichael sat behind the desk in a big low leather chair belonging to some security officer so far beneath him as to be anonymous, and Weller stood. Saying thank you, sir. I'm glad you reconsidered. You won't regret this.

Carmichael saying I don't know what got into me but there it is. A moment of weakness maybe. Looking over at Penny asleep.

Weller saying maybe it was just the car. Saying he'd understand if it was just the car he wanted and not the girl he wanted to help. It didn't matter to him.

Carmichael looking up and thinking he'd found the right man for the job. You couldn't fool this one. Not even about the thing that mattered to him the most.

Weller said, "So what's the plan? When do we get her to the doctor?"

"Oh," said Carmichael, stretching the syllable out as though he'd been required to do the impossible. The slaying of some nine-headed monstrosity. "These things take time."

"We've waited five years now."

"Some people wait forever."

"People like me. Not like you. People like you don't wait."

"There'll be patients ahead of her."

"Not ahead of Anderson Carmichael."

The rich man laughed. "It's not that simple," he said.

"I think it is. I think it is that simple." For this system was only a machine, after all. A machine that had ground him down and lifted Carmichael up.

"You don't understand."

"I do understand." Weller tapped his finger on the big walnut desk. "I wouldn't be here if it weren't that simple. I'd still be downstairs."

"Don't press me."

"I wouldn't dream of it. But fair's fair. A deal's a deal."

"I know all about deals," said Carmichael. "I know about deals if anybody does." Turning away from Weller to look out the wide black window at this city of his.

Weller pictured Carmichael as a machine himself. Inputs and outputs. Power and leverage. He looked at his own reflection in the black window and said, "I'd really like to get started for Spartanburg, is all." Stating his single condition without stating it. Applying weight where it would matter. "So how soon do we see the doctor?"

Carmichael didn't pause more than a half-second. "We'll get you in tomorrow," he said.

"Fine," said Weller. "And you'll keep her in the hospital until I get back."

"Of course. Don't be ridiculous."

"Good. Now tell me about the car."

Which warmed Carmichael up considerably. He said according to *Road & Track* there was no reason for anybody in the world to own this particular vehicle. They said there were better choices. Could you believe that? Four hundred horses and eight forward gears and all wheel drive and they said there was no reason. Of course there was a reason. It just wasn't apparent to everybody. So the company hadn't made many of them and that was reason enough right there, wasn't it? The scarcity. Plus gas went through the roof and kept going and getting fifteen miles to the gallon meant you'd spend a grand just to do a week's commute back and forth to a job that was tenuous at best, so demand dried up altogether. There were certainly people who'd had them out in the suburbs of one city or another for a while, parked in the garages of those big cookie cutter mansions they'd built with money they didn't have before the real estate bubble blew and credit went south, but one by one they'd run their tanks dry and sold them off for scrap. Steel and glass and rubber. Transmission fluid and grease. They'd held on to their cheap little Geelys and Toyotas for as long as they could, which wasn't long, and then they'd scrapped them too.

"To tell you the truth," Carmichael said, "if we'd seen it coming, I don't know that we'd have let it happen."

"We?"

"Ownership."

"Let what happen?"

"Let it all fall down the way it did. Once you've acquired everything, you'd think you should be able to keep getting more." Expressing it as simply as he could.

"So you'd be better off if guys like me were out there building new cars."

"We might be."

"I'd do it if I could. If there were jobs I'd do it."

"Unintended consequences," Carmichael said. "It's hard to predict the future."

"Hey. You've still got the opera."

"I don't want the opera. I want an X9."

"And you'll have one."

"Black. With the eight-cylinder engine."

"I'll do my best."

"I'd like something newer, but there isn't anything newer."

"I can't help you there."

"I know you can't."

"So tell me about Spartanburg," Weller said.

*

Essentially, the coasts were what was left of the country. The two coasts plus Chicago and Houston, each population center isolated from the others. Transportation was the problem, transportation and people. The lack of both made big distances bigger. Chicago would have shut down a long time ago if not for the insurance business. Family Health Partnership was all that kept it alive. People out there lived on meat, meat raised by hand in walled sectors of the Midwestern Empowerment Zone and Management-butchered generation after generation. The knowledge of how to do it passed down from father to son. Who cared how much meat you ate and how high your cholesterol spiked when you owned the insurance company.

Transportation cost money. The expense of maintaining the highways. The price of diesel. National Motors that ran the trucks and MobilGo that sold the fuel couldn't make it pay because there weren't enough markets, and there weren't enough markets because there weren't enough people. Blame that on insurance if you wanted to, but the insurance folks were getting their own punishment. Those isolated carnivores out there in Chicago.

So a couple of trucks ran back and forth each week maybe and that was that. Scarcity inducing scarcity. They ran through wastelands that had once been productive farms and wastelands that had once been manufacturing centers and wastelands that had once been cities teeming with people. The Rust Belt and the Sun Belt and the Bible Belt and every other belt that there ever was. All drained of everything and everybody when gas got too expensive to burn and food got too expensive to eat. When housing went bust and nobody could afford to visit the doctor anymore. Not even doctors. When the Great Dying came, and people buried their dead and dried their eyes and turned their backs on home and went to the cities to find work and didn't find it there either. When the last thing the federal government made stick was the division of what was left into Empowerment Zones. Suburbia plowed up. But only certain bits of it even then. Only where it made financial sense. The South was different and farther out and not worth pursuing. PharmAgra had had crops there in the old days, back when there'd been people everywhere and the need to feed them, but not anymore. A lot could have happened since. Nature could be lying dead down there or nature could have come back or something in between.

Spartanburg, then, seven hundred miles from New York and five hundred miles from Washington, was a mystery. A vacant spot on a road to nowhere if there was even a road. A place from which civilization had withdrawn, leaving behind God knew what. Maybe nothing.

Carmichael said, "Spartanburg? Hard to say. There are a number of unknowns."

Weller said if the knowns were National Motors security and old bounty hunters cut loose from Black Rose, then he'd take his chances with the unknowns. Unknowns didn't bother him.

Carmichael said *Now that you mention Black Rose.*

Which got Weller's attention.

"You know that they own Washington," Carmichael said. "White Washington anyhow." Meaning the pale limestone city. The grand old public spaces. The monuments and the Capitol building and the White House.

Weller said he knew.

"The rest of that town was never worth looking at anyway."

Weller said that's what he'd been given to understand.

"So here's what I'm thinking we'll do," Carmichael said. "We'll go straight to the experts. Get you down there and hook you up with Black Rose and let them decide what you'll need in order to make this happen. We'll spare no expense."

Penny was stirring on the couch. Weller lowered his voice as far as he could and said that he didn't think he'd need much of anything. Some kind of transportation. Food and water. Money.

"Money's no good out there."

"Money's good everywhere in the Zone." Hating Carmichael for sparing no expense with Black Rose but denying him this.

"We'll ask the experts. I'll make some calls first thing tomorrow."

"That'll be a big day then," said Weller. "Between making those calls and getting us to the doctor." Just so it didn't slip Carmichael's mind.

*

The hospital was on the Upper East Side and it was the Taj Majal except for being a shrine to the living instead of the dead. Weller and Penny went there in a limousine with a black-hatted Management driver in the front and some Management assistant of Carmichael's in the back sitting on a soft leather banquette opposite them. A woman looking doubly ill at ease, uncomfortable on the deep cushions usually reserved for Ownership and uncomfortable face to face with the two of them. Forcing herself to make small talk. The weather. The traffic. Their room at the Four Seasons. Weller said the room was fine and Penny was bursting to say more but she didn't let it out. Weller asked how far was it to the hospital. After all this time. Wondering about a few minutes after five hopeless years. She told him it wouldn't be long, and it wasn't.

To enter the hospital was to enter a palace of youth and light. Music soaring from invisible speakers and a spring in everyone's step. Plate glass and falling water and banks of flowers. The assistant led the way across an atrium that reached up thirty floors and more, her heels clicking on a white marble floor inset with precious stones and grouted with gold and altogether worthy of the Medicis, to a reception desk that was more concierge station than anything else. The woman behind it raised a tiny wireless scanner and Carmichael's assistant clasped the hand that held it and made it disappear. The subtle magic of high decorum. "This young lady is Anderson Carmichael's guest," she said, sliding a small white card onto the desk with one hand and indicating the poor urchin behind her with the other. Penny bent over attempting to pry a gemstone from the floor. Waiflike Penny cleaned up but in her filthy clothes still. A creature of the road, doctored at the last minute and perhaps made even less presentable for the effort.

"My, my," said the woman behind the desk. "What a beautiful little girl."

Penny straightened up and beamed in her direction. Her father standing behind her with one hand on each of her shoulders. "We're here about her eyes," he said.

The woman bent forward, enchanted. Those bottomless blue pools. "Really," she said.

It occurred to Weller that he couldn't guess how old the receptionist might have been. Her skin was flawless, her eyes were bright, and the movements of her compact body—sleekly clad in gray wool—were as lively as those of some small animal. She was youth and vigor made flesh, and yet there was something in her manner that suggested otherwise. Something that hinted at experience and maturity. It might have been the result of her breeding and station, but then again she was certainly Management, and therefore no higher in the scheme of things than Carmichael's uncomfortable assistant.

The woman smiled and looked at Penny.

The assistant cleared her throat.

The woman got the idea and broke away and turned her attention to a screen mounted on the desk, shaking off the enchantment cast on her by the child. A grandmotherly reflex that she could barely help. In that moment Weller decided that she was an advertisement. An old woman made young again. A reminder that in this particular world there was no need to look at an old woman. Not even among the lower class.

An orderly who could have been the woman's brother took them to a glass elevator and from there to a suite on the fifteenth floor. A suite with Penny's name on the door, overlooking Central National Park just at the level of the tented wire mesh. Three rooms and a full bath. The orderly left the assistant on a couch in the first of the rooms and showed Weller and Penny into the next, where there were two enormous beds and a wall-mounted television and tall built-in closets of gleaming cherry. Clothing in the closets just their sizes. Penny tried on everything. Spinning in front of a floor to ceiling mirror and getting in close to see and then spinning away again.

Her father let her spin and put on a three-button suit himself and fumbled with a necktie for a while. Every knot he knew, until he finally gave up and put it back and cracked opened the door to the next room. Steel and rubber and tile. Hoses hung from the wall and fittings mounted along the side of an upholstered table and machinery suspended from gimbals. Bright lights overhead and a low hum of electronics. He closed the door and took her arm and sat her down on the bed. He knelt before her and looked into her grave little face and asked if she understood what was going to happen now that they'd finally made it to the hospital, and she said she did. "I'm sorry we haven't had more time to talk about things," he said. "We've been so busy these last few days."

"That's all right," she said. Looking like she understood everything in the world. Everything they'd been through and everything to come.

"I'm not sure exactly what to expect next, but you'll have the very best doctors in the whole world. What they'll do in particular, I can't say." Feeling himself helpless within the machine of this medical system.

"That's easy," Penny said. "They'll fix my eyes."

"Right. They'll fix your eyes. And I won't leave until you're all better."

She said she knew that.

There were flowers in the front room when they came back out. Two bouquets as big as Penny herself and each with a card attached to it. The first card was engraved with a filigreed letter *C* and signed *Mr. and Mrs. Anderson Carmichael* in a hand that surely belonged to neither one of them. The second bore an embossed version of a familiar wheat stalk, and was signed *Your friends at PharmAgra.* Friends that she didn't have before, but you never knew. Both cards signed by the same hand if you looked at them together. Weller put them on the table and pulled out one tulip for Penny and gave it to her. Then he sat down at the table across from the assistant and the orderly and asked when would the doctor be coming.

The assistant said soon. It was all arranged and he should be right along.

The orderly said Penny looked lovely in that new dress.

Penny said thank you.

Time passed.

The doctor arrived, a slight man built like a greyhound, shouldering the door open as if he believed in touching as little of the world as possible. Coming in with a white coat unbuttoned and a stethoscope hanging around his neck and a very white smile that was pasted on but just barely. The Assistant's smile was pasted on too, pasted on and brittle, and the orderly rose and stepped in to negotiate between them.

The doctor had a small beard trimmed tight against his jaw and he smelled of fresh laundry and rubbing alcohol. He fastened his eyes on Penny and said, "Let's go, shall we?" but she didn't move. She just stood holding her tulip. He reached out a hand in her general direction but there was something disdainful in it even though he was plainly doing his best, and she didn't respond.

Weller stood up and put out a hand of his own toward her and said, "Come on, honey."

The doctor asked the obvious. "Are you the father?" Lowering his hand. Relieved but not entirely.

Weller allowed that he was.

The doctor said, "I'm pleased to meet you, Mr. Weller, but your daughter's the only one I'll need right now."

Weller picked up Penny and headed in the direction of the examining room. Saying, "I guess you might be the doctor, but there are still a few things you don't know." Not confrontational. Just filling him in.

*

The tests took a week. Weller didn't know why he'd let himself expect some kind of abracadabra, and he realized that he should have been tipped off by the suite with the two beds and the living area out front and the clothing, but he guessed you had to live and learn. Some afternoons when Penny was looking at the television or resting in the darkened bedroom with her eyes dilated, he'd walk around the hospital and see what was what. The hallways were vacant for the most part, empty and hushed. Everything that went on went on behind closed doors. There weren't even any scanners that he could see. Freshly shaven and showered and dressed in one of the suits from the closet, he could have been anybody. He could have been Management or even Ownership. Strangers greeted him as such, strangers clutching computer tablets and strangers bearing huge floral arrangements and strangers pushing elegant carts laid out for room service, and he decided that the operating principle was always to assume upward. If they didn't know you, then you were a patient or a patient's family. That meant Ownership. So they consulted their tablets, hid behind a bank of flowers, or adjusted the already perfect placement of a napkin. And moved on.

Ultimately the doctor said they weren't one hundred percent sure. He didn't say it in front of Penny. He told Weller at the table in the front room while she was still sleeping. Early in the morning and the shadow of the hospital still heavy over the park below. He said they'd had their very best people on it and they'd consulted with specialists in Boston and Los Angeles and not one of them was one hundred percent sure either. They weren't sure about the root of her trouble and they weren't sure about how they might correct it. They had theories, and they had a protocol worked out, but there were going to be uncertainties on every hand. They would have to see what they could see.

The doctor was apologetic. In spite of his white coat and his neatly trimmed beard and his youthful canid vigor he looked beaten. Beaten by the conclusion they'd reached, and beaten by having to confess it now to Weller. Admitting failure or the possibility to one like him. An interloper from the Empowerment Zone.

Weller asked how it could be. How it could possibly be that they weren't sure. Hadn't doctors in a hospital like this seen everything before?

"It's environmental," the doctor said.

"Environmental."

"Something she breathed," he said. He drew a long finger across the tabletop. Tracing the grain. "Something she ate. That's about all we know."

Weller sat stunned for a minute. He looked out the window at single pigeon flapping against the wire mesh of the park. He kept looking. Watching it try to escape into a world that would have eaten it alive. "Then it's definitely a mutation," he said.

"Yes. A mutation. Meaning if we correct it surgically, it might come back."

"But you *could* correct it."

"We could. As I said though, it might come back. It probably would."

"If you don't know the cause of it, how can you know that for sure?" Not even looking at the doctor. Not able to.

"We have to make certain assumptions. And I don't want to make any promises I can't keep."

The pigeon gave up and Weller turned back to the doctor. His face ravaged. "I guess I thought you'd have seen a lot of problems like my daughter's."

"We used to see them. The literature was full of these cases for years. People got into things they shouldn't have gotten into because nobody knew. Nobody knew the risks. They thought food was food." He sighed, either remembering or imagining. Impossible to tell because it was impossible to tell his age. "The system got overloaded. All of those people so terribly sick and too many variables to be sorted out, given the funding. Funding that dried up pretty rapidly, seeing how quickly those cases disappeared from the literature. They were just kind of a blip, if you look back on it now."

"A blip. They were people."

"A spike then. They came and went. Anyway, the insurance companies would have gone bust if they'd had to keep on covering all of them. It's better now."

"Better now that you don't have to look at them."

"Well." Rethinking his position. Smiling. That doglike grin. "Better now that we all know what to avoid."

Weller kept on. "But you have to look at *her*," he said. "You have to see *Penny*."

"And I assure you that we'll do everything we can on her behalf."

"Money's no object."

"That's right."

"No expense will be spared."

"Correct."

"All right then. When do you get started?"

*

The good news, her father told her, was that there wouldn't be any surgery. At least not right off. No knives and no lasers.

"Well," the doctor put in, "maybe some lasers."

Penny's jaw dropped.

"Depending," said the doctor, which didn't help much. "You won't feel a thing, though. Before or after. Not a thing, I promise."

Penny was sitting at the end of the upholstered table in the examining room. The bright overhead lights were dimmed, and screens along the walls pulsed with images from inside her skull. Three-dimensional fly-throughs in constant motion and various digital cross-sections arranged like geological records. The doctor before her smiling wolflike and her father in a chair to one side. Looking at the doctor and deciding that his mouth must have been remade that way at some point. Wondering why they hadn't fixed it. Wondering if maybe they had.

The doctor pointed to his own eyes and said he'd had cataracts taken off years ago with a laser and it hadn't bothered him in the slightest. These days he saw better than ever. Twenty-twenty. Nothing to it.

Penny asked was that what she had. *Cataracts.* Saying the word carefully because it was new.

The doctor said something like cataracts. Not exactly but almost. They'd try some other treatments first, though, and maybe they'd shine some light in there later on if they had to. That's all a laser was, he said. A little light you shined in places.

Penny nodded.

Regardless, he said, they'd use it only if the other treatments didn't work. Some injections they'd be giving her.

Penny asked what he meant by injections and he said they were like the blood that the nurses had been taking but the other way around. Putting something in instead of taking it out. He pointed to the cannula taped to her forearm and said we'll use that and it won't hurt a bit.

*

After three days Carmichael's assistant came back, not for a report but to sit down with Weller. Ten days had passed altogether and her employer was running out of patience. "He'd been under the impression that they'd operate and she'd recover and that would be that," she said. "He wasn't counting on this delay. These complications."

"I'm sorry," said Weller.

"I am too."

"I guess that'll teach him to play doctor."

It was early in the day and Penny was still sleeping. They sat on opposite sides of the table. She'd given up on maintaining the niceties of status, so it was just the two of them face to face. Weller would never have it any other way without her having to remind him, and the very act of reminding him was a loss of status right there, so what was the point. "The doctor tells me it will be a couple of weeks before we know anything," she said.

"A couple of weeks at the inside."

The flowers on the table were still blooming, but not by means of any miracle. New arrangements arrived fresh every morning, from *Mr. and Mrs. Anderson Carmichael* and *Your friends at PharmAgra*. Contractual clockwork. No flower anywhere in the hospital was permitted to fade for even a moment.

"Mr. Carmichael doesn't like waiting," she said.

"I don't care much for waiting either. But I think the results will be worth it."

"I'm not talking about waiting for Penny."

"I know you're not. I am."

"But you think it'll be worth it, you said."

"I do."

"That's good," she said. "Because we want you to get started for Washington right away."

Weller laughed.

"Tomorrow morning. First thing."

Weller laughed again.

"It's not a laughing matter."

"I know."

"Look," she said. "You're confident about your daughter, we've established that. Mr. Carmichael has been extremely patient, we've established that. But I'm here to tell you that he's not going to wait forever."

"He can wait a little bit longer."

"No. It's time."

"It's not time. Not yet."

"You're not acting in good faith."

"I'm acting in good faith toward my little girl. If he hadn't expected that, he wasn't paying attention."

She pushed her chair back a quarter of an inch. "I could send both of you home right now. You and Penny. Find you in breach of contract and stop her gene therapy and send you home."

"Carmichael would kill you if you did that. He'd lose the car."

"You're not the only individual capable of doing the job, Mr. Weller."

He thought for a minute. "Something tells me I am."

"Then go home." Rising. "I'll speak to the staff and have her released."

"Carmichael will have your head."

"He relies on me too much," she said, pushing in her chair. "If he has to have somebody's head, he'd rather have yours."

She was out the door and down the hall and signing something at the nurses' station when he figured it out.

"My wife," he said. "Send somebody for my wife. Get her here to look after Penny, and I'll be on my way." He knew that the assistant would go along with it. And he could hardly wait to get back and wake up his daughter and give her the news. Her mother was coming.

*

The reunion was too brief. Liz was exhausted from travel and aghast at the needles in her child's arm and amazed at how her husband looked in those suits. The three of them couldn't get enough time together. They sat up talking too late for their own good and they slept halfway through the morning like a pile of housecats or emperors and when they finally roused up there were clothes hanging in the closet for Liz as well. Clothes and a half-dozen pairs of shoes in just her size and a soft white bathrobe that matched Penny's and made the two of them feel like twins. As if they could have felt any closer at just that moment.

Weller didn't ask Liz how she felt about the progress Penny had made in spite of her old doubts. He didn't need to, and it wouldn't have been kind. To turn such a good thing into the results of a contest. In return, Liz didn't say how worried she was about everything it might take for him to hold up his end of the bargain. He'd done so well so far. Letting hope give birth to hope.

Careful of Penny's arm, her mother bathed her in a tub. Both of them knowing that she was too old for this kind of thing but what of it. You made exceptions. The tub was like nothing she'd seen before, big enough for two people and plumbed all over with nozzles and air jets that they didn't try. The supply of hot water was endless, and even with an exhaust fan whirring overhead the mirrors steamed up. Weller sitting outside the door listening to them. To the squeak of his daughter's skin against porcelain. To the soft murmur of his wife's voice. That second a thing he hadn't even realized how painfully he'd missed. The particulars of her. Each little aspect. You get started on something and you go where it takes you and you set aside other things because you don't have any choice. Because if you didn't set them aside you would never be able to go on. And then if you're lucky enough you get back to where you started and you realize your mistake. You realize how difficult it is to keep everything in your heart at the same time. How impossible. You can only keep so much and still go on. You come back for the rest if you're lucky enough.

The tub drained and the door opened and Penny emerged in a cloud of white terrycloth inside a bigger cloud of white steam. Borne up by both of them. Her mother staying behind and drawing more water for herself, and Weller coming to his feet and stepping inside and closing the door and embracing her. Helping her out of her clothes. Her warm skin in the warm room. He wondered why he hadn't thought of this before. Thought of having her brought down here to be with Penny. To be with both of them. Another of those thoughts you can't keep in your mind all at once, there are so many. He latched the door and they heard their daughter turn on the television and in the front room the buzzer sounded, meaning someone was at the door. Penny switching off the set and the sound dying and the damp slap of her feet on hardwood. Silence, and then her voice coming back high, *Daddy Daddy it's Mister Carmichael he says it's time.*

They took their own pace anyhow. Opening the door a crack and saying tell him to have a seat and latching it again.

"He's waited this long," Weller said low, "he can wait a little more."
Letting the water run.

Seven:

Make Straight in the Desert A Highway

It was just a little chopper. A little Black Rose chopper that darted and gleamed like a bug. Land anything much bigger on the roof of One Police Plaza and it would be the fall of Saigon all over again. Everybody going nuts. Plus who knew if the building could take the weight. The concrete work had deteriorated and lengths of rusty iron rebar were showing through in places with cement crumbling away and falling and there wasn't anybody left to inspect anything anymore. All of those city offices had been closed up for years. Nobody trained to staff them and no money to keep the lights on and civil engineering itself a thing of the past. National Motors had a few oldtimers around who could still use a transit, but they were jealous of them and you couldn't subcontract them out for anything. That old knowledge just draining away.

Weller was in his old clothes. The engineer striped coveralls, cleaned and pressed by some invisible hand but entirely beyond salvage. The scarred workboots burned and cut as if they'd been worn throughout some invasion. The baseball cap, its logo that of a team that hadn't played a single inning in his lifetime. You couldn't go on the road in a suit and a dress shirt. You couldn't get any real work done in a suit and a dress shirt. Anyone knew that. When he'd gotten back into his old clothes and said goodbye to his wife and daughter, Liz had said that seeing him dressed that way made it worse. She'd said if he'd gone wearing a borrowed suit it would have been a little bit like saying goodbye to somebody else, while this was saying goodbye to the man she loved. No question about it and no disguise to shield her from the truth. The only man she'd ever loved.

Planes still flew out of Newark now and then, a few rattletrap commuters plying the old trade routes between Washington and Boston. The mighty coastline megalopolis that had never quite materialized and was now breaking back down into its constituent parts. The commuters were unreliable and dangerous, and their schedules were uncertain, so the helicopter was bound for the remains of a military airfield near Lodi, New Jersey. A Black Rose outpost off limits to civilians as a rule, but money bought exceptions. The trip would take minutes. Weller sat inside a gleaming bubble of glass strapped tight to the seat, and he didn't know where to look first. The helicopter rising up with the harbor in view and the ocean beyond that and the coastline stretching away to the south. No significant traffic on the water at all. Nothing in motion except a couple of little power boats. Big ships docked like shackled ghosts at abandoned piers and others rusted through and sunken into deep water dragging entire wharves into the drink after them and a handful of others lying in dry-dock half broken. The industry of these places having reversed itself for a while. Dismantling great ships for raw materials until the market dried up and the dismantling ran out of steam and the work was over.

The helicopter swooped into a wide semicircle and they banked to swing west over the Hudson. This part of New Jersey greener than it had been in a hundred years or maybe twice that. Nature recovering faster than anyone could have imagined. Enormous oil tanks draped with greenery like antique places of learning or remote jungle redoubts. Refineries themselves refined by weather and years to raw steel and rust, making their slow journey back into the ground. Most remarkable were the networks of empty roads, crumbled and grassed over smooth and stretching into vast distance like carpets for some green world-consuming king whose arrival mankind had awaited forever. *Make straight in the desert a highway.* Of all of these roads only Ninety-five, fenced in and maintained by National Motors, endured intact.

The pilot wore black sunglasses and spoke into a radio when he spoke at all, an intermittent stream of codes and numbers, low terse talk incomprehensible to Weller. Both of them wore thick padded headphones that blocked some of the hammering of the rotors and the wind but did little to improve the other side of whatever conversation was under way. The hard numerical language of robots.

Weller spotted the airfield from a distance. The runway a single thin stretch of pavement unmolested amid the greenery, with a little tower and a long low hangar standing close to it alongside what looked like a barracks. The rest of the buildings all collapsed to the ground or dismantled and hauled away. Not a single road leading in or out. No car or truck traveling the concrete runway or parked alongside any of the structures. As if every earthbound vehicle had been raptured up. Weller looked north and east and saw another highway joining Ninety-Five, an east-west strip veering away into the unknown. He pointed and made questioning noises and the pilot shouted *Eighty*. Where it passed by to the north it couldn't have been more than a quarter mile from what remained of the runway, and yet all connections to it were gone. The men who lived here lived here for one purpose only.

The pilot chose a painted circle on the concrete and lowered the helicopter toward it, and six men emerged from the hangar. Moving quickly and with purpose, no motion wasted. Grim by practice and inclination. They wore black boots and dark green uniforms and soft dark berets cocked identically over identically shaven heads, and their weapons were holstered tight. One of them waved the helicopter down. A formality but what wasn't. Everything done by the book.

A pair of them escorted Weller out of the helicopter and back toward the hangar. The pilot bending over his paperwork and no more acknowledging his leaving than he'd have acknowledged a cargo container. Not lifting a hand. He had spoken one word to him altogether. *Eighty*. And even that word wasn't really a word but a number.

Weller was certain that a look was passing between the men on either side of him. Something judgmental. Something about his fitness for the job he was undertaking. His thick glasses and his raggedy sparkburnt coveralls and his greasy baseball cap. The way he walked, like a different kind of beast from the two of them.

The beating of the rotors slowed and stopped, and he hazarded a question. "Either of you two fellows ever been to Spartanburg?"

They laughed without a trace of humor. It was just air coming out. The same laugh that wasn't a laugh came from each of them as if they'd been practicing it.

"I guess that's a no," said Weller.

"You bet your ass it's a no," said one of the men. It didn't matter which.

"Nobody's been to Spartanburg for ten or fifteen years," said the other.

"How come?"

"Nobody goes there anymore."

It didn't seem like much of an answer. They walked on.

After a little, one of the men spoke to the other. "I knew a guy who served with Marlowe once," he said.

"I don't believe it," said the other.

"Believe it."

"You knew somebody who actually served with Marlowe?" He said the name the way a person might say the name of God or the Devil.

"I did. This was Afghanistan. Back when Marlowe was Navy."

"Marlowe was Navy?"

"SEAL."

"Right." Nodding his head as if that explained something.

They stepped out of the sun into the shade of the hangar. Weller stopped short and they went on. "Who's Marlowe, anyway?" he asked.

"He's an old man," said one of them. "Come on."

"What's he got to do with Spartanburg?"

"Simple." Heading toward an airplane that looked like a bullet with smaller bullets hung underneath it. A fighter jet. Weller catching up. "Marlowe is the reason nobody goes there."

"Nobody? Not even you? Not even Black Rose?"

"Not even Black Rose." Kicking a wheeled set of steps over to the plane.

One of the men climbed in and Weller followed him. "So let's say Mr. Carmichael wanted to hire you fellows to go down there and bring him back something he's got his heart set on."

"I don't believe we'd take the job."

"You wouldn't."

"No sir. I don't believe we would." Belting himself in.

"Because of one old man," said Weller.

"Because of one old man."

*

Weller had time to think on the plane to Washington. Buffeted by the roar of twin engines and cutting through the air at close to the speed of sound and wondering why there should be any sound at all. There was nothing to see through the canopy but sky and clouds and water beading up on curved glass. Drops of it accumulating and sliding back leaving thin trails behind them and then the drops disappearing and the trails disappearing too. Then more water beading up and the process continuing. Over and over.

They landed on the Mall at the center of the grand pale public city, Washington become an immaculately preserved memorial to itself with only the monument to its namesake missing. That mighty obelisk cleared years ago to make way for this landing strip, torn down stone by stone and the pieces used to pave the reflecting pool. Crews drained the pool dry and filled in the lower depths with a substrate of sand and crushed granite and then laid on the square gray marble blocks one after another. Fitted with the utmost finesse by artisans imported from Italy in the cold bellies of military cargo planes, a score of the oldest men on earth brought here to build a cobbled pathway for fighter jets and finish it off as smooth as glass. While they were at it they rebuilt parts of the World War II memorial to support a network of arrestor wires rather than risk the collision of a landing plane with Black Rose headquarters in that grand domed building at the far end of the mall. The old Capitol.

Two men in a black jeep roared up to meet them. The driver up front indistinguishable from the fighter pilot or any of the six men who'd greeted the helicopter or the helicopter pilot himself. As if they'd all been made on the same assembly line. Seated directly behind him was an august old gentleman, bright of eye and upright as a flagpole, wearing a full dress uniform with a peaked service cap. His little steelgray mustache was cut too narrow to hide the least fraction of his delight with the entire world.

The old man's breast was paved with medals, and they jangled as he leapt from the car. "Henry Weller," he said. "Welcome to Washington, my boy." Pumping his hand without letup.

Bainbridge was his name. General Bainbridge. The only five-star general in the entire Black Rose organization and proud of it. "I told that fellow Carmichael we'd make a man out of you," he said, "and I'm relieved to see we've got something to work with."

The driver kept an eye on the proceedings from behind his sunglasses. Looking as if he weren't so sure.

Bainbridge didn't own any part of Black Rose, but he ran it. Ownership was invisible inside the old White House on Pennsylvania Avenue, surrounded by guards and barricades and armored vehicles of all kinds, with rooftop snipers stationed up and down the block for a mile or more in each direction as if the entire city weren't a fortress already. Bainbridge himself lived in the mansion at Number One Observatory Circle, home for more than a century to a succession of officials of increasing authority. From observatory superintendents on up to Vice Presidents of the United States of America. A place so grand and lovely that not one of them would permit a lesser individual to live in it for long.

They drove there with Weller and Bainbridge side by side in the back, Weller's old rucksack thrown into the front alongside the driver. The open-roofed jeep making its own breeze and the hot sun beating down and the summer air wet. Bainbridge talking steadily all the way, avid as some paid tour guide. Washington was the most beautiful place Weller had ever seen, far more beautiful than Manhattan with its grim skyscrapers and walled parks. This was a white and open city populated by a race of supermen and fitted ideally to their use. A kind of Elysium. Every lawn a parade ground and every building a palace.

"You'll be bunking with me," Bainbridge shouted as they roared up the hill on Observatory Circle and veered into the drive.

"I appreciate your kindness," Weller said. "But honestly, if you can just point me toward the gear I need and send me on my way—"

The jeep stopped abruptly and Bainbridge sprang out of it. "We'll see to that in due time, son. Right now let's get you to your quarters."

For all of its grandeur, the house was spartan inside. Whitewashed plaster walls and hard furniture. Faded photographs of presidents and generals on the walls in the barest of frames. Marble floors and hardwood floors and linoleum floors all polished alike. There wasn't a shred of comfort to be had unless you redefined comfort. At the top of the front staircase was a monkish cell with another identical monkish cell right beside it, each one containing a small bureau and a straightbacked chair and a writing desk squared underneath a screened window. A clock on the desk and a cot against one wall made up drumtight, with white cotton sheets and a scratchy wool army blanket in spite of the jungle heat that blew in through the window. Mosquitoes buzzing against the screen. Over the head of the bed not a crucifix but a photograph.

Weller took off his ball cap and mopped his brow with the back of his forearm.

"The founding fathers built this city on a swamp," Bainbridge said. He stepped inside his own door and hung his cap on a peg and stepped back out, not the least bit troubled by the heat. Dry as the sound of his own voice. "Come summertime, we pay the price."

"I can see that." Weller tossed his rucksack onto the cot and the cot gave no more than a marble slab. He sat down on it and it still didn't give. Great. At least he wouldn't be here for long. "Let's get started," he said. "I'm in a little bit of a hurry."

Bainbridge stood in the open door with his legs spread and his hands folded behind his back. Not moving. Not doing anything except studying Weller and smiling. "I like a man with a sense of urgency," he said.

"I've got that in spades."

"Good. You'll do fine."

Weller took a few things out of his pack and put them on the table. The photograph of himself with Penny and Carmichael. Balled socks and underwear. The Zippo he'd taken from the old man in the bunker. "I guess there'll be some kind of vehicle involved," he said.

"We've lined up a nice vintage Harley from the motor pool. World War II issue. It goes like a bat out of hell."

"I was picturing something with four wheels."

"Four wheels means four tires and four tires means twice as many opportunities for failure. It's all about the numbers, son. Trust me. You'll do fine."

"I will."

"That Harley's tough as nails. The simplest transport in the world."

"Simple is good. If it breaks down, I can fix it."

"Let's hope it doesn't come to that."

Weller looked at the photograph of his daughter. He had half a mind to reach out a finger and touch it to her chin, but he looked up at Bainbridge instead. *"Let's hope?"* he said, "The way you fellows work, I wouldn't think hope would figure into it ."

"You'd be right," he said. "We strategize, we train, and we execute." Letting himself look at the photograph and then looking away. Just enough to let Weller see him do it. Seeing that it mattered to Weller. "Hope is a weakness," he said. "Operationally speaking."

"Operationally," said Weller. Standing and taking up his ball cap. "So anyway—the Harley. What else were you thinking I'd need?"

Bainbridge tilted his head and stuck out his lip and looked him square in the eye. "Most of what you'll be needing, sonny, is *you*. And that's what we're going to work on, starting first thing tomorrow."

*

The picture over the bed was of the last chief executive of the old United States. the one that AmeriBank and MobilGo and Family Health Partnership had resurrected from the dead to tear down the federal government once and for all. The born again president. Another miracle of science. In the picture he was on a trout stream at sunrise in some western Eden, craggy mountains in the background and clouds streaming overhead and mist rising from the water into the cold dry air, casting a fly line. His famous reedwork creel hung around his neck, the one that held the heart pump and the battery packs and the dialysis equipment and whatever else it was that kept him alive. Top secret, all of it. A matter of national security.

Weller lay half asleep on the hard bed with the moon outside the window and the lights on in the hallway and Bainbridge moving around in his room next door. The clock on the desk said four something. Recorded music played somewhere, a march with a full military band. Trumpets and trombones and big bass drums, with a piccolo soaring above it all birdlike. He lay in the bed and the light from the doorway fell on the picture and he looked at it upside down for a while, listening to the marching band, until he remembered where he'd heard Bainbridge's name before. Whom he'd associated it with. The last president himself. General Bainbridge had been chairman of the Joint Chiefs under him. The last man to hold the job, and the first to hold it as a civilian subcontractor.

A shadow passed across the door. Something emerging from it, moving into the room at speed and unfolding itself as it came. Something on the order of a bat but heavier. "Rise and shine, young fellow. Put these on." Fatigues of his own landing on the bed. Weller pushed them aside and pointed to the photograph before Bainbridge could go on his way. Wanting to seem alert at this hour if nothing else. Wanting to seem ready for anything, which he was, but still. Pointing to the picture and saying, "Friend of yours?"

Bainbridge went soft if he ever went soft. Leaning against the jamb. "You bet your ass he was a friend of mine. A fighting man never had a better ally than that individual right there." Tilting his head down and raising his eyebrows to indicate. *"Angler,* we called him."

Weller had his feet on the floor now, and even in the chiaroscuro of the hard hallway light and the blackness of his cell he could see the sentiment written upon the general's face. A softness. A softness permissible here perhaps because it was home and perhaps because the mingling of light and dark concealed it some but a softness nonetheless. Undeniable. The tough sentiment of an old soldier. "That's interesting to hear," Weller said. "I always understood he didn't like the military all that much."

"Au contraire." Straightening up. "He loved the military. He loved every man in it. What he didn't care for was how the U. S. government ran the operation. He didn't trust the government to handle anything that important."

Weller was up and sliding into the fatigues. The lamp still switched off in the room and Bainbridge still blocking most of what light came in from the hallway. He was having trouble finding the buttons or snaps or whatever they were, trouble even determining *what* they were, at the same time listening to Bainbridge talk and studying the picture of the last president on the wall. That little bit of light finding it and bouncing off and making it gleam like an icon. "But that doesn't make any sense," he said. "He was Commander In Chief."

"And he *still* was, even after he'd outsourced the whole business to people who knew what they were doing. He was always in charge. Don't you forget it. He never did."

"I'll bet he didn't." Looking at the figure standing hip-deep in the trout steam, braced against the moving water with every bit of his fractionally restored strength. The rising sun like a halo and his ghastly face dark under the shadow of a longbilled cap. Still intent. Still pursuing the old pleasures. Still angling.

*

Bainbridge said they'd eat at the officers' mess. The jeep was out in the circular drive but they didn't get in. They ran instead. Five miles or so to the Pentagon with the jeep rolling alongside them in case Weller should falter. A driver behind the wheel who may or may not have been the same driver as before. Old man Bainbridge remarking on this and that the whole way and hardly breaking a sweat. They ran down the hill from the observatory and into Georgetown and then made a little side trip through the old university with its endless red brick barracks. Morning drills under way on broad lawns trimmed crewcut short. They passed by with the general utterly anonymous and they stopped in the middle of the Key Bridge so Weller could catch his breath. Not quite halfway to the Pentagon. Weller doubled over gasping and the driver stopping to offer him a bottle of water and

Bainbridge saying what did he tell him last night, eh? About how the most important equipment he'd have would be himself? Saying Weller probably understood now what he'd meant by that. Saying he bet Weller was a fast learner. Weller ashamed of himself and not looking up. Bainbridge shaking his head and helping him into the back seat and getting him arranged with his head down between his knees. Giving the driver orders to go on without him. He'd be right along.

Weller had recovered when Bainbridge arrived. Sitting on a bench in front of the building, cooling his heels and finishing up his bottle of water, watching a small army of men mowing the enormous lawns. They weren't the automatons he'd seen everywhere else. Just ordinary men with ball caps and sunglasses and overalls not that much different from his own. Each one wearing headphones against the small engine roar. All of them working quickly and carefully.

Bainbridge slowed to a trot when he spied him on the bench and he came up steadily but he didn't stop. Saying, "Take a look at those boys with the lawnmowers if you want to understand the beauty of the military. It's the one place left where a man can rise up from humble beginnings." Still talking as he went past, and Weller having to get up and keep pace if he wanted to hear.

"Every single one of those recruits came in from the outside. Straight from the Zone. They found their way here and they enlisted because they had a dream, and if they keep their noses clean that dream will come true. They'll be Management. Just like me. Do you know anyplace else where that can happen?"

"No sir, I don't."

"Damn straight you don't. Because there isn't anyplace. Nobody's born into Black Rose, son."

"So I see."

"A man can still work his way in and work his way up." Arriving at the main entrance and taking a thick white towel from a soldier waiting there for him and waving Weller through in his wake. "God bless Black Rose," he said as he took off across the lobby, and the soldier at the door said, "Amen to that, sir." Coming to attention and saluting for a second time. Apparently just because it pleased him to do it.

*

The Pentagon had seventeen miles of hallway, conference rooms of every size and description, and offices almost literally without number. Target ranges and running ovals and weight rooms. A pair of competition swimming pools in the basement and an obstacle course spread over the open central pentagle in five wedges of ever-increasing impossibility. The motor pool was linked by a secure underground tunnel to the old Ronald Reagan International Airport, where most of the runways were still functional and a glass-walled museum housed the last lumbering twin-rotor Chinook helicopter in the whole world. Better than seventy-five years old but still in working order, its belly full of empty drums stenciled all over with the word NAPALM for verisimilitude. Jellied gasoline. Airborne destroyer of worlds.

"Now then," said Bainbridge when the tour was over. Standing at ease, stiff as an ironing board. "I'm only here to facilitate. You're in charge."

"In charge of what."

"In charge of preparing yourself. I'll be with you every step of the way, son, but exactly where we go is up to you."

Weller said he'd always thought they'd just give him a set of keys and a tent or something and send him on his way. Some road maps and some food and what have you. But that run from the house this morning had opened his eyes a little.

Bainbridge smiled. "Good thinking," he said. "So take all the time you need. It's your call. We're billing the bank a fortune every day you're on board, plus the bonus when you turn the car in, so I don't care how long it takes." Lifting his eyebrows and giving Weller a look. "The longer the better, actually."

Weller said, "You get a bonus when I deliver?"

"You bet. That was the lesson of Vietnam, and the lesson of Iraq too. You promise to fight, but you don't promise to win. Not if you're smart. Winning costs extra, if you can do it at all."

Weller said he guessed he understood now why Bainbridge took such a personal interest. The general had a lot of duties, but the most pressing of all were financial.

It wasn't just that, the old man said. Sure, he had something of the mercenary about him. That's what they were, after all. Mercenaries. But Weller's case was different. There was the little girl. It just about broke your heart, didn't it?

Weller nodded.

Bainbridge said he'd seen Weller with that photograph he'd brought. The way he'd looked at it.

Weller smiled.

Plus there was the adventure, he said. One man against the world. Against the unknown. "I'd go down there with you if I could. It'd be just like the old days."

Weller saw that he meant it. Anyone could have seen that.

"I wouldn't mind crossing swords with Marlowe again, either."

"Marlowe. You know him?"

"*Knew* him." Turning away then, heading toward the showers and changing the subject. Saying Weller had a hard decision to make, didn't he. He'd have to balance preparing for what he kept calling *the mission* against getting back home to that little girl of his. Saying he couldn't offer any particular counsel on that one. His own children were grown and scattered. Two sons and two daughters and neither of the boys had had the least interest in the organization that had always meant so much to their old man. Which was just as well. As he'd said, you didn't get born into Black Rose. They'd have had to endure the same hard time as everyone else. He wasn't sure they'd have withstood it.

*

There were satellite phones with big screens in the communications room. The officer on duty showed him how to work one and located the number and helped him call Penny's suite at the hospital. The satellite phone there was mounted alongside the door and the camera over it was aimed down at the table as if for some kind of commercial function. A consultation maybe.

Penny looked good. Her mother looked good. The sight of the two of them made him heartsick but he tried not to show it. The weird and troubling miracle of their disembodied presence was harder to endure than the still photograph on his little writing desk, the urge to reach out and touch their images stronger. Penny leapt from her chair at the table and ran toward the phone and got so close that she disappeared from view on his end. First going out of focus and then dropping out of the frame entirely. Her father saying, "Hey, hey, back up a little bit, all right? I can't see you." His daughter coming back into focus and walking backwards. Returning slowly to her chair, one step at a time, leading with her little butt. Looking disappointed, but recovering.

He asked her how she was doing and she said fine but why was he wearing that uniform. She didn't like it. Plus how come his hair was all wet. He smiled to reassure her and said he was staying with some soldiers who were giving him a hand and he'd just gotten out of the shower was how come. He'd just gotten out of the shower and he'd been in a hurry to come talk with her and her mother. Thinking while he was saying it how fine it was that she'd noticed. She'd noticed what he was wearing and that his hair was wet. It seemed like a good development.

Penny said if he was in such a hurry to talk with them, then he should just finish up what he was doing and come on home. Her mother laughed but there was sadness in it. He laughed too and said that he thought that was a good idea. A first-rate idea. He'd come on home just as soon as he could.

*

A month would pass before he was ready to move on south. A month spent in the weight room and on the road and at the target range. A month spent studying under tough men who'd devoted their lives to tough jobs. And a month spent chowing down on the healthiest diet he'd ever eaten, dishes absolutely unknown where he'd come from, in quantities beyond his imagination. Banquets, one after another.

Above all, it was a month of being torn in multiple directions. To stay or to go, to keep improving himself or to be tested, to persevere or to risk everything. He let himself call the hospital no more than every third day, because it was too difficult to see Liz and Penny for a moment and then to stop seeing them. Each time he pushed the button that ended the call, he thought he might die. Some of the soldiers said that to toughen himself he shouldn't call at all, and others counseled that he should call every single day if it hurt all that much because the pain would keep him sharp. But they didn't know what they were talking about. They weren't Henry Weller. They weren't Liz's husband and they weren't Penny's father and they didn't know. So he called every third day. It was the compromise that pained him the least.

Toward the beginning of the fourth week he noticed a definite change in Penny. Her eyes didn't seem to have that swimming quality they'd always possessed. Not so much anyhow. There was more purpose to their movement. It couldn't be his imagination. She had a stack of crayon drawings she'd been making, some kind of therapy her mother said, and she was showing them to him one by one. Pointing out details. This one showed the view out the window and the next one was a portrait of one of the nurses and the one after that was their house back in Connecticut. What she could convey of it. Some of the details were more imaginary than real and all of them were colorful. He marveled as she chirped on in her high voice. Not only over what she'd drawn, but over her mere presence. The breaths she took. After she ran out of pictures she disappeared into the other room on some errand and he asked Liz if she'd seen what he was seeing. Was their daughter actually improving?

She said she was. Most of this had happened in the last couple of days. A corner Penny had turned. She'd gone crazy waiting for his call. And had he noticed the other thing? Had he noticed that she'd grown three or four inches?

No, he hadn't. Blame it on the television. The lack of any context.

Trust her, she had. She'd grown three or four inches and she was filling out some and getting stronger than she'd ever been in spite of being indoors all day out of the sun and the fresh air. Lying in bed half the time, hooked up to an IV. But getting stronger. As Liz leaned toward the camera he couldn't help noticing that she was looking stronger too. There was more color in her cheeks. Her hair was glossier. A little bit more meat on her bones unless he missed his guess. Half of him wanted to run back to her and the other half wanted to put it off as long as possible. Let her keep on eating whatever it was they were feeding her in New York. Build up her strength for whatever lay ahead. The rest of their lives.

*

Liz and Penny weren't the only ones getting stronger. "I must say you're looking fit, my boy," Bainbridge said as he joined Weller in the mess one morning. Finished with their run and out of the showers and stoking up for the day.

"You think so?"

"By all means."

"I'm giving myself another week," Weller said.

Bainbridge nodded. "Suit yourself. May I add that you're doing nicely with that .38 special."

"I guess. Thanks." Reaching for more toast. "Honestly, what do you think are the odds that I'll need it?"

"They'd better be slim. If there's any serious shooting to be done, you're going to be outnumbered and outgunned. Marlowe'll have guard towers, snipers, the whole nine yards. Then again, maybe not. Nobody's done any recon down there in years. He might have given up on all that stuff. He might have put a welcome mat outside the front door. Your guess is as good as mine."

"Right."

"My money's on the middle ground, though." Starting to tick ideas off on his fingers. "Tripwires. Listening posts. A handful of men on the roof, lightly armed but well trained and wound up tighter than ticks."

"That's how you'd do it."

"That's *exactly* how I'd do it."

"But you're old-fashioned."

"Marlowe's old-fashioned. Plus he's got to be getting a little complacent by now. Put yourself in his shoes. His men haven't taken a shot at anything more upright than a black bear since you were in short pants. Never mind the manpower it would take to mount a full watch twenty-four hours a day on a facility like that. My hunch is he's gotten a little bored, and found some better things to do with his men."

"But it's just a hunch."

"A solid gold, forty-year, five-star hunch. They don't come much better."

"How well did you know him, anyhow?"

Bainbridge was suddenly captivated by his oatmeal. "Well enough."

"What does that mean?"

Bainbridge looked up. "What it means is that he was my friend. We went to the Naval Academy together, and the minute the shit hit the fan we both got hustled off to Iraq. I hated it. I hated the heat and the sand and the wind. I hated the noise worst of all. We lived in house trailers stacked up inside a big warehouse on an airfield in Qatar—can you picture that?—and the noise in that place never stopped. Generators going night and day. Lights everywhere that wouldn't go off. The work wasn't bad, son, but the living conditions were hell."

"Right."

"The thing was, Marlowe couldn't get enough of it. He just thrived on that stuff. Some men do. I've spent a lot of years trying to figure out why that is, what traits might make a man go one way or the other. It would be useful to know that kind of thing, especially with an all-volunteer outfit. If you could figure that out, you'd have something."

"So?"

"I still don't have a clue. I'll tell you one thing, though. I always thought that when I went one way and Marlowe went the other, he took the tougher road."

"Maybe your road would have been harder for him."

"That's a lovely idea, buddy, but it doesn't wash. I went looking for a great big desk to hide behind, and he went after the dirtiest work a person could get his hands on. Five years later, where were we? I was back in Washington on the way to my second star, and he was flying top-secret missions for SEAL Team Six. In case you don't know, that means he was one tough sonofabitch. As hard as they come."

"Is that so."

"The stuff of legends. Marlowe may have reported to a desk jockey up the chain of command, a desk jockey like me, but he was never that man's inferior. Not for one minute."

"It sounds like he knew it."

"You bet your ass he knew it. They all do," said Bainbridge. "And the problem is, so do we."

"So what happened?"

"Afghanistan happened. By which I mean Pakistan. He was one of the boys who went over the border in a couple of choppers and took out that fellow bin Laden. Remember him? Remember bin Laden?"

"It rings a bell."

"Jesus. People always say that the victors write the history books, but there aren't any history books anymore and there isn't any history either. Nobody remembers anything. This bin Laden was a very big deal. A major terrorist, a major target. *Numero uno.* There were parties in the streets when we got him."

"When Marlowe got him."

"Right."

"Then what?"

"Then Marlowe thought it was time to go home. He thought he was done. *Mission accomplished* and all that. He figured he'd bagged the number one target in the war on terror, and they ought to let him turn in his dog tags."

"I can understand that."

"Worst of all, he decided he had it coming. He let his ego get involved, which never ends well. SEALs aren't even supposed to have egos. They're supposed to do their jobs and maintain their anonymity and leave the hero worship for Superman." He buttered his toast and stared at it. "Not Marlowe. Not after bin Laden. He wanted a goddamn ticker tape parade, and Uncle Sam didn't give him one."

"Aww."

"*Aww* is right. And do you know the saddest part? He sat right down and wrote me a letter. His old pal the general. It said he was up for another tour of duty and he didn't think he should have to serve it on account of what he'd accomplished, but he couldn't find anybody who'd let him out. He wondered if I would be so kind as to put in a word on his behalf."

"Did you do it?"

"What do you think? He served two more consecutive tours whether he liked it or not, and then Uncle Sam made up his mind to get out of the soldiering business. Marlowe cashed out rather than going to work for Black Rose. It was beneath him. He wrote a book instead. I guess he thought it would sell a million copies, but nobody gave a shit anymore. Everybody was on to the next thing by then and Marlowe was old news."

Weller shook his head.

"So there you have it. He broke cover and gave away everybody's identity and not one person in the whole wide world even gave a damn. So much for his ticker tape parade. Next thing you know, he was knocking on the door at Black Rose with his tail between his legs."

"Old soldiers, I guess."

"Old soldiers. Exactly. What the hell else could he do?"

*

According to Bainbridge, outsiders called it Marlowe's Retreat. The place and the action both. Where he ended up and how he got there. Word was that when he'd quit Black Rose he'd taken the toughest men with him. The misfits and the hard cases, culled from an operation where misfits and hard cases were the top of the heap. The men who understood that he'd blown his identity and blown everybody else's identity in the process and didn't care. The men who'd have done it themselves, given the chance. They'd have followed him into Pakistan and they would follow him now wherever he was going. All the way to Spartanburg.

Everybody in the Pentagon spoke of Marlowe's Retreat with a mixture of derision and fear and grudging respect. He was a turncoat and a quitter, but he'd had the courage to be both. He'd risen through the system and then he'd thrown it all away, and then he'd risen through the system again only to throw it all away once more. The SEALs first and then Black Rose, and now he was freelance. Independent. A mercenary's mercenary, when you got down to it.

But why Spartanburg? Why the hills of South Carolina of all places, when men that hard and that capable could have gone anywhere at all. Spartanburg certainly wasn't paradise. Marlowe could have taken Cuba if he'd been after paradise. He and his men could have thrown out Castro and claimed the island for their own and nobody would have denied them. They'd spent their working lives overthrowing regimes like his and for what. A paycheck in the SEALs. A paycheck and immunity from criminal prosecution in Black Rose. Big deal. Try prosecuting Marlowe if you think he needs immunity. Try prosecuting any of them. Try giving a single one of of Marlowe's men so much as a traffic ticket, and see how far you get.

Bainbridge said Marlowe had grown up in Spartanburg or somewhere right around there. He had a southern accent. The accent of a good old boy who wasn't a boy anymore and wasn't much good either, except by his own lights. Bainbridge had come to Annapolis with a diploma from Choate, and Marlowe had come from some regional high school south of the Mason-Dixon. A great big football-playing gum-chewing southern-fried tarheel, and Bainbridge had befriended him. Worse than that. He'd looked up to him, for possessing something that he didn't. Something internal that drove him to achieve at the academy independent of Choate and the Bainbridge family tradition and the expectations of Beacon Hill society back home in Boston. And later on, too, for the mysterious quality that Bainbridge had spent all of these years trying to name. The personality trait that made a person take the most difficult path there was, simply because he couldn't help himself.

Marlowe and his men had moved to Spartanburg when everybody else was moving out. When the car plant shut down and the other plants that had grown up around it shut down too. When the UPS trucks stopped coming and FedEx tailed off and then the mail. The U.S. Postal Service outsourced entirely and deliveries cut back to weekdays and then just two days a week. Mostly junk coming then, and soon enough not even junk since nobody had the money to buy whatever somebody else might be selling. There was nothing left but the Wal-Mart and the dollar stores selling imported goods that people used to make here better, like this was the third world. Like they'd had to invent a second third world since they'd worn out the first one. Other than low-end retail there was only fast food and health care, and those two seemed to go together. A match made in heaven. Until Medicare ran out and Social Security went bust and nobody had any use for the government anymore anyway. Why should you keep paying your taxes when there's nothing coming back. How can you pay taxes when you've got no income. Congress tried, but it was blood from a stone. Then the people with the real power brought Angler back and called it quits. That was the signal for Marlowe and his army to go AWOL for good. To leave their Black Rose bases, both the new headquarters in Washington and the old place in Kill Devil Hills, and close in on what was left of Spartanburg. Like teams of murderous angels, swooping to their own rescue.

*

"I've got money." Weller was talking to Liz on the phone. Penny in bed and Weller planning to leave before she was up. Not having told Liz much about the journey ahead, not eager to tell her much about it now, and keeping it as simple and upbeat as he can. "I've got plenty of money, but I don't really think money's going to do me much good."

"You mean cash or credits?"

"Both. Cash and data. Better than cash, really. A whole pile of Ameri-Bank scrip. They sewed it into my pack just in case. The trouble is, the fellow in charge doesn't seem like he'll care all that much about money. If he'd wanted to sell those cars, I think he'd have parted with them a long time ago."

"So?"

"So all I can do is talk with him. Appeal to his sympathy and see what it'll take. Whatever he wants, Carmichael will make happen. Anything with a price tag on it. I've got a letter." Not mentioning everything else he had. A carton of water purifying tablets and food to last a month and nearly enough parts to build a second Harley from the ground up. Tool kits and inner tubes and spare gas cans. A pair of .38s and a half-case of ammunition. Plus a satellite phone for calling in air support as long as the satellites weren't down, and signal flares and smoke canisters just in case. Not mentioning that the air support counted only if he'd gotten his hands on the car he was after. They'd come for the car but they wouldn't come for him. It was part of the package and he accepted it.

"So how long do you think you'll be?"

"They're flying me to Richmond, and after that I'm on my own. I figure a couple of days down and two or three days back, depending on the roads. Then there's dealing with this Marlowe and fixing up the car if I need to fix it up. Which I probably will."

"You'll call, though."

"I'll call Bainbridge when I can. This phone doesn't work on a civilian band. He'll call you. He'll let you know how I'm doing."

"I'll miss you."

"I'll miss you too."

"I miss you now, Henry."

"I miss you too."

"Be careful."

"Of course."

"Come back."

"I will."

Eight:

Old Royalty

The helicopter pilot asked if he had anything for snakebite, and Weller said he figured there must be something along those lines in the first aid kit. He'd been inoculated against tetanus, hepatitis, rabies, encephalitis, and typhoid, so somebody must have thought about snakebite. The pilot shook his head and said Weller must not know anything about using a snakebite kit if he didn't even know what a snakebite kit looked like, and Weller said he guessed that that was so. The pilot yawned and said training in this outfit had gone straight to hell. Letting a man die of snakebite from pure oversight. Weller said he'd just look out for snakes, how about that. He said he'd put up with all of the training he could stand, and if somewhere along the way somebody'd forgotten about a little thing like a snakebite kit then so be it. The pilot said you won't think it's a little thing when one of those rattlers gets hold of you. Copperheads and timber rattlers and diamondbacks hanging from the trees like Spanish moss. Hiding under every outcropping that didn't have a bear living in it.

Then Weller kickstarted the Harley and it roared to life and the pilot headed back toward the chopper and they parted company. The pilot turning on the iron step and hollering *watch out for alligators while you're watching out,* and Weller not hearing him. Just smiling and waving him off.

The outskirts of Richmond looked bombstruck. Looted and hollowed out and used up entirely. The chopper had put Weller down in a rest stop near where Ninety-Five had once intersected with Eighty-Five, and he had a job scrambling past the barricades. Eighty-Five would take him to Greensboro and then straight on to Spartanburg. Three states or what passed for them, Virginia and both of the old Carolinas. He sat the Harley and watched the sun move across the ruins of a distant roadside industrial complex and drank the last of a bottle of water. Threw it over the guardrail and watched it vanish into the trees below. Then he set out.

The road had seen use for a few years longer than the greened-over highways around north Jersey, but the climate here was warmer and wetter and PharmAgra had been gone from the cultivated fields for a generation and the return of everything to some modified version of its of pre- or post-natural state had been faster. A chaotic green aggression overwhelming the rectilinear work of man. Willows and cottonwoods and vast sycamores arched over the highway, hung with peppervine and Virginia creeper and supplejack. Screening the world beyond the margin of the road and screening the road itself. He found that large sections of the pavement were more or less undamaged, but the track beneath his tires was roped over with vines and roots and after the conversation he'd had with the pilot each one of them looked like a poisonous snake. He wondered how great a striking range such a thing might have, and every time he stopped to hack clear a path through dogbane or kudzu he was careful not to waste the slightest time or motion. Crawling down the jungle road on a throttled-down motorcycle, dressed in his old engineer striped coveralls and a Black Rose helmet with his baseball cap jammed underneath it, a machete tucked into a pair of bandoliers crossed over his back. Glad of the food he'd brung and wishing he hadn't been half so optimistic to Liz regarding his time on the road. If only he'd known.

Under the dark forest green it was always a kind of night, but true night came at last. When he couldn't see to travel farther he set up camp in an open space and built a fire from deadfalls and stoked it high. He took out food for supper and slung the rest between two trees at the margin of the clearing, beyond the reach of the black bears that were common here once and had no doubt returned. He left the pup tent rolled up and lashed to the back of the Harley, thinking he'd sleep under the stars. Saving himself the time needed to stow it in the morning. Get back to Liz and Penny that much faster. He drew up a log and ate his supper and sat listening to the crackle of the fire. The burst of pine knots one after another. Looking up at the numberless stars and wondering how many more nights before he made Spartanburg.

Beyond the circle of firelight, the uncontaminated darkness was loud with life. The scratching of insects and the creak of living green branches in soft wind. Small scurryings in dead leaves, and the underbrush crackling beneath some stealthy tread. The sudden rush of wings. He made up his bedroll and lay down and listened to a bullfrog calling from a culvert. The water in the culvert was stagnant and when the breeze was right it filled his nostrils with the stink of green mold and rusty black rot, and once from down in that dark place there came a dark splashing. A sudden movement of water and the chime of something hard raked across corrugated pipe.

If it was an alligator, he didn't want any part of it. He didn't want any part of it whatever it was. He got up and stoked the fire and unlashed the tent from the Harley. Switched on the flashlight and made his way to the edge of the woods, where he chose two trees to hang the canvas between. It made a makeshift hammock six feet off the ground, which he figured was enough. He scrambled in and looked up and saw no stars. Just the black canopy. So he dropped back down again and got another rope and shinnied up higher and slung the rope between the same two trees and draped his bedroll over it to keep off snakes.

*

Four days and nights of it altogether. The only change a cycling of the forest density that he could attribute to nothing in particular. Open stretches followed by stretches clogged with growth. He made time where he could and he chopped his way through where he had to. For the most part the road ran flat, rising up only now and then to accommodate some underpass or cloverleaf, and in these rhythms he felt the presence of the men who had come here before him. How they had built up one place and left another untouched. He began to sense the pulse of their engagement with this world, a faint but regular pattern that was the only sign remaining of their old dominion.

He noticed a rhythm to the way that his mind and his heart worked as well. How he awakened each morning thinking of Liz and Penny, how they drifted from his consciousness as the mechanics of the road took over, and how they returned to overwhelm him once more when the day's work was done. Then the blackness of sleep and the night and the dawning of the day again and with it the two of them rising up. As if they were there already. As if they had awakened before him and drawn forth the day for his benefit. As a gift. A way of reminding him of their presence in the world.

On the third morning he dug out the satellite phone and called Bainbridge. The connection went through on the first try, which got him thinking how there were different satellites over different places on the earth and maybe he'd gone far enough that he was underneath a better one.

Bainbridge didn't even say hello. "For Christ's sake," he said. "What's the fascination with North Carolina?"

Weller had forgotten about the GPS chip in the phone. How they'd know right where he was. "No fascination," he said. "Just slow going."

"What'd I tell you?"

Weller didn't answer. He didn't mention that Bainbridge and his people hadn't actually said the first useful thing about how rough it might be down here in the wilderness. They'd been too busy obsessing over Marlowe.

Bainbridge was going on anyhow. Shifting gears. Bainbridge the motivator. Bainbridge the cheerleader. "You can handle it, though, son. No question about that. You can handle whatever North Carolina throws your way."

"I'm doing my best."

"We're counting on you. Slow and steady. That's our man."

Weller watched the sun come up beyond the trees. This day that his wife and child had given to him. "Tell me the latest with Penny," he said.

"Penny!" said Bainbridge. "Oh, my goodness. You ought to see the progress she's making."

"Honest?"

"Honest. Just these last few days."

"Tell me."

"The doctors are calling it a miracle."

"How about the specifics?"

"Not off the top of my head. There were numbers. Measurements. You know, doctor talk."

"Sure." Watching that sun rise. His spirits rising with it. "It's never the same as seeing for yourself."

Despite the satellite connection, Bainbridge could hear the change in his voice. "Exactly," he said. "So you've just got to buckle down now, buddy. Get your ass back home."

"I will."

"See your little girl."

"I will."

"ASAP."

"I'm on it."

"Because one thing I do know. She keeps on saying that she wants to see her daddy."

*

There was thunder on the third night and hard rain. A protracted and furious storm that broke the humidity and the heat but not for long. A lightning strike woke him in the black middle of it all and he lay underneath his suspended bedroll with the rain pelting down in spite of the cover of trees, and in the morning when the storm was over the pelting went on. Rainwater dripping everywhere nonstop. He rolled his gear up wet and put everything on the Harley and filled the tank. Half of the gas used up already. Maybe not quite half, but close enough. He went on. He got up some speed on a bare stretch of road that arched high over a cloverleaf and spotted something he hadn't seen in forever. A thin column of smoke rising, maybe half a mile away. In the stillness after the storm there was no wind and the smoke went straight up. Like a solid thing. He cut the engine and rolled to a stop and looked at it. Feeling himself badly exposed on the high road, but deciding that the feeling was only a reflex. He was just spooked. Accustomed to his solitude and taking any interruption of it as a personal intrusion. He watched the smoke standing grayblue against the green woods and decided what it was. The lightning strike that had jolted him awake. A tree set afire and still smoldering. That was all.

He went on. The underpasses were the hardest. Blind and overgrown caves where some other road ran above the road that he was on. Road or railroad trestle or both. They were black and ominous places, places absent any hint of distant light, places like mouths, and every time he passed through one of them without incident he could feel his luck diminish. As if he were using it up.

*

Noon on the fourth day. North of Greensboro, with the tallest of her buildings just beginning to creep into view, he found the highway blocked entirely. Concrete barriers thick with lichen, and vast piles of broken roadway heaped up behind the barriers and crumbled and treed over, and behind the trees and screened off by them a chaos of upended shipping containers and gaping railroad cars and ruined automobiles all rusted into one solid thing. All of it strewn like the aftermath of some terrible accident, except there hadn't been any accident. This was willful. Man had done it. Weller climbed the barriers and stood among the young trees looking out over the sea of jumbled iron and thought *Marlowe*. Marlowe at work this far from Spartanburg. Wondering exactly how long it had been since Bainbridge's men had seen this place from the air. They'd said years. They'd meant it. This cover of trees and underbrush hadn't grown up overnight. This lichen that carpeted the concrete barriers. It all took time.

He'd have to go straight through Greensboro proper, so he got back on the Harley and turned it around and headed back for the last ramp. Thinking he might have difficulty spotting it and relieved when he didn't. The directional sign had collapsed into the dirt on the shoulder and rusted down to nothing, but another smaller sign still advertised lodging and food and pointed which way to go for what. The Courtyard and the Hampton Inn. Burger King. Places that sounded like destinations in a foreign country. Places frequented by old royalty in a lost world.

The ramp was grassy and absent of trees and he took the long open curve of it down into a broad dry canyon of ruined commerce. Car dealerships and restaurants and grocery stores on either side of the road. Great square castles barely glimpsed through greenery, their broken signs reading Target and Staples and Petco where you could read them at all. He rode along under the trees toward the city, marveling that people had once been rich enough to have filled up these buildings with merchandise and taken it all back home with them at will. Filled it up again and kept on going. They had been royalty indeed. Kings and queens, and every last one of them gone now. Weller their poor bastard child, penniless and in possession of nothing. Not even their memory.

He pictured their children. Children raised up amid such impossible abundance. What were they like? How did they think? What did they know? They couldn't possibly have recognized their privilege for what it was. Not when privilege was commonplace. It must have been an Eden of fine fat children as healthy as horses, not one of whom would have known hunger for a moment. Not one of whom would have eaten something homegrown instead of storebought and paid the consequences. Not one of whom would have been given such a treacherous thing by her own unknowing father. It must have been a paradise.

The road grew more difficult. Greenery closed in again. He passed through intersections wider than any he'd seen before but still choked. Intersections wide enough for four cars in each direction. Roman roads. In some places traffic signals still hung overhead on long galvanized steel beams miraculously intact, but the beams were wrapped and enmeshed now with vines and branches and creepers. The road was straight for the most part and he checked his compass to stay oriented and he kept on, thinking to stay parallel to Eighty-Five. Stay on the commercial road or the access road or whatever it became and keep close to the highway and get back on it as soon as he could. Not that he was making any worse time down here than he'd been making up there. It was a strategic matter. A matter of principle. You could get lost down here even if he wasn't lost yet, which he might have been for all he knew. He caught glimpses of the highway through the canopy of trees only now and then, and sometimes what he thought was the highway wasn't the highway at all. Just some concrete building. The ramps of a parking garage. Keeping track of where he was going and where he wanted to go divided his attention, a thing that could get him into trouble faster than anything else.

An overhead sign with an arrow pointing to the northwest said Greensboro Commercial District, but he didn't follow it. He kept on for a mile or two until Eighty-Five swung west by a few degrees and the road he was on veered south and cut straight underneath and went God knows where. He didn't like the look of the underpass either. He came close to it and stopped and switched off the Harley's engine to save gas like always and he got out a map that he knew would prove useless. It'd have been one thing if he knew what exit he'd taken and could tell from that which road he was on, but he didn't. Maybe someone in a Black Rose helicopter could have correlated the maze on the map to this deeper maze, but he doubted it. His natural impulse was to go back to that last intersection and follow the sign pointing toward the commercial district, but he didn't. He needed to recon. A word he'd never even heard before Washington. His month with Black Rose turning out to be good for something. So he leaned the Harley against the concrete of the overpass and drove the tip of his machete into the ground and took off the heavy bandoliers and laid them on the saddle. Checked the pistol at his hip and shook out the map and folded it again into his pocket and found handholds and footholds in the vines meshed over the concrete and began to climb.

He was nearer the city than he'd thought. The vista from the high roadbed suggested he'd arrived in Greensboro without even knowing it. It wasn't like any place he'd seen before. It was low-lying, for the most part. And small, at least compared to New York. Small but spread out in all directions including this one. The city becoming the suburbs and the suburbs becoming the boulevards of commerce. It was bigger than Hartford back home but not as dense. Empty, though. Emptier than Hartford, which got emptier every year but wasn't quite empty yet. Greensboro was empty because nobody could live here. There wasn't any commerce. There wasn't any safe food coming in. The Great Dying that had winnowed down the population and left places like this unsustainable as markets. The few people to survive had moved out, taken the last train or the last truck or gone on foot. In search of what, only they knew. Each other. Likeminded souls capable of building something up together. Only the most stubbornly individualistic of them could have stayed on once everything public closed down, once the cops and the firemen were gone, once the hospitals were shut for good, once the final delivery truck had dropped off the last loaf of untainted bread.

He checked his compass and studied the roads and when he had his bearings he climbed down. Got on the Harley and doubled back and took the turnoff for the commercial district after all, trading this maze for that one. Roads for streets and all of it green. The American South, recalled to itself now that there wasn't even an America anymore.

*

Movement on a rooftop. He was certain of it. It wasn't some branch shifting in the wind. There wasn't any wind. The roof was four or maybe five stories up, although it was hard to say exactly how high the building was since the outside of it gave few signs. A church, he thought, or maybe a theater. He'd seen it for only a second as he'd passed through an intersection and the view to his right had cleared momentarily. A big building with a big space inside instead of regular floors with windows you could count. It was surrounded by other buildings of similar size or lower and there was definitely a church behind it with a steeple so maybe it was a church and maybe it wasn't. The top was flat, so probably not. His mind ran. Whatever the building was, there had been movement on it. Definitely. A flat roof with a parapet at the edge and movement along the parapet like someone looking over and then ducking back down.

He kept going, his speed steady. He put city blocks behind him. Every inch here had been paved over with concrete and blacktop, and there was less of the jungle about it than there had been on the outskirts. It was a harder environment that had put up a better fight. A place without many footholds for nature. He drove on, feeling glad for the clear pathway and telling himself that he'd imagined that figure on the rooftop. Either he'd imagined it or else it had been some animal. Surely it wasn't a man. He passed intact buildings and crumbled buildings one after the other, and he wondered why some stood and the rest fell. He passed by buildings that had been dismantled for raw materials with some of the raw materials still piled in front of them. Iron beams and copper wire in loose coils. Wallboard and plumbing. Alongside one a midden of raw garbage, a great spreading heap of food scraps and bones and excrement and what have you. The tailings of something like civilization. But he didn't think about it. He was distracted by a figure going through the pile. Something mansized and black and furred over. Something secretive that crouched as the Harley neared but didn't hide itself completely, a simplicity about it that seemed like a kind of fearlessness. The fearlessness of a creature unaccustomed to man and untamed by him and thus unafraid.

Greensboro was a city taken over by bears, he decided. It must have been a bear he'd seen on the rooftop, and now here was another. They'd moved in when the people had moved out. Bided their time and returned when the city had been empty for long enough and made of these concrete caves new caves of their own. He wondered how many there were. Hundreds maybe. Possibly more. He wondered how large a territory such an animal required and how much proximity to one another they could tolerate. Whether they had been out prowling by night on Eighty-Five when he'd been asleep in his hammock. Thinking he ought to sling the hammock higher next time, rig a pulley with some spare motorcycle parts and climb in and haul himself up just as high as he pleased. No sense making it easy for them. Not now that he'd seen how big they really were.

Which was when he hit the wire. It was strung tight across the road at chest height, heavy gauge copper wire salvaged from someplace, and it swept him clean off the motorcycle. The Harley kept on, tipping over and going into a slide and the engine slowing to an idle without his hand on the throttle anymore, momentum carrying it on down the empty street in a shower of sparks. Weller landing flat on his back and his helmet clanging against the machete and the bandoliers cutting into his shoulder blades. Nothing broken by how it felt when he rolled over onto his side and sat up a little. He was scraped and cut everywhere though, and the first aid kit lay open and scattered on the street with everything else that had come loose from the Harley. His pack burst wide and his gear strewn. One of the gas cans unlashed and crumpled and torn open, emptying itself onto the pavement. He came to his feet and heard the motorcycle coughing and saw the drive wheel rotating erratically and the front wheel crushed against a curb, absolutely beyond straightening. Turned away furious and despairing at once and rubbed at his chest where the copper wire had taken him and lifted his eyes from the street to find himself surrounded by men. Men wearing castoff rags and men wearing bearskins, primitive men looking hungry and desperate and ready for anything. Dead silent in a half circle.

The pistol held six rounds. There were that many men. He raised his hands above his head, and they came toward him.

Nine:

The Approaching Storm

With his wrists tied behind his back, Weller was the only one who went empty-handed. The men mobilized as if they were used to this kind of work, and he guessed they were. The way they'd strung that copper wire and waited for him to run into it. The way the one who looked like he might be the leader helped himself to the pistol and snapped opened the cylinder and spun it. Hunters. They'd seen him coming and they'd set a trap. They worked together silently now, and in a moment the street was picked clean. Everybody carried something. One of them had a rolling cart and the wrecked Harley went onto it. Two men to push. Nobody spoke. Nobody except Weller, who said go on take what you want and you can even keep the motorcycle it's no use to me now. As if he would have any say in the disposition of his belongings. As if he were in charge. They didn't so much as dignify him with a denial. The ropes cut into his wrists, and they ignored him.

They took him to the building he'd noticed before. It was an old theater turned into a fortress. No windows at all, just a hole sawn through the roof to let in light. Late as the afternoon was, the light in there was dim but for a gleaming column in the middle full of dust and smoke. Most of the seats were torn out and the floor slanted down in the direction of the old stage and trash was piled high down there. Not piled exactly. Just come to rest. They came into the lobby through big glass doors. Two of the men staying out front with the Harley and three of them beginning to sort through his belongings on the moldy carpet and the last one, the one with his pistol, pushing him toward a narrow stairway going up. From a landing on the stairway he could see the auditorium below and a balcony cantilevered out. Scrap lumber nailed over the doorways that led onto it by way of precaution. Everything smelling of rot.

There was a fire going in the auditorium right under the ceiling hole and figures moving around it. Every now and then getting one another's attention and pointing or jerking their hands in abrupt gestures as if signaling. Communicating without words. From this vantage he calculated that there might be a dozen people altogether, counting those who'd taken him. Mostly men and a couple of women. How they worked out that detail he didn't want to know. There might be a child or two but it was hard to say. A dozen people living like animals in animal skins and their own filthy skins too, one as bad as the other. The man walking him up the stairs directed him through a small doorway and up a couple of steps and into the projection booth without saying a word. The booth had a heavy stubborn wooden door that opened hard and locked from the inside and the outside both. Some slots cut into it high and low for ventilation and a square window on the opposite wall that looked down. The rest of the room was raw cinderblock and concrete, unfinished and utilitarian. Trash everywhere and garbage decaying and decayed. Ragged bedsheets and rotten foam rubber on the floor bunched into a pallet that he couldn't look at, and a teetering pile of old movies in steel cans rusted together into a leaning tower. In the center of it all was the big projector itself, an antique twice over because it had been old even when the theater was in business, two big vertical reels and a housing finished in pale green enamel and a maze of chromed metal parts. Thick with dust and black with soot from the fire they kept going down below.

The man with the gun pressed him to the wall face first and untied the ropes from around his wrists and backed out the door. Locked it behind him. Weller put his ear to the ventilation slots and listened to him go. The man muttering to himself as he went down the steps. Or maybe growling. Something low and harsh that didn't sound like words. Not human words. Weller wondered if people could lose the capacity for spoken language. He thought that if it were possible it would take longer. Longer than they'd had. He thought it would take a few generations if it could be done at all. Talk was like machinery and the longer you were human the more complicated you made it, ideas getting more complex and words and tools keeping up with them. One feeding the other. Then again maybe these people had some mutation. It was possible.

He kicked his way through trash and squeezed between the projector and the wall to get near the square window, through which he could see everything below. He saw the fire going in the center of the auditorium and he saw something big roasting on a spit over it. Someone in heavy skins giving the spit a half turn now and then. A halfhearted half turn. The person was small and he figured it was a child but it didn't move the way a child moves. It moved slowly and as if it were in some kind of pain that was offering it constant resistance. Like an old person, although how a person would get old out here he didn't know.

The smoke from the fire burned his eyes and the scent from the roasting animal made his stomach growl. He hadn't eaten since breakfast and he didn't know when he'd eat again. Not with his supplies gone and the men from out in front of the theater bringing them in now and storing them among the various piles of wreckage and salvage and trash down there. His tent and his sleeping bag and everything else. Dividing everything up and distributing it all with the rest of the junk they already had. His pack and his satellite phone and his Black Rose rations. Arguing over one thing or another with their hands. He watched long enough to see the small figure give the spit another half turn and then he began searching his own cell before the sun went down and the light died entirely.

*

The main thing was that the door opened in, so the hinges were on this side of it and he could get to them. They were rusted from a leak in the roof, but so what. He just had to find a tool. Something to work at the pins with. A spoon or a screwdriver or a knife or just about any stiff piece of metal that was flat enough and thin enough.

The problem was that there was nothing. Nothing made of metal but the stacked film cans and the projector and the hinges themselves. The film cans were too perforated with rust to hold up and the projector was monolithic and he got filthy hunting through the rest of the garbage. Bat shit and rat shit. Slime from the corpse of a possum or a woodchuck or something along those lines, a corpse whose bones were too weak and flexible to be of any use although he tried because he didn't have any other choice. The leg bones were too fragile and the ribcage was too soft and the skull just crumbled. He stood against the door and watched the bits sift down onto his shoes. Dropped the skull and searched some more. In the gathering dark he blundered into an abandoned hornets' nest and the papery dried mud from it stuck to the slime on his hands and his clothing and everything else. Got in his nose. If it had been a bees' nest he could have broken it open for honey, but not a hornets' nest. A hornets' nest was just an impediment.

He went to the window and watched the last of the light fade from the little circle of sky and watched the fire below take over. Its orange light rising and shapes flickering on the walls. Accidental shapes that lurched and wavered. Black shapes against black walls filmed with soot. He imagined how this auditorium must have been in the old days, the days before the collapse of the economy and the Great Dying and the exodus of the survivors from cities like Greensboro. When families would have come here in the evening and filled this place up and a different light would have flickered. A bright light from up here, making images on the screen opposite. He turned his head and sized up the projector, now just a scattering of little gleaming points and arcs reflecting the variable dark like the burnished weapons of a distant army, and he decided that one of those parts would have to come loose and serve his ends tomorrow. Wishing he'd started there instead of digging through everything else, but knowing that he'd been reluctant to tear apart anything so beautiful and complete.

He smelled meat from below and thought about calling out for some in case they'd forgotten about him and he imagined how his voice would sound to the people down there. Coming from the high dark. It would be the voice of a god in a world that didn't have room for gods. Better to stay forgotten. He pushed the pile of film cans toward the door by way of an alarm and kicked a place clear in the middle of the floor and went to sleep. Thinking of Penny and Liz. That old rhythm returning. Sure that with the dawn he would come up with something.

*

A child arrived in the morning. A soft rap on the door and a plastic plate pushed through the lower ventilation slot. The plate hanging there balanced and a presence outside waiting for him to take it. He scrambled awake and went to the door. Thinking at least they let him eat. At least they ate from plates themselves. They hadn't lost that. It could have been worse. He leaned against the tower of film cans and wiped his fingers on his pantlegs and dug in. Cold meat cut cleanly with something sharp. His own knife or some other knife. The presence outside lingering. He leaned forward and narrowed his eyes and looked through the slot and saw it was a child. Girl or boy he couldn't say. An animal child looking at him as at an animal. Fascinated but afraid. He leaned back on the pile of cans and the child stayed put. The meat tasted good and he said so and the child didn't respond. He said thank you for bringing this to me and the child just stared at him through the slot. Blinking but that was it. He finished the meat and licked the plate clean and slid it back through the opening in the door, saying are you trying to fatten me up or what. Smiling. The child taking the plate and turning its back and running like mad.

He didn't despair. He had two aims for the day. First to work some likely bit of the projector loose, and second to mind the schedule of the people in the auditorium. Family or colony or whatever you'd call them. Tribe maybe. He did his best to identify individuals by size and demeanor and the particular rags and skins they wore. The one who'd brought him up here at gunpoint still seemed to be in charge, judging by his manner and by the subservient pose that others fell into when he was around. He kept Weller's gun clipped to a leather thong tied around his waist and he wore the bandoliers as if they signified his status, which Weller guessed they did. He'd need to keep an eye on him.

They left the premises early and they stayed gone, keeping the kind of schedule any working person kept. The child went with the rest. Two by two and three by three they passed through a fire door close to the front of the auditorium, up by the stage. A couple of them staying behind to finish up one chore or another and then those two going as well. Only one stayed behind for good, the one he'd seen turning the spit. The one who'd moved so slowly and painfully. Left behind here to circulate all day, sorting this and that, tending the fire. Clearly of no use in the harsh green woods and perhaps revered in some way for his or her age. Her age, he thought. But he couldn't say for sure.

He worked silently and steadily on the projector. Freeing the housings and prying the metal trim loose. Mice lived in each of the housings and they scrambled away at his touch in a shower of sawdust and shit that turned into a torrent when he pulled the covers away. The decorative trim was thin chromed metal too weak to be of any use. It broke when he folded it forward and back on itself enough times, but a short length of it doubled over and flattened on the concrete beneath the hammer of his boot-heel made a good flat-bladed screwdriver, which was something. The spool on the top of the projector was vacant but the spool on the bottom had an empty reel mounted on it, a skeleton of galvanized steel that looked useful. It was held on by a locking mechanism that had seized up a long time ago, but the mechanism was held together by screws and now Weller had a screwdriver.

He had the reel off and taken to pieces and had begun filing one arm to a sharp edge when he heard the fire door open down below. He stood and went to the window and watched. People coming back in, silent as monks, bearing skinned animals and scrap wood and salvage. A stringer of fish. Dropping everything and settling in and signaling to one another with those hand motions again. The old woman, for he had grown certain that an old woman is what she was, put more wood on the fire. Weller counted them all again just to be sure.

The child appeared at his door again, carrying another plate. Slipping it through the ventilation slot and balancing it there until Weller took it, and then waiting. Weller ate and burped and said I feel like Hansel and Gretel in here or don't you know about Hansel and Gretel. Nothing back from the child. The gingerbread house and all, he said. He finished and licked the plate clean, wondering if he could make this child a friend. Saying come on now, didn't anybody ever tell you that old story. The woods and the breadcrumbs. The wicked witch and the gingerbread house that turns out to be just a trap in the end. The child listening, drawing ever so slightly nearer. Blinking. Weller deciding that it was a girl after all but not being able to put into words why he thought so. Thinking of Penny. Maybe that was all.

The girl took the plate and tilted her head to one side and didn't move otherwise. Weller got the idea that she was waiting for something else. For some word. He came slowly to his knees and the girl pulled away again. He held still and the girl didn't come back. She was just a shadow out there against the dusty light that rose up from the lobby. Come on, Weller whispered. Leaning forward slow. Cat got your tongue?

At which the child came forward and showed him. Showed him through the slot. Came near and opened wide and let him see the reason that she hadn't spoken. She had no tongue at all. Just rotten teeth and the black pit of her throat and a hard wet knot pulsing. Weller drew breath. She clamped her mouth shut and dropped the plate and ran.

*

Later the old woman came. She stood outside banging on the door with something hollow as if she were demanding that he open up when she was actually warning him back. And back he went, as far away from the door as the little room permitted, dropping the metal arm that he'd been working on into his pocket. Hearing the hollow banging on the door and seeing her legs blocking the lower ventilation slots but not seeing anything through the upper slots at all and guessing who it was. He hollered all right come on in I won't try anything. For all the good talking to her might do. She sprang the lock and pushed the door open a crack and slid through. The door opening hard and the old woman stronger than she looked, using her shoulder. She kept an eye on him and put down a red plastic bucket. Just inside. Closing the door behind her but not locking it and giving Weller a look like don't you come near. Like don't you dare. The red plastic bucket a warning and its missing wire handle proof that someone had been circumspect. Weller felt the arm from the take-up reel in his pocket and wondered who. Who had been careful about what he might do with a length of heavy wire and who knew she was up here and who might be waiting for him to make a mistake and push his luck.

The woman leaned forward in a crooked way that made her seem both smaller and more threatening, and she looked Weller square in the eye. Steady and unafraid. Almost taunting. She was bent and wizened and lined all over like a map of someplace nobody had visited for a long time. Filth in those lines and puckers. Every pore and cut and eroded place plugged up with dirt. But she looked at him evenly and calmly and with serious intent. Holding out an accusatory finger. He thought she might begin signaling something to him the way he'd seen them signal to each other down below and he felt at a loss on that account, ignorant, but she didn't signal anything. She just held out her finger quivering. And after a moment, in a nearly inaudible voice that hissed and creaked from disuse, she said, "You leave my grandchild be." Five words that took all her breath.

"Your grandchild."

"Shhh." Her finger to her lips. "I still carry a little weight around here is all."

Nothing from Weller.

The woman backed up and unlatched the door and toed the bucket toward him. A peace offering or something. Who knows. "We can save you for the cold weather or we can eat you right now," she said, "it's all the same to me."

"I'm—"

"That child's got troubles enough."

"Yes, ma'am. I'm sure she does." For what child doesn't.

*

In the morning he rose and went to stand by the square window, patiently rubbing his bit of steel on the cinderblock and watching the day unfold below. Work details forming just as they had yesterday. The old woman tidying up and not looking toward the projection booth even once, as if he weren't there. A couple of the men, the leader and one other, kneeling together over what looked from his elevation like one of his road maps, poking at it with their fingers, disagreeing about something from the way they looked at each other and the way their hands flashed. Tight little movements at chest height. Something belligerent about them. A disagreement. Weller thought he knew who would win.

The other man folded the map and put it in Weller's backpack along with a few other things. The leader took some of those things back out and the other man let him. He didn't look happy about it, but he acquiesced. He knelt and dug around underneath a pile of junk and located the bag with Weller's spare pistol in it and the half-carton of ammunition, and the leader shook his head. No. He patted the weapon hanging from the leather thong around his waist as if he were the only person in the world entitled to wear such a thing. The other man shrugged and hoisted the pack onto his back and they both made for the door. Separating once they were outside, the leader going left and the other man going right and the fire door clapping shut behind them.

Soon everybody was gone except the old woman. The granddaughter leaving with the rest of them. Weller made a point of watching her go and he saw no sign of affection pass between those two. No sign of any connection whatsoever. Just two animals. Not even animals. Animals showed affection or something that you could mistake for affection, particularly with their own young. Dogs and cats, foxes and deer. No doubt even bears, which he'd thought these people were when he'd first seen one of them. He got thinking about that moment and about the narrow column of smoke he'd seen rising out over the forest earlier that morning. He'd thought then that the smoke was from a lightning strike, but now he wasn't so sure. Maybe they'd been watching him all along. Maybe he should have been more careful. It was too late now. Standing alongside the wall scratching his bit of steel against the cinderblock and checking his progress and watching the last of the people in the auditorium below filter out. Like bees, he decided. Like some kind of insect. Insects working together toward some automatic aim. They'd made themselves that way.

Lucky him, he thought. The place emptying out every day except for the old woman. Plenty of food coming in, just in case she was right about what they had in mind for his fate. Every day that they came back with rabbits or birds or fish he had another day to work on freeing himself. And whenever he finally pried the pins out, all he'd have to do was wait until it was just the old woman home before he opened up the door and left. As simple as that.

He thought of how easy it would be and he thought of getting home to Liz and Penny and it gave him the patience he needed. Plus now he knew where to find his spare pistol.

Later on she brought his food. She didn't enter this time. She stood outside the door while he ate and that was all right because it meant she didn't see when he soaked up a pool of grease with a part of his shirttail and saved it for lubricating the hinges. She just bent to slide the plate through and then stood outside the door. He talked to her, though. Said he hadn't meant any trouble by speaking to the girl. By seeing if she knew some old fairy tale. It wasn't anything. He hadn't meant any harm. Certainly not by asking if the cat had her tongue since who knew. It was just an expression people had.

The woman didn't answer. Weller just talking to the idea of her outside the door. Talking and tearing off a piece of his shirttail with his teeth and sopping up grease and continuing to talk. Telling her he hadn't meant any harm. Not to a poor little girl. Not when he had a little girl of his own back home who was the whole reason he was down here in the first place.

Just planting that seed. Sliding the plate back through and thanking the old woman kindly, and planting that seed.

*

She brought him his breakfast the next day and he talked to her some more. Told her why he was on the road, if she was interested. Why he'd come so far from home. How that daughter he'd told her about was blind and how he was going to get her cured if it killed him. Not looking for sympathy but just telling his story, the way a person would.

Around noon, when they were all alone in the building, he stepped away from what he was doing and called down to her from the square window. She glanced up at the sound of his voice and quickly turned her back as if to pretend she hadn't heard him. Busying herself. He called down asking her name. Saying his name was Henry and what was hers. She didn't answer.

*

He had his tools ready, and he began working on the hinges. Working on the top hinge for a while and moving to the middle when his back started to seize up and then kneeling to work on the bottom. Repeating that. Thinking he'd like to get far enough today that he could work a little grease into each of them and have that going overnight.

Between the noise of his scraping and his deep concentration and the old woman's light tread, he didn't hear her come up the stairs until she was there. Outside the door saying, "What in hell do you think you're doing?"

"Nothing."

"Don't tell me nothing. I've got ears."

"I'm working on your movie projector," he said. Not sure where the lie had come from but glad to have it.

"You can lay off right now," she said.

"No," he said. "I want to see if I can make it work."

"We got no use for a movie projector."

"I know that," he said. "The bulb's busted anyway and you don't have any juice, so you'd be in trouble if you wanted to start watching a movie."

"Nobody here needs to watch a movie."

"I know that."

"So leave it alone." That cracked voice sounding hurt. "It's been ages since I seen a movie, and I don't guess I need to see another one."

"All right. I'll quit."

So he had to work quietly. He kept his motions small. He wrapped his scrapers with rags. He untangled the bedsheets and the foam rubber that someone had made into a pallet and he shook out the mouse droppings and folded them double and he worked underneath them. There was no air and it was hot and it stank, but everything stank. A man using a red plastic bucket for his toilet doesn't trouble himself about that. He only considers how long it might be before he's free of the whole business.

When they all returned that afternoon he hadn't scraped away enough to use the grease, so he waited. The old woman brought him his supper and he ate it and saved some more grease in case. She whispered to him through the slot once he'd handed it back. Said she was glad he'd made up his mind to behave himself. Said if he kept it up he might last until his people from Black Rose came and got him.

He whispered back what was she talking about.

She was gone.

*

By that same time the next afternoon he'd broken through to raw metal in three places, one at the top of each hinge where the pins went down through, and he worked the sharpened steel into the crevices he'd exposed. Rubbed in some grease and let it work.

She came and slid him his supper and he whispered to her. What was that she'd said about Black Rose? He wasn't any Black Rose.

She said not to kid her. That motorcycle. The helmet. His gear. All of it Black Rose and all of it brand new and nobody got hold of that stuff who didn't have a claim to it. You try stealing from Black Rose you don't get very far so don't try to kid her. She said they'd sent one of their own to negotiate. To cut a deal and sell him back home where he belonged.

He said, "You mean that fellow who left."

She said, "That's the one."

He said, "So he's going to Washington."

She said, "Wish him luck. You still might get out of here in one piece."

It was ridiculous but he didn't say so. Black Rose would come get him if he'd taken possession of that car he was after, but until then he was utterly dispensable. The man was chasing down a dead end. Probably fixing to get shot. He felt some sympathy for him but not enough to say so. Not enough to say so and let the old woman see how little value he actually had in the world. So what he said was, "That's a good plan. You folks think of everything."

And what she said was, "Don't get smart." The fellow who'd left was her son-in-law. She'd lost her daughter in the Great Dying, but still. Family was family.

"Not to mention he's the little girl's father," said Weller.

"You might not be as smart as you think," said the old woman.

*

He worked on. The more progress he made, the more he saw that he hadn't guessed how aggressive the rust might have been. It had eaten right through. So thoroughly that when he'd cleared the head of the top pin and worked a sharpened bit of steel underneath it for a lever the lever just sank into the metal like into something soft. And when he put a little pressure on it, the head tore off clean. The little round disk popped away and ricocheted against the door and nearly hit him in the eye. All right, he thought. Fair enough. He could still drive the pin through, and he could do that with one of the other pins as soon as he had one out.

He moved on.

The pin in the center hinge broke too.

The third one, the one at the bottom where the water leak had done less damage and the rust was lighter, came out clean. It took some patience and it took some time and it took all the rest of the grease he had, but it came out. Weller wiped the grease from it. Standing in the projection booth holding it up like a prize for just a moment, the pin gleaming darkly in his hand. Fragile and a little bent. He wanted to straighten, it but he didn't dare.

He rubbed the grease from it again. Took off his boot to use the heel for a hammer, not caring that the old woman would hear. He positioned the pin above the middle hinge and began tapping on it. It bent more, but he kept tapping. The other pin starting to inch free. Red rust falling.

The sound of his tapping drew the old woman. She said you quit horsing around with that projector and he said what do you care if I do or don't. He said you worry about your granddaughter and her father of hers that went off. You worry about them and leave me alone. Not pounding then because she was right outside the door and she'd know exactly what he was doing.

She said, "That one who went off isn't her father. He married my girl but they never had children. Her father's my own son. My own son by blood."

"What happened to him?"

"Last thing I knew, he was carrying a six-shooter around."

Weller understood. "So he's the boss."

"You could say that," she said. "The boss is usually the one with the six-shooter." Using that old word again. That old word from the western movies that almost nobody had ever seen.

"I had a gun like that myself once," Weller said. "But I lost it."

"I guess that's why you're not the boss anymore." The old woman laughed. Laughed like she thought Weller was funny, not like she was rubbing it in. And then she stopped. Turning away. Getting ready to go on down the stairs. "Now you leave off on that hammering," she said. "Don't cross me and don't cross my boy. People who cross my boy don't come out of it happy."

Weller standing behind the door with his boot off, waiting. Saying, "I understand." Saying, "I guess if a fellow's got what it takes to run a crew like this, he might leave behind a little bit of a wake." Giving him his due.

"They're only alive on account of him," she said. "They'd do anything for my boy."

"I'll bet."

"Every single one of them had his tongue cut out because he said to do it."

Nothing from Weller.

"That boy of mine," she went on "You're either with him or against him. That's how he knows."

"How about you?"

"I've got seniority."

"What about the girl?" he said. "His own daughter?"

The old woman began to move off at last. "She's with him," she said. "What did you think?"

*

He woke in the morning to another day drawn out from nothing by the dream of his wife and daughter. Thinking this was it. This was the day he would set himself free. He got the middle pin out right away. It was broken into a million pieces and the shards of it were all powdered down into a little heap on the floor, but it was out. One more to go. He stood with one boot off and stretched up on his toes to reach the top hinge and he breathed in the thin trickle of rust that leaked down with every strike. The angle was awkward but there wasn't anything in the room he could stand on. The projector was bolted to the concrete and nothing else was solid enough. He tried the stack of film cans but it just toppled over. Crashing down. Spilling out streamers of celluloid.

The old woman came with his breakfast but she said he wasn't going to get it unless he laid off. He said didn't her son want him fed and she said yes and he said then maybe she'd better not start making his decisions for him. A man who'll have his own child's tongue out. How did he get started on that anyhow.

She told him. It was as if she'd been waiting for him to ask. For anyone to ask. For anyone to be able to ask and now Weller had shown up and raised the question and made himself her father confessor.

She took responsibility for everything. This was before the Great Dying, she said, but they didn't have any insurance so it was really the same thing as the Great Dying and even if they'd had insurance nobody could have fixed what happened. What she'd done and what she'd caused. She'd eaten something while she was pregnant and the next thing she knew her son had come out damaged. Maybe it was the beginning of the Great Dying. Maybe her son was one of the first. Regardless he'd been born damaged and she and her husband God rest his soul had raised him up as best they could but he'd turned out crooked in spite of them. A child who looked all right on the outside but whose insides were damaged. It had made him crooked. And in the end, she was the one to blame. Which made her to blame for her grandchild too. She took it all upon herself.

Weller said he understood. He understood all about that.

She said oh sure I'll bet you do.

Weller said no. Really. Kneeling down and letting his boot drop silently to the floor and talking to her through the ventilation slot. Saying how it was the same way with him and his daughter. How he was on this terrible trip not just for her sake but also for his own when you got right down to it. Taking something he did wrong and killing himself if he had to in order to make it right. Something that wasn't any poor child's fault.

After a while saying how about my breakfast. And the woman sliding it through.

As soon as he'd finished and she'd taken the plate and gone back down the stairs, he started hammering again. Up on his tiptoes in that cramped position. Blame it on that because you might as well blame it on something. His strike was off and he was still thinking about what he owed Penny and the pin bent itself at an angle of about thirty degrees. He tried straightening it, kneeling and daring to give it just one single tap, but a rotten break opened up in the middle, leaving just two useless pieces left. Short pieces not much more than shards themselves. And him kneeling on the floor with one boot off and one boot on, cursing himself and looking everywhere for some other possibility. There was nothing else to use on the hinge. He'd already determined that. As for ways out other than the door it was hopeless. There was a ventilation grid overhead but it was only about ten inches on a side. The square opening that looked down over the auditorium wasn't much bigger than that and even if it had been picture window he couldn't have gone out through it. Not without some way to lower himself down. These rotten sheets and rags would never do. And even if he'd lowered himself to the balcony what then. He could feel it collapsing underneath him already. He could feel everything collapsing underneath him.

He stayed there on the floor and sank back on his haunches and thought of Penny and Liz. What a ruin he'd made of everything. How he should have left well enough alone. The two of them were stuck in New York now without him, without him ever, and with no way to get back where they belonged. He'd made no provision for that. He thought maybe Carmichael would take pity on them, but he knew that was a pipedream. Carmichael would feel that he'd been duped. Taken advantage of. Caused to waste the tiniest fraction of his fortune on Penny, on something that meant nothing to him and never would. Weller knelt there on the floor thinking about what he'd said to the old woman. About how he'd kill himself if he had to in order to make Penny's blindness right. Thinking he should be content, because as far as he knew he'd done just that.

*

The woman came with his supper and asked what was that crash before anyhow, you can be honest with me. Maybe feeling some kind of common cause or maybe not.

He said it wasn't anything. Just those movies in the cans. He'd bumped into them and knocked them over and the old woman said you'd have to bump into them pretty hard and Weller said he did. Saying they were all over the place now. A mess of film everywhere.

The old woman asked what movies he had in there and he said what did it matter if they couldn't watch them. They were just film.

She said the last one she saw here was some western. That famous one. Not John Wayne but after him. John Wayne was dead when they made it. The same character but a different actor, she couldn't remember who. They used to have senior citizen specials for a dollar and now that she was old enough to qualify as a senior citizen they didn't have them anymore. Just her luck.

He said she was welcome to come in and take a look if she wanted. See what he had.

She said no. Not no thanks, just no. Like she could tell he was angling for her to unlock the door. She just left him his supper and waited to take the plate back. A thin chipped plate made of plastic and no use to him but she always waited for it anyhow.

He got thinking. He asked her how many movies she'd seen here.

She said hundreds. "I lived in Greensboro my whole life," she said. Her voice was less cracked and labored now that she'd been using it a little from time to time, coming in softer through the ventilation slot. The two of them whispering so nobody could hear. She said she'd seen everything in those days. Nature movies and animated cartoons when she was a little girl and James Bond when she got a little older. James Bond always keeping the world from coming to an end. It was a nuclear bomb or a death ray or something like that every time with James Bond. Remembering put a lightness in her voice, but there was a weariness there too. "James Bond never saw this world coming," she said.

Later on, in the smoky dark, Weller lay on the hard floor thinking about the end of the world. Thinking that thanks to him his daughter would see the world winding down at last, the way it had been going for his whole life and he hadn't even paid attention. Crumbling and winding down and Penny seeing it clearly but not really recognizing it because nobody did. Not really. Regardless of how good her vision became she wouldn't know where the world had been and where it might have gone and how far down it had come. Not the way that the old woman did. The old woman remembered. He watched the firelight flicker up from below and he studied how it made the projector loom up out of one kind of darkness and into another and he had an idea.

*

After breakfast he began to work on the projector. Cleaning the various surfaces with rags and blowing off dust and freeing up stuck parts. Working gently and steadily. The big lens was screwed on tight but he got it loose. It was meditative work that gave him time to think. It was quiet work too, and the old woman didn't know he was doing it, so he told her when she brought supper. Just to see if she'd object this time and this time she didn't. Instead she asked again what movies he had in there and he said again that he didn't know. She scoffed, asking how he thought he'd show one without power anyway, and he said he hadn't figured that out yet.

*

The man who'd gone to Washington wasn't back, and it had been a week at least. Enough time, if he hadn't gotten in trouble. Weller asked about him while he ate his breakfast and she didn't have any answer. She didn't know how long her son would wait before he'd make some decision as to Weller's future without him. Until then there was still hope, she said, but Weller didn't feel hopeful.

He said remember that six-shooter he used to have and she said yes. He said he used to have a satellite phone, too. He said a condemned man usually gets one phone call. She said she remembered that from some movie. Except she thought it was a cigarette he got. The condemned man.

The rest of the day he kept working on the projector. He had it pretty clean now and he began breaking off lengths of film and attempting to wind them through the various pins and clamps and gates. A maze of them. There was a diagram inside the cover but it didn't help much because the printing on it was faded and the paper was brown and generations of mice had chewed away parts of it. The film was fragile and it kept breaking. Bits flaking off and getting stuck and Weller blowing at them and sometimes pushing them deeper into the works and having to take everything out and start again.

The frustration nearly killed him.

He took off his glasses and held up the big projection lens and squinted through it to see what he was doing up close. He figured out the drive mechanism and used the broken hinge pin as a crank and made it turn. Greasing it a little and cranking it more and limbering it up. Working himself into a kind of hypnotic rhythm, and rising out of it only when he heard a voice.

It was the old woman down below, singing to herself. Making her rounds with her voice raised up wobbling in the absence of her son and his silent followers, going over some old song that Weller didn't know. He looked out through the square window and saw the dusty sunlight streaming down through the hole in the roof and the woman down there working with her voice lifted up. The song had the word baby in it a few times but it wasn't a lullaby. It was some old love song. He listened, wondering how many years it had been since these walls had heard such a thing and guessing that the old woman probably wasn't even aware of what she was doing.

Before the rest of them got home and she went quiet he tried threading some film through again and this time he had it right. It didn't break against the sprockets now that he could turn them with the makeshift crank. There was a little gate or window that opened and closed when the film passed in front of it and at first it didn't want to open or close at the right time, but he got that worked out. He settled on a speed that seemed good. Just feeding the same length of film through again and again and looking through the gate to watch the shapes on it move in the light from the hole in the roof. She sang some other songs, one of them a religious one that he knew, and then the light began to fade and her son returned and that was the end of it.

*

She came in the night with the satellite phone. She must have. It was there in the morning, right beside him. It was dented and cracked from the crash of the Harley, with the battery pack loose and the antenna cocked to one side, but that was good news. About the battery pack anyhow. Because as long as the phone had been without power, Bainbridge didn't know where he was.

*

While he ate his breakfast he told the old woman he'd been looking over some of the film from the cans. The labels were ruined so he couldn't tell what was what but he'd been studying what he had. Time on his hands and all.

She asked was there anything like that movie *National Velvet,* and he said he didn't know. She said it was a horse movie with a girl. She didn't remember if she'd seen it here or on the television but it was a nice story and nobody told stories like that anymore. She'd had a horse herself when she was young, and thinking of the movie made her think of her own horse. He said he hadn't seen any horses so far but he'd keep an eye out. He'd let her know if he found *National Velvet.* She said it would do her heart good just knowing it was there. Just knowing it was somewhere and not only in her memory.

He told her thanks for the phone, and she said what phone.

It turned out later that the battery was weak but still good. Locating the satellites took a couple of minutes and the phone beeped a number of times in the process and Weller was glad that everybody down below was gone except for the old woman. Clamping his hand over the little speaker grate and realizing how much trouble he could have caused her. Thinking that her son might have gone ahead and taught her not to talk to strangers as a result.

The phone connected, but Bainbridge didn't answer. Some assistant instead. Weller said, "Hurry up and get him. My battery's about gone."

The general came on saying he could plug that into the cigarette lighter on that fancy car or had he forgotten.

Weller said, "How did you know I've got the car?" Glad that the other man had come up with the idea himself. It was easier than lying.

"What a kidder," Bainbridge said. "You're in Greensboro. You're on your way home."

"I'm sorry I've been out of touch."

"No shit, sonny. We were worried sick."

"All for nothing."

"I can see that," Bainbridge said. "So tell me about my old friend, Marlowe."

"First you tell me about Penny. Given how well she was doing before, I'd think she'd be making really good progress now."

Bainbridge hesitated. Weller got uncomfortable when Bainbridge hesitated. It meant he was thinking. "The main thing to keep in mind," he said, "is that *you're* making good progress."

"I am."

"Keep it up, then. Keep it up because—to tell you the truth—she's had a couple of setbacks."

"What kind of setbacks?"

"Her mother didn't give me the details. The only thing she said was *setbacks.*"

"I don't like hearing that."

"Who does? Bottom line is it's time for you to put the pedal down and come on home. That's all you can do."

"I was thinking you could talk to Carmichael and have him get the two of them home without me."

"Just come back and see her with your own eyes. Get yourself home with your little girl."

Bainbridge the motivator. Weller picturing himself dying here without ever knowing how Penny's and Liz's stories would end. Cursing himself for having made this call and broken his own heart.

Bainbridge asked about Marlowe again. How he was holding up. What kind of arrangements he'd made for himself down there in the wilderness.

Weller wanted to hurt him. "You wouldn't believe your eyes," he said. "He's living like the king of some tropical island."

"No."

"He's so happy it would make you sick."

"Honest? I can't believe it."

"Believe what you want," said Weller. "But tell those doctors it's time to get serious. And have Carmichael get them home the minute she's ready, in case I get held up." The battery was blinking red and the blinking was getting slower, dying out. "Tell everybody I'm on my way."

*

Later on, running the film between his fingers and holding it up to the light, he found a sequence with a barnyard in it. No horses, but at least a barnyard. People moving around in a dirt yard in front of a house and going in between the house and a barn. Black and white images but brown with age. A storm brewing and a snakelike cloud whipping the sky and a little girl hurrying down a path with a suitcase in her hand. He didn't know if maybe this was part of that *National Velvet* the old woman remembered. Most of the film was sticky and rotted and glued together at some molecular level and he'd never get the loops of it separated from one another so he'd never know for sure, but there were still parts of it that he could make out. He fed one length into the projector and got it clicking along and looked through the gate. Watching the girl hurry down the path. A dog alongside her or maybe a cat that she stopped to pick up. Shooting a desperate look around and getting that dog or cat before she dared go on. Weller thinking she looked like she wanted to get home. Looking at the girl and thinking of Penny. Thinking that if he ever got home he'd get her a dog or a cat. Whichever she wanted.

The film ran out and slid into a pile on the floor and he bent to retrieve it. Stood up and put his arm out the square window holding it like a caught snake and called down to the old woman. Saying he'd found something.

She came up and asked what it was.

He told her. He said he had no idea if it was that horse movie she'd seen once upon a time, but it had a little girl in it and a barnyard so it might be the one. Either way it was only part. A few seconds. But he had the projector sort of going and you could see the pictures move against the light that came in from the hole in the roof, so if she wanted to take a look, now was the time. Her people would be back soon. Her son. And then she'd have to wait.

She made him promise. She made him swear on his daughter's heart that he wouldn't do anything rash, by which she meant trying to slip out while the door was unlocked or striking her over the head and tying her up or something on that order. Saying her son would kill her if Weller got loose before they had the chance to make a deal with Black Rose and Weller didn't want that on his hands did he, no matter how much she deserved it. Even though she had made her own bed a long time ago. Both of their beds it turned out. She just wanted a look at that *National Velvet* if that was what it was. Just a look.

He said, "All right. I promise."

She said, "I think we understand each other."

He said, "I believe we do."

She said, "I'll work on my son if that deal with Black Rose doesn't turn out."

He said, "I know you will."

She said, "I can't make any promises."

He said, " I know you can't."

She let herself in. Latched the door behind her and saw him feeding the film into the machinery. She said, "Careful now," as if he might be otherwise. Weller not even turning to see her come in. Not even turning to see about the door behind her.

He lined her up alongside the projector and slightly behind, where she could see best. Clouds passed overhead and the column of light in the room below went dim and she squinted. He said, "Wait." Reaching out a hand to her shoulder to put her in the right spot. While the light was dim he gave the pin a half-turn and asked her if she could see the picture move, and she said she could. It was blurry but she could. He moved her back a few inches and gave it another little turn and she said it was worse. He gave her the big lens and she looked through that. Experimenting for a minute until it was clear as a bell, she said. Clear as a bell. Right there.

He pulled the film and set it back to the beginning and they waited until the clouds passed. "All right," he said. "Here goes." The film beginning to pass over the sprockets. The gate snapping open and shut.

The old woman held the lens up to her eye and gasped. People moving about in a barnyard. "I believe I've seen this one," she said.

"Wait," said Weller. "Wait for the girl."

"Oh, my," said the woman. "A storm's coming."

"I don't know about any storm," said Weller. "I never looked through that big lens myself."

The woman was motionless. Rapt. "Here she comes now," she said. "The little girl." Her mouth dropping open as the child turned and bent to gather up her dog. "A storm's coming," she said, woeful and full of panic, as if it were coming right here. "She'll be caught out in it."

"It sure looks that way," said Weller.

The last frame snapped through and he quit turning.

The old woman lowered the lens. Tears in her eyes. Tears for the resurrection of this long dead story and tears for the rebirth of this poor suffering child. Tears for the storm that was coming, and for the storm that had already come. "You make that phone call?" she asked.

"I did."

"And what'd you find out about your girl?"

"Not much," he said, "But I guess I'm still hopeful."

"Then go," she said. "Go on right now."

And he went.

Ten:

Salted Earth

He stayed off the highways and kept his profile low. He took the dead battery out of the satellite phone rather than risk any trickle of power that might betray his lie to Bainbridge. He ate what he found, not touching the handful of Black Rose rations he'd snatched up, holding those in reserve in case he had his bearings wrong and the trip to Spartanburg stretched out.

He was careful to stay away from any green thing that looked as if it had ever been cultivated, sticking instead with mulberries and blackberries and bitter acorns, feeling his energy waning. He ate his way through the banks of kudzu that grew rampant everywhere. Toward evening on the second day he killed a two-headed mud turtle in a reedy slough and started a fire and boiled it in its own shell. It made dinner and breakfast plus some extra to carry along in his pack. He spent most of the next morning skirting a broad acreage of ripe feed corn that beckoned him with its numberless bobbing heads. The hardiness of it smelled powerfully of PharmAgra intervention. That mud turtle had likely fed here and he had fed on the mud turtle but you couldn't control everything. He went on.

The woods were dense with game trails but not with game. He had the spare pistol and some ammunition and he was halfway hoping for a wild boar but he found no sign of one. They were supposed to be everywhere in these hills. Good eating but fierce. Aggressive and impatient with man. He began thinking a deer would be easier, although he didn't have any interest in shooting a deer. He would rather shoot a boar than a deer unless he had to, but he guessed he might have to so he kept his eyes open.

Alongside a dry creek bed some fresh prints crossed the trail, coming out of dense woods and vanishing back into the same. Not game, but men. Two and a half days out of Greensboro and more than halfway to Spartanburg with Charlotte not even visible to the south from the highest points. Willfully in the middle of nowhere. That far away from anything like a city. And yet here they were. He thought he'd been going quietly but he went even more quietly now, thinking they might have seen the smoke from his fire last night. That fire he'd lit with the old man's Zippo. Wondering what else that two-headed mud turtle might be about to cost him. Walking on and wishing he hadn't seen those prints and glad he had. Calculating his odds and not liking them and figuring how to change them to his benefit.

Damn it if he'd be ambushed again. He stopped and doubled back to the place where the prints crossed the trail. They pointed south, toward Charlotte. He stepped off the trail and followed. Drawing his pistol and vowing that if there were any ambushing to be done, he would be the one to do it.

He found the men in a grassy place where their path went under a road. One of those big dry culverts that were starting to seem like part of some secret underground transit system. He came out of the woods and saw two men sitting face to face just inside the lip of the culvert, eating. Passing a canteen back and forth. Out of the sun the way a person would want to be when he ate his lunch, but still visible. Weller didn't need to know everything they'd taught him in Washington to see that if they got up and ran they'd have to come either toward him or straight down the culvert, and either way he'd have a clean shot. Either way he had them. He clicked back the hammer of the gun to announce himself, and they raised their hands.

These men weren't like the people in Greensboro. They were rough but businesslike in the way of soldiers or pioneers. Experienced traveling men who'd made a mistake out here where they'd thought they owned the place and it turned out they didn't. They carried backpacks and duffel bags and they had pretty fair hiking boots from someplace. They were lean but not starvation lean. They weren't the two runners he'd seen in Connecticut, but they could have been their twins.

Weller said, "Don't worry, I'm not PharmAgra."

The men didn't lower their hands and he didn't lower the .38 either.

One of them lifted up his chin and said, "No shit." His mouth full. Like PharmAgra didn't come out here anyhow, and like they would be better equipped if they did. Better equipped and more formidable than Weller, who was standing there like some kind of lightly armed scarecrow.

Weller kept on. "I don't want that stock you've got. Those seeds or whatever. Those plants."

"I don't know what you're talking about."

"Sure you do."

"All right. Have it your way." Like Weller was crazy and he was humoring him.

"I'm a friend of that plant doctor. Doctor Patel up in Connecticut."

"Good for you," said the man in the culvert. Staring down the gun. "I ain't *nobody's* friend." He tilted his head toward the other man, who hadn't said anything yet. "I ain't even *his.*"

"I'm talking about that doctor you work for."

The man shrugged, but with the heel of his boot he pushed back his duffel bag to conceal it behind him. "I don't work for anybody."

"Fine," said Weller. Figuring he knew who paid at least some of the freight, and not caring.

"Fine," echoed the man. Actually echoing in that culvert. "So now we know what you *don't* want, what is it you *do* want? We got places to be."

"I'll bet you do," said Weller. "Charlotte, maybe."

"None of your business."

"Spartanburg."

The man blew air through his nose. Not quite a laugh. Hard to say what it meant.

"What do you know about Spartanburg?" Weller asked. Thinking whatever these two had seen from ground level would trump all of the airborne reconnaissance in the world.

The other man answered this time. His voice was low and cracked and he had to work to make it come out. Like there was something wrong with the parts of him that made it. "Spartanburg ain't what it used to be," he said.

"Is that right? What'd it used to be?"

"It used to be a nice friendly town."

Weller smiled. "You find a nice friendly town out here, you let me know about it."

148

The man wasn't amused. "My people come from Spartanburg. Way back. Generations."

"Lucky them."

"I guess. They got evacuated a long time ago. Some by the dying and the rest by the mercs."

"Marlowe."

"Right. Shown the door. I was a teenage boy living in my grandfather's house. They took everything useful and barricaded themselves inside the old car plant. Bunch of locusts swarming through."

"Sorry."

"Me too."

Weller scratched his forehead with the butt of the .38, and the first man spoke up. "Are you going to put that thing down one of these days?"

"I just didn't want anybody getting the drop on me."

"Mission accomplished." Both of them lowering their hands.

Weller watching them. Lowering the gun too. Releasing the hammer easy and saying, "There's just one more thing."

They shrugged.

"I could use a little bit of that food you've got." Hanging the pistol in its rope sling and drawing near.

*

They went their separate ways. Weller back through the woods to where he'd left the game trail and the other two down the culvert. They wouldn't say where they were headed. He thought Charlotte, or someplace in that general direction whose name he didn't know. Maybe a place without a name at all. Patel had said that there were stations like hers scattered everywhere. Who knew how many or where.

The landscape opened up. Hills rose to the southwest and he rose with them. Mile after mile of green spreading out below, great expanses of it visible from certain open vantages, more shades of green than a person might have thought possible. Different greens from up north.

He kept close to the highways but not on them. Not again. Progress was slow but it was progress, and it was secure or if not secure then at least more or less secret. Eighty-Five was his touchstone and he kept to it, not even seeing Spartanburg proper when he passed by to the northwest. Just an exit ramp labeled with the name of the city suspended high overhead with the last five letters of the word shot out. The work of a machine gun by the look of it and no ammunition spared.

He crept up the ramp and reconned and saw that the highway itself was in fair shape. Carpeted in green but no doubt passable in that car he was after. If he got the car and if he got gasoline for it and if he got out. He thought of Greensboro. How that barricade of ironwork had driven him off the main road and down into the remains of the city, where people he'd taken for bears did their hunting. He thought now that he should have suspected something. He should have wondered why someone would divert people off the road.

He descended and walked on through a forest of pine and hardwood with a high canopy and not much undergrowth. Looking up once and seeing in a stand of hickory the husk of a two-man helicopter dangling down. The rotors gone and white bones in canvas harnesses picked clean. Not even skeletons, just bones. Birds nesting up there. Birds that must be finding something to eat someplace.

He walked on thinking that there were dangers here beyond the natural.

When he came near the old car factory twenty miles west of town, the woods ended abruptly. He hesitated in the protection of the trees, reluctant to step out, finding himself on the perimeter of a circle so scorched and surgically cleared that not one blade of grass grew. Death radiated a mile in all directions. At least a mile and maybe more. Salted earth. Within it stood a maze of fence and wire. Razor wire topping sixteen-foot hurricane fence, and barbed wire in tangled gusts strewn everywhere, and nearly invisible lengths of trip wire running from fencepost to fencepost.

The day was growing late. He unshouldered his pack and emptied it out and went back into the woods to gather up rocks for checking his path against landmines come morning. He located a straight tree limb half again as long as he was tall. Then he gathered dry wood and sorted kindling and started a fire. Planning to warm up those last Black Rose rations and let the flames climb as high as they would and spend the night here at the edge of the clearing.

The people in the factory may as well know he was here. They'd find out soon enough. And if they came out to get him, so be it. It would save him the trouble of passing through the minefield come morning. He stuck the pistol in his boot just in case, and lay down underneath the stars.

*

But they didn't come. He sat up half the night and he slept the other half and nothing whatsoever happened. Lights came on at full dark way up high on the roof of the distant building. One or two of them moving around as the night went along, as if someone were carrying them. Someone on guard duty. Then again they may have been nothing but stars. He kept the fire going and made himself obvious and nothing came of it.

In the morning he set out, scoping a course through the fences and wire. Climbing where he had to. Crossing wide retaining ponds drained dry and gray asphalt parking lots cracked to pieces. Testing the path ahead with the tree limb and sending rocks thumping on ahead of him. He didn't care if he made a racket and he hid behind his backpack each time in case something blew, but nothing did. Nothing tripped and no matter how exposed he was on those sixteen-foot chain link fences nobody tried to stop him.

As he drew near the factory he could see why. It was a blank fortress of cast concrete and steel. Impregnable and uncaring. The forward section had once been a great sweeping horseshoe of glass as long as a city block, but it was just a skeleton now. Something for the wind to whistle through. All of the glass was gone and birds nested in the steel framework, coming and going unmolested. It was practically an exhibit of birds, framed there uncaged. He caught himself marveling at them and wondering how they lived. What they ate. Nothing from that mile-wide wasteland so well maintained. Something else. Bugs and worms but from where. They fluttered and sang in the ruined building and he listened to them for a moment and then he walked on. Around the side and down a pathway, keeping close to the wall. Toward the place where the real work must have happened in the old days before the factory closed. Where it must still happen now.

It wasn't a place meant to be entered. The circuit took him an hour and change and he saw no way in or out. No sign of people having come and gone. Running along one side of the complex was a series of loading docks, but they were welded shut. Not just locked or rusted over but welded. The place was a tomb, a pyramid meant to bury something forever and ever, a grave or maybe a prison. There wasn't so much as a roofmounted camera to keep an eye on things out here. He began to see why no one had noticed his fire last night or his movement across the cleared zone this morning, why no one had come out to warn him off or bring him in. There was no warning off because there was no entry. There was only this vast and complex relic of an earlier age, maintained and expanded and sealed up into a monolith.

Birds circled over it, coming and going by way of entry points well beyond his vision. The walls were many stories tall and unscalable, at least without the ropes and tackle that he'd set out with from Washington and lost in Greensboro. On the other hand he hadn't imagined he'd need to break in. Nobody had imagined that. He looked up at the high blank walls and thought of the wrecked helicopter he'd seen dangling from the forest canopy a hundred miles back. That was probably as close as Black Rose had ever gotten. He cursed his luck and considered how little those people in Washington really knew. How it was all guesswork even if it was professional guesswork, and how nobody'd guessed he'd find nothing here but a blank wall shutting out the world.

Still sewn into his pack was everything they'd given him for negotiating with Marlowe. Paper scrip and electronic credits. A promise from Carmichael written down in a letter, saying that whatever Marlowe wanted he'd deliver. Money being no object. He stood in the shadow of those high walls with the birds circling overhead and he thought that Marlowe not only wouldn't want money, he probably wouldn't want anything at all. He wondered how you'd negotiate with a man like that. If you could. How you'd negotiate with a man who'd already rejected everything.

He kept walking. He found himself in front of the old visitor entrance with the birds and came around again toward the welded-shut loading docks. Climbed up and tried a couple that he hadn't tried before. Regular man-sized doors alongside every second one of them but they were locked tight and their windows were boarded over from the inside. Little square windows with chicken wire and glass but not much glass anymore. Wood fastened from the inside instead. The last of the doors was the main one. It had a little shingled roof over it to keep off the weather, but the shingles had mostly blown off and the tarpaper underneath them was tearing loose in sheets and the whole business didn't look as if it kept off much. Alongside the door was a scanner, mounted at neck height the way they always were. There must have been a specification for that. Something architects used or contractors anyway. Another thing you could count on in a world that people had made regular.

He climbed the concrete steps to this last door and plucked little crumbles of safety glass from the tiny window and rapped on the wood nailed up behind it. Taking the pistol from his belt and using it to hammer on the wood and then hammering on the metal door itself. Gonging with the butt of the pistol. As if anyone who might hear would go to the trouble of answering or the further trouble of letting him in.

After a while he slung the pistol and turned away. Disgusted. Picturing the car he was after inside there someplace and wondering how he'd make it home if he never got to it. Hoping now that he was back in motion that Carmichael would hold onto Liz and Penny until he returned, and hoping on the other hand that he'd send them safely home to Connecticut just as soon as he could. Either one would be fine, now that he was a free man in the world again.

He punched at the scanner for good measure and the scanner lit up, a little blue light pulsing beneath a film of dirt. It still had power and it still worked. He didn't know which impressed him more. He stood there marveling at the blue light until it stopped pulsing and then he pushed at the face of the scanner again and the blue light pulsed some more. A little low-pitched electronic hum coming from somewhere now that he noticed it. Nothing else, though. No audible alarm or bright flashing lights or anything else. He imagined a readout on a screen somewhere in the belly of the factory blinking away to mark his intrusion, and the thought came as a relief. He might get inside after all. He stood there waiting on the concrete stoop and the sun went higher and the edge of the building's shadow crept nearer and nearer across the blasted earth and he punched at the scanner from time to time to keep it going and he stood there waiting on the concrete apron. He wet a fingertip and wiped the film of dirt from the blue light and nothing changed.

Then he remembered. He dug in his pack and found the lighter. The old man's Zippo. He worked the bottom cover off and dug one finger into the wet cotton wadding for that old Black Rose brand. The little gleaming square with a metal prong mounted on each side. He found it and clamped it between his teeth and slid the cover back onto the lighter and put the lighter away. Then he swept the brand past that pulsing blue light, and all hell broke loose. A klaxon barking from somewhere behind the wall. Footsteps inside running. What sounded like an army but was probably six or eight men, heavy boots pounding almost in unison and probably heavy armament to go with them.

Weller stood at the door and wished that the little square window with the chicken wire weren't blocked with wood. He was blind this way and he didn't care for it. He stepped back and nearly stumbled from the stoop but didn't quite. Caught his balance at the last second and backed down the steps nice and slow. No surprises or as few as possible. Staying clear of the door and keeping his distance from it for all the good that might do.

The klaxon choked itself off and the sound of the boots came closer, rapid and purposeful but certainly not panicked. Not by any means. People running but not running away. Running toward. They stopped just behind the door and everything went silent. A throat cleared. Some clicking from inside and a reciprocal blinking on the scanner. A key turning in a stubborn lock. Weller thought if they had wanted to see him before they opened up they could have done something about the wood covering the little window, but apparently they didn't. Apparently it didn't matter to them. To them it was all or nothing. Another key turning in another lock and metal falling on concrete and the clanking of heavy chains drawn through their own loops. Then the door opened.

An old man pushed it with one hand and leveled an automatic weapon with the other. The weapon large and well-oiled and heavy as death. The kind of thing that ought to stand on a tripod and here he was aiming it with one hand. The old man looked as if he'd been put together out of alligator hide a long time ago. As if he might have taken such an alligator himself with his own bare hands. Skinned it alive if he'd had to.

"Well, shit," he said. Frowning underneath the drooping gray mustache of a gunslinger. "You're not Patterson." But he didn't lower the weapon. It had a laser sight and the red dot of it hung steady on Weller's forehead. Cooly burning there.

"I guess you shouldn't have gotten your hopes up, major." The next soldier back. A woman, hard as the rest of them, reaching out to hold the door open with one hand. She was younger than the major by far, but then all of them were younger. "Patterson's dead," she said.

The major looked disappointed. "I suppose he's dead enough if this fellow's got his brand." Taking his eye from the scope to look hard at Weller. Sizing him up and finding him wanting. This poor wayfaring stranger, footsore and heartsore and looking it. He shook his head and put his eye to the scope again and moved the red dot from Weller's forehead to the little gleaming brand that he held, saying, "How about you toss that up in the air just as far as you can throw it."

Weller did, and at the top of its arc the old man aimed lazily up and squeezed the trigger just once. A burst. Nothing up there anymore but vapor.

"So much for Patterson," he said. "Another man gone." Lowering the weapon and looking Weller in the eye. "Now hand over that popgun and get indoors."

Weller didn't even think he'd noticed. But he took the .38 from its rope sling, and held it out by the barrel, and came on ahead.

*

He hadn't been given such hands-off treatment since PharmAgra back in New York. There at One Police Plaza with everybody wearing hazmat suits and that sealed-up glass room with the air being drawn out of it. Nobody here touched him either. Not a single one of those hard soldiers was hard enough for that. The major saw to it but he didn't really have to. Weller being hustled at gunpoint through long narrow corridors and across big echoing spaces, untouched and untouchable, like he was made of poison. In a warren of rooms that he took for the brig, one of the soldiers broke off and ordered him into a little concrete booth with showerheads on the wall and a drain in the floor and told him to strip naked and put everything in a plastic bag. The serious young woman who'd stood behind the major. She took the bag through a sliding glass panel and turned a valve that Weller couldn't see and the valve creaked and she kept on turning it until some kind of noxious chemical began to spray from one of the showerheads. There was no hiding from it in the little booth. The soldier could see him through the glass panel and she was going to keep the spray on for as long as it took. The chemical smelled like insecticide and it stung Weller's bare skin and it stung a hundred times more in all of the places where he'd scraped or cut himself over the last few weeks. Which was most places. Including that little incision on his throat that he thought had healed up completely. Even now the throb of it stirred his memory and made him think of his daughter. He cried out in his pain and in his sorrow, audible through the glass panel, and the soldier very nearly took pity upon him.

Plain water came next, from a different showerhead, and the soldier slid the panel open an inch to push through a washrag and a sliver of soap. The water heated up. The drain was slow. Weller shivered and scrubbed himself clean of the insecticide as best he could, standing in a pool of

chemicals and soapsuds and his own running filth. The mixture still sting-
ing his feet for they were blistered and broken and bursting with the early
stages of jungle rot. Bleeding and suppurating and turning the water a rusty
orange.

"Sorry about the drain," the soldier said when she'd cut the water and
opened up the panel to push him a towel. "I can't remember the last time
anybody really used this thing."

*

A young medic wrapped a sheet around him and took him away. He
sat him on a table and bathed his feet in alcohol and bandaged them. Said
he ought to have a course of penicillin, but it would require approval from
higher up. He'd see what he could do. Penicillin didn't grow on trees.

He had Weller lie down on the table and started up a saline drip, the
old kind with a graduated glass bottle and a rubber tube. He said Weller
was lucky to have made it here. Lucky to have made it here from wherever
it was he'd started, given the dangers out there in the world. But in any
event he was safe now. Safe and sound. "I guess you could tell us all a story
or two," he said.

"I guess I could," said Weller. He hadn't realized how exhausted he
was.

For the next hour the medic studied him like a specimen. Poked him
all over. Looked into every single orifice as if he expected to find something treacherous lurking inside of him, dying to get out and ruin everything they'd built here. He worked from an old Black Rose field manual
that had been passed down from one generation to the next. The highest
medical authority they had. He laughed to himself about the jungle rot
because it was something you found in the field manual but not in real life.
In real life you saw pregnancies. There wasn't anything about pregnancy in
the Black Rose manual, as Weller could imagine. As for jungle rot, the
manual said you could lose bone. You could lose the whole leg. He held the
book up to the light and paged through. Checking the index and going
back and reading closely to refresh his memory. His finger underlining.
Yes. It was a combination of sanitation and nutrition. What you ate played
a big part. No doubt whatever Weller had found to sustain himself out
there in the world hadn't done him any favors.

"Then again," he said, "Food was the least of your troubles. You've seen things that would give all of us nightmares."

"I suppose."

"Marlowe still goes out there sometimes, you know."

"Marlowe." Raising his head.

"He goes out all by himself." Shaking his head. "Out there where you've been. He's the fellow who runs this place."

"So I've heard."

"And he *still* does solo recon. A week at a time. Sometimes longer." Stricken by Marlowe's courage and selflessness. "Out there among them."

"Among who?"

The medic said Weller didn't have to pretend on his account.

*

He fell asleep on the table with the saline dripping into his arm, and when he woke up the major was there. The one who'd done the trick shooting. Time had passed but Weller didn't know how much. His belongings were on the chair in a sack, everything studied and sorted and his clothes put through the laundry. An old pair of boots from somebody's closet standing on the floor below them at least two sizes too big. The major had a tray in his hand with a plate of food and a cup of coffee. A .44 in a black Kevlar holster slung diagonally across his chest. He set the tray down and pulled the needle from Weller's arm like he was unhooking a fish and had Weller sit up. Told him his name was Oates. Standing there with a long face, watching Weller get dressed, saying he'd been disappointed when his team had filled him in on the Black Rose gear they'd found in his pack. The satellite phone. A knife and a compass and those rotten boots he'd been wearing. Not to mention the .38 special. He shook his head and consulted a list of Weller's belongings on a slip of paper and said in other words they'd pretty well established his *bona fides,* hadn't they? He said if Weller didn't mind, he sure would appreciate hearing whatever story Black Rose had cooked up to explain why he was down here in the first place, instead of up in Washington where he belonged.

Weller said there wasn't any cooked-up story.

Oates said fine. He said have it your way. He said the only other time they'd sent a scout down here he'd come complete with a nice cooked-up story, was all. He'd been a raggedy-looking individual like Weller and he'd seemed as if he'd lost his way and the story he told was just as pretty and sorrowful as it could be. But it hadn't smelled right, and in the end it had done him more harm than good.

Weller said he didn't have any story. Thinking about Penny and deciding that it would be best not to mention her just yet.

Oates said fine. That was all right with him. The last Black Rose scout should have saved his breath and maybe Weller had more brains than he did. Maybe he wouldn't try getting smart like that last one had.

Weller said getting smart how.

Oates said never mind that. He said if Weller didn't have a cooked-up story or had decided not to tell it, then why didn't he just skip right to the facts and save everybody time?

Weller touched the breast pocket of his coveralls, the pocket where he kept the picture. Whoever had done his laundry must have taken it out and cataloged it and put it back once his clothes were clean. He touched the place near his heart where he kept it and the touch itself was a kind of apology for not seeing fit to mention Penny. Reaching for the tray with his other hand. "For Christ's sake," he said, not even looking at Oates, determined not to have a story if Oates didn't want to hear one. "I just came to see about a car."

Oates laughed out loud.

Weller took that for a good sign, and he started working on the plate of food.

Oates quit laughing. "If it weren't for all that Black Rose gear, I might almost believe you."

"That old junk?" Weller didn't even look up. Talking with his mouth full. "I took it from your friend Patterson."

"Patterson was no friend of mine."

"You knew him."

"I sure did. We served together in Afghanistan. Afghanistan or Iraq, one or the other."

"I can't help you there." Looking over the rims of his thick glasses instead of through the pale shroud they'd become over this rough passage. "I get those two mixed up myself."

"Of course you would," said Oates. "You weren't even a gleam in your old man's eye back then."

Weller nodded. "I appreciate what you fellows did, though." Sitting there looking ruined. Unshaven and bone-thin. His bandaged feet bleeding through in patches and his fingernails black and broken. Those great thick lenses that magnified his eyes and magnified the weariness in them.

Oates thought about it all. How hard the journey had been on the poor bastard. How he'd lacked rations or anything else in the way of food out here a million miles from nowhere. How those eyeglasses he wore were anything but a prop. He thought for a minute and then he asked, "You came for a car, huh?" Because you couldn't get into Black Rose with vision that lousy. No way.

Weller nodded.

"We're not exactly in the car business down here."

"I can see that." Smiling up. "I was hoping I might change your mind."

"Right, right. All that money sewn into your pack. That chip full of credits."

"You noticed."

"We notice everything. Like how you don't seem to be the kind of individual who'd be walking around with that much money burning a hole in your pocket."

"It's a long story."

"I've got time," said Oates. Leaning against the wall. "Let's start with Patterson."

Weller was cautious. "What do you want to know?"

Oates smiled at him and maybe he meant it. "How you got that brand of his, for one thing. He sure as hell didn't give it away."

"Oh, that." He waited a beat. "I thought it might come in handy, so I helped myself to it." He waited another beat. Letting a light come on in his eyes. "The rag full of ether helped."

That got Oates's attention. He smiled from behind his big mustache. "I'm sure it did."

"Besides, I figured he could spare one little brand. He had a whole pile of them. A whole collection he'd cut out of other people."

Oates erupted. *"I knew it."* Slamming a hand against the iron door. "A bounty hunter."

"Correct."

"Counting coup like some damn Indian."

"You could say that."

"All his training, and he threw it away. For what." He made a fist and unmade it. "With all due respect, time was a civilian like you could never have gotten the drop on him. But a man gives up the structured life of the service and heads out on his own, next thing you know he's in trouble. First his training slips and then he loses his moral compass. Everything falls apart."

Weller said he guessed so.

Oates smiled a tight smile. "Then again," he said, "you look like you've had some experience with things falling apart."

Weller sat up straight in the chair. Squared his shoulders. "Yes sir, I have."

Oates nodded.

"That's how I ended up signing on for this trip."

Oates shook his head. "After a car."

"Oh, it's not just *any* car." As if that were the only thing he had to think about. A man with a singleminded and mechanistic mission. Just another mercenary like the rest of them.

Oates chewed his mustache. "You did the right thing taking that bounty hunter," he said, as if he'd forgotten the old man's name already. As if he'd willfully set it aside, just like that. "No hard feelings."

"I appreciate it," said Weller. Reaching for his things. "Now can go see about that car?"

"I'm sorry, but that's a few notches above my pay grade. You need to see Marlowe, except nobody sees Marlowe."

"Nobody?"

"Nobody but me."

"How about that money I've got. All that credit. That ought to get his attention."

"Money's no good here. Whoever gave you an idea like that wasn't using his head. It's not like we're on the old spice routes to the Orient."

"I've got more than money." Thinking of the letter from Carmichael. The overarching promise. Still hopeful.

"Not that we found." Oates consulting the list on his slip of paper. Folding it over and jamming it into his pocket. "Besides, we've got a funny belief in pulling your own weight around here. You want something, you work for it. Tell me: What do you do when you're not counting coup and stealing cars?"

"I wasn't stealing cars."

"It's a manner of speaking."

"I do a little of this, a little of that."

"Meaning."

"Mechanical work mostly. Machinery. Small engines. Repairs and whatnot."

"What kind of call is there for that out in the wilderness?"

"More than you might think."

"I wouldn't think much."

"You'd be wrong."

Oates gave him a look that said he didn't like being wrong and probably wasn't. "I've got a spot in mind for you," he said. "A couple of little jobs. Do as you're told, I'll go see Marlowe and get you that car. For all the good it'll do you."

*

The factory or compound or village or whatever it had become over the years must have occupied a square mile under roof, maybe more. It sure seemed big to Weller, clomping along with his bandaged feet hurting in those oversized boots. Some parts of it were original, and other parts had been expanded and modified far beyond the plans of the engineers who'd built it in the first place. Again and again until it had taken on an organic life of its own, fitted to the people who lived within it and tended it and modified it to suit their lives as their lives changed.

The character of the place shifted with each turn they made, and the more ground they covered the more Weller saw how complex and well-regulated it all was. A city-state in the antique mold. A world unto itself. Oates showed him hospital rooms and schoolrooms. Facilities for power generation and water treatment. In one place, a corridor they walked along opened up as wide as a street in some ordinary town. Facades of single houses and double houses and row houses springing up one after another on each side, with a few vehicles parked in front of them. Old cars like the cars he'd seen up north, Toyotas and Subarus. A couple of muddy old American pickup trucks looking hard-used. There were little lawns in front of the houses, a reel mower leaned up against one front stoop, and some porch swings hanging from light gauge chain. The factory ceiling was high here and there was glass overhead that opened for ventilation, letting in the air and the light and the day. The street if you could call it a street reminded Weller of where he'd come from, exactly the way it was meant to.

"Home sweet home," said Oates.

Weller asked how many people lived here.

"Just over five hundred," said Oates. Raising a hand in greeting to a middle-aged man who was emerging from behind the screen door of a little bungalow, dressed for farm labor and heading toward one of the pickups. "Running late, Harry?" The man looked abashed and didn't answer.

They walked on, Weller keeping his eyes open and noting the places where these houses had been knitted together at the seams. There were no yards at all between them. No alleys and no driveways for the cars. Just a solid surface built up from pieces. Fronts of one house butted up against the next and patched together, not so much like a real town as like something made to suggest one. The pickup truck rattled past, and Oates pointed back toward the little bungalow the driver had come from. "For all intents and purposes," he said, "That's the house where that fellow grew up."

"Honest?"

"We dragged them here board by board," Oates said. Waving his hand to take in the entire street. "Every single one of these houses. Marlowe's idea was to make things as homey as possible. If America insisted on going to hell, then by God we'd have our own little America right here."

There was a crossroads up ahead. A commercial district, with a grocery store and a diner and the rest of it. The necessities. Around the corner a public library and a three-story apartment building side by side, each of them made of actual red brick. "Housing for the younger crowd," Oates said, pointing at the apartment building. "Folks born after we got here. It turns over, of course. There are still a couple of spare slots where we can put you up."

"I'm not staying long." Not to reject a kindness, but just to keep things clear.

There was a white marble building across from the library. A cube in some simplified version of the Federal style with a sign out front saying Town Office. It was on the scale of an ordinary two-story house, no doubt far smaller than whatever municipal building old Spartanburg had once had, and with its ghostly face and its blank windows and its sealed door it looked like mausoleum. Weller pointed his thumb toward it and raised his eyebrows, and Oates said that's where they'd find Marlowe. Except they wouldn't. He was as secretive as the last president in his secure and undisclosed location. He came and went when you least expected it. Weller stopped and looked at the building. Oates saying Marlowe lived there and worked there both. Lived upstairs and worked downstairs, like an officer on campaign. Like old George Washington himself in his sleeping tent, with a desk in front of the bed and a carpet spread out on the grass. Spartanburg pretty much ran itself, he said, but Marlowe liked to be close to the center of things just in case.

People came and went on the street. Children in baby carriages. People smiling at Oates and eyeing Weller with something that he couldn't quite put his finger on. Suspicion or admiration or something else. Like they were looking at a giant come to life from a fairy tale. An ogre. An old woman walked past with a net bag full of groceries. Fresh vegetables of every description, round and fragrant and brightly colored. She lifted the bag to her chest with both arms and gave Weller a wide berth. He tried not to look at her but he looked anyhow, questions growing in his mind.

"The food," he said to Oates. "Where does it come from?"

"You'll see."

"What do you use for money?"

"Everybody works, everybody eats."

"This isn't what I was expecting," said Weller.

"Good," said Oates.

They came under an archway into another vast roofed space that must have been an assembly line in days gone by. Long fluorescent fixtures hung on chains at what would have been ceiling level, although the ceiling itself was much higher. Seventy-five feet up and buttressed like a cathedral, only with iron. The lights themselves were either switched off or dead, and in their place big glass panels ringed with razor wire let in the sun. Some of the panels were open to the sky, and birds came and went. Nests up there in the high iron. Back down on the floor, people worked at machines spaced at regular intervals. The hiss of compressed air and the hard flat clack of relays closing. The whisper of steam and the whir of thread over bobbins. People making clothing, not cars.

They angled in between a couple of machines and passed into a roaring hallway that stank of combustion and grease. Getting near the heart of the place.

Oates stopped at a closed door and poked his finger at the scar on Weller's neck. The faint red spot still angry from the insecticide. "What are you, anyhow? Branded or generic?"

"Generic."

"I mean for real. Not that crap you fellows put in and take out."

"Generic. Honest. Bred and born."

"So what's with the cut?"

"Nothing. I've been empty my whole life long." Touching the spot himself. "Your friend Patterson was just a little less polite than you about getting information."

"Cut first and ask questions later, eh?"

"Cut first and ask questions later."

"That's Patterson." Laughing but not because anything was funny. A sound that was rueful and full of accommodation to a hard world. "No wonder you ran out of patience with that old bastard."

*

They pushed through the door into a low place where the factory revealed its origins. A workshop, part garage and part high-tech hospital room. Certain things about it made Weller feel right at home. Impact wrenches and hydraulic lifts and grease guns. Tool carts on wheels and high-pressure hoses coiled like springs and the low pulse of an air compressor working. On the other hand there were plenty of things unfamiliar to him. Video displays mounted flush to the walls and thick gray cables snaking everywhere and bright flat touchscreen surfaces like relics from the elevated past brought back to life. A young woman with her back to them, poking at one of the screens and reading a stream of numbers that meant no more to Weller than birdsong. There was a car behind her with its hood open and a cable running to the screen. Some old Honda. Even though there were a number of cars in here—cars and other machinery too, broken-down tractors and golf carts outfitted for hauling and heavy equipment slung from overhead chains—even though there were plenty of cars, none of them was the one he was after. Not even close. For the most part it looked like New York. All that old Chinese and Japanese iron. All of it on life support.

They went across the shop floor and the young woman turned. Raising her right hand to Oates in a kind of half salute that she turned into a wave for Weller. Just being polite he figured, until he realized that she was the one who'd been in charge of the delousing. She wasn't a full time soldier after all. A volunteer army. It made sense. They kept going to a dim corner where a tractor stood neglected. A little antique John Deere missing most of its green. Oates climbed up and turned the key and it started up but it didn't seem to want to. Its upright exhaust throwing off a flurry of sparks and black smoke. Running but just barely.

Weller clucked and shook his head.

Oates shouted over the noise of the engine. "These babies were never meant to run on what we put in them."

"What would that be?"

"Ethanol. Homemade. We've still got a little gas around, but prudence requires that we conserve it." He cut the engine and waited until it shook itself quiet. Standing there while it coughed away for almost a minute. Tilting his head toward it when it finally died, and saying, "Think you could correct that?"

"I believe I could."

"Excellent. Do that for me, I'll do that other thing we were talking about."

"Deal."

"Start tomorrow morning."

"That suits me."

"How long'll it take?"

"Not long," said Weller. "I'm in a hurry."

Eleven:

The Garden of Eden

He ate supper in the diner at the intersection and his money was no good, just the way Oates had said. Everybody was fascinated with him. He was the only stranger they'd seen in forever. The talk of the town and already a legend, already bigger than life, so big they probably would have given him his supper for nothing even if everybody else had had to pay. But nobody paid. Oates had been right about that.

People acted like he'd been through a war and come out fine. Like he'd been through worse than a war. The end of the world and what came after. They weren't specific. Mainly they were speechless. Weller sitting there at one end of the counter eating a by-God hamburger with a slice of by-God tomato on top of it and by-God fries on the side like it was the most ordinary thing in the universe and people studying him like they couldn't believe their own eyes. Imagine that. Imagine what he'd passed through in order to eat that hamburger in their presence. Not one of them asked him a single question, though. He had never impressed anyone in the world that much. Not even his own wife or daughter.

Weller looked at the plate in front of him and asked the fellow behind the counter how safe this food was and the fellow laughed. A laugh like Weller must be kidding. He had an old-fashioned paper garrison cap on his head like in a diner in the fifties, the nineteen-fifties, almost a hundred years ago now. That folded wedge of bright white paper cocked forward. Whether someone had found a store of them during the ransacking of old Spartanburg or whether it had been made right here he didn't know. You could make that kind of thing easily enough yourself. It was just folded paper. Either way the counterman in the creased garrison hat looked like something out of an antique photograph in a magazine. Old. Older than the photograph in Weller's pocket by what may as well have been a million years.

Weller winked at him and told him he was starving and he wasn't going to turn down this hamburger if that's what he was driving at, but a person couldn't be too careful.

The counterman scoffed. Said there was no safer food in the whole wide world than that hamburger right there. He stood up straight and made a muscle to prove it. He was a few years younger than Weller but not many. Flexing a bicep and saying he was born right here and he'd eaten nothing but homegrown all his life and it hadn't done him any harm. They'd built this place on homegrown. Grass-fed cattle and open-pollinated vegetables like that tomato right there. Those very spuds. He stopped and put his knuckles flat on the countertop and showed Weller his teeth. Either demonstrating that he was still in possession of them or else just smiling big. Then he turned away to draw a cup of coffee, saying what did it matter to a tough guy like Weller anyhow. He'd eaten what he'd had to out there in the world, right? Before he'd found his way here. Before he'd found the Garden of Eden.

*

Weller didn't volunteer any information about his life up north and how he'd come to be here. Word had gotten around that he was a rough-shod mercenary on a job for pay, and he left it at that. He let them believe it because it served his purpose. The young ones had grown up idolizing old mercs like Oates and Marlowe because they'd saved them from the fate suffered by the rest of the world. They'd set them up like little gods. The older ones felt the same way, even though they knew their leaders' personal weaknesses from having worked alongside them at the outset. Nonetheless sufficient time had passed that even the oldest of the originals, the toughest and the most resourceful individuals who'd been handpicked by Marlowe for his march to Spartanburg, had forgotten the founders' weaknesses or at least forgiven them. To each of them, then, young and old, Weller might as well be another little god. That was fine with him.

After he finished the hamburger he went out into the street. A few people were out there on porches talking low in the failing light or standing around jawing on the street corner such as it was. A street corner with an actual working lamppost, he saw now. A mercury vapor lamp up there buzzing. There was one familiar face, the young woman from the machine shop. She was just a girl, really. He could see she wasn't much beyond that. A girl barely into her twenties. Out there smoking all by herself. Grease on her hands under that mercury vapor glare. He went to her and she said she was glad to see he'd recovered from the delousing yesterday. His tormentor then but not without reason. Apologetic now but not entirely. Like he knew how things had to be. Like everybody knew. She said she understood he'd be working in the shop.

He said yes. That tractor. Which he figured must be important since they were eating and all. Eating food grown around here somewhere. Agriculture required a tractor or two and it seemed he'd gotten here just in time. He sounded like this was another reason he ought to be treated like some kind of little god. Not meaning it that way but sounding that way because this was something he knew about and being proud of it came naturally.

She pulled on her cigarette and took him down a notch or meant to. Told him the problem was that there wasn't anybody in the shop old enough to work on that equipment. The old-timey mechanical stuff without an interface you could plug into. That antique machinery. Looking at him like he was a relic of the deep past. An antique himself.

He didn't even notice. It wasn't his way to notice but she didn't know that. He was too busy thinking. He said he didn't intend to stay around long, but if she kept her eyes open she might learn a thing or two. He'd show her if she wanted. Thinking as he said it that he could show Penny the same things one day, now that she'd be able to watch. Thinking that now that he'd given her a future he could give her a little of the past too. The knowledge that he carried with him. Feeling good about the future for a change, and realizing it.

The girl ground out the cigarette under the toe of her boot and picked up the leavings. Wadding the paper and carrying it to a trash bin a few steps away and coming back. Weller saying as she came, "The first thing you ought to learn is that tobacco's bad for you."

"Come on. Nobody lives forever." They were all tough around here.

"Live forever?" he said. "You never know. Why take chances?"

"You're a fine one to talk about not taking chances," she said. "At least I haven't gone outside."

More people were entering the diner and more people were leaving and there was a little group of folks milling on the curb. People down along the way in the dimness of their porches lighting candles in jam jars and glasses. Setting up folding tables and dealing out cards. Weller said the candles looked nice and the girl said she hadn't thought much about that since for the most part they just kept the bugs away. Weller said there weren't bugs where he came from. There weren't birds and there weren't bugs because the whole world was sterilized. He said bugs were mysteries to him.

She said, "If you show me what there is to know about that old tractor, I'll show you where those bugs come from. Work starts at eight in the morning, but meet me here at seven."

*

A cornfield. An actual cornfield under a yellow sun that blazed down through a rent in the roof that seemed just about the size of Kansas. An opening outlined with razor wire and what looked like electrified fencing but an opening nonetheless. Ripening green plants below it in long rows, tended by someone riding another cantankerous tractor. Different rectilinear fields surrounding this one like a patchwork quilt, ramifying out in all directions, teeming one after another with soybeans and potatoes and sorghum, green beans and red peppers and peas. Acre after acre of green in every hue. He thought he saw what looked like cotton in the distance and it probably was. Along one side were pastures fenced off for cattle and sheep, and there was dappled shade down there where trees grew, live oaks and maples and weeping willows clustered around irrigation channels dug to direct runoff. A vest-pocket apple orchard beyond that.

Something buzzed past his cheek and he swatted at it.

The girl looked at him like she'd told him so. She laughed and said her name was Janey. They walked through the field with their boots sucking mud and the tractor still coughing away in the middle distance. It crossed Weller's mind to think Oates might push his luck and require him to modify that one too. He wondered how many more of them there might be. How many more tractors and what all else of that vintage. He hoped Janey turned out to have a quick mind, because it looked like he was going to need an apprentice who could take things over.

In the shop they worked alongside one another but not together. Demonstrating things to each other when they could. Revealing secrets. Old magic on her part and older magic on his.

Janey attended to a blinking screen in her bay, tuning up the engine of a rusted-out Volkswagen Beetle without so much as touching it. The car was a generation newer than the dull red one Weller had in Connecticut. Loaded with electronics. He watched the screen and imagined the numbers flowing between the car and the computer along those cables, thinking if he'd found a car this new up north he'd have never gotten it running. He'd have had to leave it at the dump. Thinking he was a creature suited to an older time and maybe a worse one.

He showed her what a carburetor was. Going piece by piece through how these things actually worked. Where the fuel mixed with air and how you could tell a lean mixture from a rich one just by looking. This competent young girl who didn't know a float pin from a ball joint. Weller took the tractor engine down to its bones and she marveled like this was something that had just now been invented.

They talked about other things too. She said the drill they'd gone through yesterday was something that she and the other volunteers had run a million times. That drill where after the perimeter alarm goes off and you open up and it turns out to be just a regular person out there. What to do with him. It wasn't as if the alarm ever went. It had gone only once before in her lifetime. But they drilled anyhow, just in case. Just in case it went and it turned out to be a regular person out there needing to come in. Needing sanctuary.

Weller guessed she meant a regular person as opposed to some kind of armed force on a mission. He said, "I'll bet you were glad it was just me."

She said sure.

He said, "I don't mean me personally. Just that I wasn't some Black Rose squad. Like that helicopter you folks shot down way back when." He fitted some modified parts back together but they didn't go. It didn't bother him. He kept at it slow and steady.

She shook her head. She didn't even look up from what she was doing. She said nobody ever shot down any helicopter that she knew of.

He said this was before your time, I'll bet. It was just an old rusted shell. An old shell hanging from a tree a couple of miles north, just swaying back and forth in the breeze it was so light. So desiccated. The tree grown up around it and through it.

She said it didn't matter how long ago it was. She knew her history. Military history especially, which was big in Spartanburg. She said never once had they had to fire a single shot surface to air. Everything was electronic. Radio gear scrambling the signals that other radio gear relied on. They had a few surface to air weapons, sure—RPGs and a couple of old drones that ran on high-test gas and jet fuel they stockpiled in a shed down by the loading docks—but those were strictly for use as a last resort.

In other words. she said, Black Rose never saw what hit them. Just zap. Zap and their screens went dark and their helicopter turned into a piece of metal in the air with noplace to go but down.

Weller shook his head. What a world. He asked her where they did that kind of thing. Scrambling radio signals.

She said the comm center. Communications. They had drills they did with the comm gear too. She knew all about it. She'd brought down a couple of hypothetical helicopters herself, if he wanted to know. They were all hypothetical now. You couldn't prove by her that Black Rose even existed anymore.

He said he hadn't seen any comm center when Oates had shown him around. Hammering away while he said it. A little propane welding torch hissing and him tap tap tapping with a ball peen hammer on hot steel that he couldn't get quite hot enough. His thick glasses glowing yellow and red from the flame of the torch. Back in his element.

She said that's because the comm center was off limits to pretty much everybody. There was a scanner at the door and it was tied to Oates's brand and Marlowe's brand and that was all. Oates let the team in for drills.

She asked if maybe Weller had heard about that other fellow who'd shown up out of nowhere one time, and he said he had, that Black Rose scout, and she said right. They'd let him inside rather than leave him to die out in the world, and before they knew what he was up to he was trying to get into the comm center. Some kind of sabotage.

*

The counterman had mentioned the Garden of Eden, and he hadn't been exaggerating. The food here was overwhelmingly good, and it was plentiful, and it was everywhere for the taking. In the diner and in the grocery store across the street and at lunch counters set up where people worked. Heirloom tomatoes that looked monstrous and tasted like heaven, as opposed to the PharmAgra variety he'd gotten accustomed to at home. Out there in the world you could almost believe that the chief purpose of a tomato was to fit squarely into a carton for shipping. Here, in the absence of the historical imperative that bent the natural world to fit the mechanical world, a carrot tasted like a carrot and an apple tasted like an apple and a roast chicken tasted like a roast chicken. Every bite came with its own little shock of long-delayed recognition.

Nothing had a brand name, either, which took some getting used to. Nothing was vacuum-sealed and stamped with the PharmAgra logo. There were no labels glued to the apples and no brands inked into the fatty edges of the meat, nothing to reassure you that all was well, no proof that the bred-in poisons had been blasted or nuked or burned out via the proprietary techniques that gave PharmAgra such leverage in that other world. PharmAgra had beaten or bought every one of its competitors over the long haul, and out there in the Zone it was easy to assume that they'd triumphed on the basis of superior technology. Down here in Spartanburg, it was easier to believe that technology just got in the way. That it crippled people who depended on it too much.

And it didn't just cripple them the way it had crippled Penny, whose thin frame and freckled face and vague eyes he pictured with every bite of every meal. Had she been raised here, she would still be whole and perfect. There would have been no need for everything they'd been through. No need for her to undergo the struggle of treatment and recovery, no need for Liz to have left home to help, no need for this long journey he was on. Its endless struggle and its uncertain outcome.

No wonder the people here were happy.

When they spoke of Marlowe they spoke as of a generous deity, and when they spoke of his man Oates they sounded only slightly less reverent. Oates suffered under the burden of familiarity, though. He was a real human being with real human faults, an individual known and witnessed among them on a routine basis, and thus a figure less easily worshipped. Marlowe, on the other hand, had developed an air of mystery as the years had gone by. The old-timers who recalled the founding of this place remembered his many acts of vision and heroism and plain hard work. How he'd led his renegade forces all the way from Washington and Kill Devil Hills to Spartanburg, way out here in what was rapidly disintegrating into a no-man's land of the mutated and the dead. How he'd realized his dream of preserving the simplest slice of old-time American life inside the walled security of a German automobile factory. How he'd bent his own back to the unrelenting work of tearing down and building up.

His followers had both remembered these things and added to them, the way people will. Expanding them and elevating them and lifting them up rung by rung from fact to memory, from memory to history, from history to myth. And finally from myth to the untouchable realm of pure belief. Creating for themselves a structure whose sustainment no longer even required the presence of Marlowe himself.

*

People were leaving the library as Weller stepped out of the diner after supper on the second night. Not just a few people but a crowd. A mass of them scattering down the street and into the various houses and buildings and storefronts, slowly losing density as it went. Infiltrating.

Weller recognized some of them as members of the team that had brought him inside and taken him off to be deloused. Young men and women with a certain military ranking, he guessed. The rest were older. Upstanding citizens. Pillar of the community types. Each one of them, young and old alike, had a scrap of paper in his hand.

Everywhere these people went, others approached them and pointed to the papers in their fists and cocked their heads as they began to speak. Lifting up their eyebrows and pursing their lips and nodding. Weller watched the people from the library answer other people's questions, sometimes referring to the papers and sometimes not. Gesturing with an upraised hand or running a finger beneath a line of words. He watched the others listen to them and he saw their eyes go big and their heads shake and he decided that he was witnessing the distribution of some kind of news. Looking back over his shoulder as the last of them came down the library steps and seeing Oates coming behind them. Oates not talking to anybody. Walking fast to the curb and jogging across the street with a vigor belying his years and disappearing into an alley past the town office building.

Weller wandered through the crowd until he saw Janey at the center of a dozen people, a scrap of paper in her hand. "The bottom line," she said, that old phrase still possessing some currency in spite of itself, "is that Colonel Marlowe has elevated the threat level from Four to Five. It wasn't an easy decision, but it had to be done."

An intake of breath all around. An old gray-headed man saying that never in his lifetime had he seen a Five. An old gray-headed woman who was probably his wife saying good heavens this must be serious.

"Marlowe?" Weller asked. "I've been asking to see him, and it's like he's a ghost or something. Was he at the meeting?" Thinking he'd missed his chance.

"Oh, no," said Janey. "He's up in his quarters." Indicating with her chin the town office across the street. Dark windows below and a light burning above, behind curtains. Marlowe up there all by himself. Maybe with Oates if Oates had gone in around the back. "It's Major Oates who always does the quarterlies," she said.

"The quarterlies."

"The quarterly reports. The threat assessments."

"What kind of threats would that be?"

"The usual."

"Give me a for instance."

"You've been out there. You've seen it all. The mutations. The contagion."

Weller thought of what happened to Penny's vision, and of how enormous the burden of repairing it had been. A burden so great that nobody undertook it anymore. Nobody could, nobody dared, nobody even dreamed of it except for him. Henry Weller, the only poor man in the world who hadn't given up. And even he hadn't finished the job yet. "I've seen what there is," he said.

"Then you know."

"I know you've got reason to be happy here."

"Especially," said the old gray-headed woman, just about pointing her finger, "with the threat level up to Five and all."

Weller paused. "What does that mean, exactly? Five?"

"Five's the top," she said. "Five's as high as it goes."

"So it can't get any worse than a Five."

"God help us if it does."

"Because what then?"

"Then," Janey put in, folding the scrap of paper and putting it away, "we seal up. We close the holes in the roof, which means the crops fail. We can live on our stores for twelve months and not a minute longer, after which we have to open up again, hoping that everything out there has returned to normal."

"Normal being a Five or below."

"Five or below."

"How low has it gone?"

"Three," she said. "It was always Three when I was a kid."

"What happens at One?"

"At One it's over. We open the doors."

"But it's never gotten to One."

"It's never even gotten to Two."

*

He finished the tractor after a few more days and had it running at least as smoothly as it had ever run on gasoline. So he went to see Oates. Said he'd done his bit. Said he'd done valuable work that nobody else around here seemed to know anything about and he was happy to have accomplished it. He'd even shown Janey how it was done. He'd broadened her limited horizons and set her up so that with any luck she could carry on without him. "Now it's your turn," he said. "It's time for you to go see Marlowe about my car."

Oates had his feet up on his desk. Sighting in between them. "I'm way ahead of you," he said. "Been there, done that."

"Thanks." Brightening.

Oates shook his head. "Don't thank me," he said. "You're not going to like the answer."

"How do you mean."

"Didn't you get the memo?"

"Apparently not."

"We're at threat level Five."

"Meaning?"

Oates picked at a tooth. "Meaning the boss says no."

"No."

"No. No car, no leaving the premises, no nothing. I can't give you any access to the outside whatsoever. Too big a risk."

Weller standing dumbstruck. Thinking of those boarded and chained entrances. The loading dock doors welded shut.

"Consider yourself lucky," Oates said. "We opened up to let you in, but it's just too damned dangerous to open up and let you out. You understand."

"No. Frankly, I don't."

"You've been out there. You know how it is. I'm saving you from yourself."

"You're not."

"Then I'm saving my people from your lousy judgment. From the things you'd have me expose them to."

"And what things would that be."

"Come on. Just because you didn't run into them doesn't mean you don't know."

"Try me."

Oates threw up his hands. "Good God, man. All of it. Mutants. Infestations. Monstrosities of every kind."

"It's not that way."

"And I'm supposed to trust you over Colonel Marlowe."

"It's not that way. Truly it's not."

"That's comforting, coming from a fellow who'll do anything for money. You're as bad as Patterson."

"I'm no mercenary." Taking out the photograph. The Polaroid that had been through the mill and looked a hundred years old. The image on it just a dream of itself. Carmichael's signature gone entirely. He put it on the desk in front of Oates and held one finger on it and slid it forward. Saying, "I came because of her."

Oates picked it up. Saw the faded traces of a blue sky and green grass. The yellow Hummer and the two fathers and the two children. Smiling, all of them, out there in the world somewhere.

"That's my daughter," Weller said. "She can't see very well, and that fellow there is getting her vision fixed right now. Real doctors and everything. No expenses spared. I said I'd bring him back a car in payment."

Oates looked quizzical. Opening his drawer and taking out a magnifier. "This is your daughter?" he said. "The one looking off to the side?"

"Yes sir. She began losing her vision the minute she was born."

"That's a very sad story." Looking through the glass.

"I'll tell you what, though," said Weller. "That's the kind of mutation you'll find out there. Little children going blind. Not monsters. Just little children like Penny. Damaged by what grown-ups have done to the world."

"Really." Putting down the glass and reaching into the drawer again. "Little children," he said. His hand coming back with something silvery in it.

"No matter of what you think," Weller said, pointing to his daughter, "regardless of what you've told yourselves, that little girl right there is the reality."

"Not according to Marlowe it isn't," said Oates. In his hand was Weller's old Zippo. He spun the wheel and touched the flame to the corner of the Polaroid, which went up instantly. Vaporized. Oates letting it go and then just sitting there with his pistol in its shoulder holster. Smiling and waiting for him. Daring him to contradict the accepted wisdom.

*

He vacillated between cursing Oates for burning the picture and telling himself that it didn't matter. That he didn't need it anymore because he'd be back north soon. Back north delivering the ransom and taking Penny and Liz home where they belonged. All he had to do was find where they kept the cars and get one running and hit the road. Steal it right out from underneath them since that's how it had to be. Oates could burn anything he liked. He could burn the whole place down if he wanted and everybody in it, if that was what it took to sustain Marlowe's lie.

Once he freed himself to begin looking, the cars weren't hard to find. They were impounded together in a concrete lot thick with weeds, out where the outskirts of town would have been if there'd been a town. Near where they'd come off the line and not far from the loading docks. Past a grassy lot where kids were playing a game of softball in the light that died early inside these walls. The boy at home plate sizing up a pitch and swinging for the bleachers if there'd been bleachers and the ball arcing into ironwork overhead and bouncing and clanging around scraping loose rust and falling back to earth close to where Weller stood. He caught it and tossed it back overhand like he was some kind of natural. His youth returning. Even his feet feeling better. Every particle of him invigorated now that he was through depending on somebody else's promises. Now that he was back to relying on himself one hundred percent.

The cars were beautiful. Sleek and smooth and darkly gleaming. Some of them wrapped in clean white paper like the most elegant of gifts, each glowing in the gathering night. There were probably a hundred of them altogether, row after row, two or three different models by the look of it. He walked among them, a countryman moving among cattle, and he dared not touch a single one. Not until he'd found the one he was after.

It was almost dark by the time he saw it. The X9 he'd been sent for. In this light he thought it was black and it would turn out that it wasn't but it was close enough. A kind of dark bloody maroon. It was smaller than he'd expected. Not like that big Hummer. Sitting lower than the Hummer had and lower still on tires that had gone flat years ago. There was something feline about the shape of it. Leaning forward like it wanted to run. A white paper sticker still hung inside one rear window with a price printed on it representing more money than would pass through Weller's hands in a lifetime. Ten times more. A hundred. He opened the door on the driver's side and the change in air pressure made the white paper came loose and flutter down. He picked it up and began folding it over as a souvenir, and it crumbled in his fingers. Brittle where he creased it and falling apart. Weller deciding he didn't need a souvenir anyhow. Not with Penny and Liz waiting at home. Then he popped the hood and took a look to see what he was up against before the light went out for good.

*

They'd wheeled in a huge water pump for him to work on the next day, part of the sanitation system, and Janey was helping. He gave her chores that kept her busy while he slipped away on vague errands, pretending to go measure something or consult with somebody while he was actually ransacking back rooms and storage areas for wherever it was they'd put the batteries belonging to the cars in the lot. The batteries and whatever else he might need. By and by he found everything, stored away on pallets and shrink-wrapped in clear plastic, gathered up and fitted together and entombed like the treasures of some pharaoh. Everything was grouped and tagged by serial number. Manuals and empty batteries and shipping instructions. Brake fluid and transmission fluid and motor oil. Keys and remotes and touch-up paint in little vials, along with carpeted floor mats and fancy spring-loaded trim pieces that he didn't recognize and didn't care about. Thanks to Janey, he'd already scoped out the shed where they kept the high-test.

For the next couple of weeks he worked two shifts. By day in the shop and by night in the lot. He used borrowed tools and worked by the beam of a flashlight, propping it on an oil can or holding it in the crook of his arm or gripping it between his teeth in the time-honored way of mechanics everywhere.

Whenever he got the opportunity, he brought equipment he'd need for the trip north and stowed it away. Gas cans and water bottles. Cartons of food that would keep. A chainsaw and a hand axe and a short-handled shovel. He liberated a couple of mounted tires from another car of the same model and tied them to the roof, and one night he labored for seven straight hours with a hand pump just airing them up. Seeing Penny and Liz in his mind the whole time, there before him in the dark. He didn't finish even then, but he had to get back to the shop for the start of the workday.

He never told Janey what he was up to. He just let her believe that maybe he'd found the same kind of sanctuary here that everybody else had. That he was happy to have come in from the cold. That he might never go back.

When he was finished, when he'd topped up the reservoirs and gassed up the tank and adjusted the brakes and charged the battery, when he'd checked and double-checked to make certain that he'd followed every step in every manual he could get his hands on, he got in and put the key in the ignition. Dawn just beginning to gray the sky above the ballfield. He sat in the driver's seat with the door open listening to something chime. A soft insistent tone like a bell telling him to close the door but he didn't close the door. He sat with one foot on the concrete and the other on the soft gray carpet watching the sky turn the color of a pearl and seeing lights coming on someplace down a little lane past the ballfield where people lived. People waking up and going about their business. Watching the signs of their lives such as they were and thinking he was almost done. Thinking this was it. There'd be some fine-tuning maybe but that wouldn't amount to much and then he'd just load up the car and vamoose. Sitting there half in and half out of the driver's seat, watching the sky and watching the lights and picturing the acetylene torch that he'd hidden underneath the car, the tanks and the hoses and the protective helmet lying there just waiting for him to cut open one of the loading dock doors.

But the engine didn't start. All he got was a low ticking sound from under the hood and a sequence of images on a big bright screen mounted in the dashboard. A picture from the backup camera mounted in the rear, and some words scrolling past about a hands-free cell phone connection, and then a long series of numbers in some hexadecimal code. An error message never intended for human eyes, streaming past and past and past.

*

"I need your help," he told her. As much as it hurt to say so.

Janey stood silhouetted in the door of her little apartment. Soft lights inside and music on low. It looked like the kind of place where a person could live his life and grow old and not have too many regrets about it. A world of its own inside another world of its own. Janey's world inside Marlowe's world.

She looked at him and saw his need. The weariness he'd been covering up in the shop all week and the abrupt failure that had just now followed it, both of them conspiring to bring him low. She asked what she could do.

"It's the car."

"No." Slumping against the door.

"It is."

"I thought you'd given that up."

"I didn't. I found one. Oates wouldn't give me one but I found one anyhow and I've been working on it. The problem is I've gone as far as I can go."

"You can fix anything." Kidding him and not kidding.

"I can't fix this. It's got one of those screens. Digital stuff. It's beyond me."

"Then maybe you'd better just let it rest."

"I can't."

"Let it go."

"No."

"It's a terrible world out there and you're not meant to go back out into it."

"It's not terrible and I am. I'm meant to go back. I have to."

"There's a place for you here."

"No"

"You're crazy."

"No."

She stepped back and made to close the door. If she didn't help him, no one would. He'd be stuck here. "It's not worth whatever they're paying you."

"It's not about what they're paying me." Weller stood outside the doorway wishing he hadn't trusted Oates with the picture. Thinking that if he were going to tell the truth to somebody, he'd picked the wrong person when he'd picked Oates. It was too late now. "Look," he said, "if we can get into that communications center, I think I can show you something you won't believe."

"What would that be?" she said.

"The reason I'm here."

Her whole frame went slack. "I know why you're here."

"Right. I came for a stupid car. But there's a reason behind it and it's not money. It's not anything like that. It's my daughter."

"Your daughter."

"My daughter and my wife. Oates won't let me go back home to them."

"Your daughter."

"I wouldn't do this for any other reason. She's in a hospital in New York."

"You're kidding."

"I'm not."

"You're insane."

"I'm not."

Janey stood up straighter. "But New York's gone," she said.

"No. It isn't gone."

"It's infested."

"It's not."

"It is. It's infested with mutations and worse. The new breeds. The ones that won't die and the ones that can't."

"No. None of that's true. Its all fairy tales."

But she knew her history, or what passed for history here. "Come on," she said. "Everybody knows New York was the first to fall."

"It didn't fall. And if it's infested with anything, it's infested with rich people."

She cocked her head.

"Nothing fell, Janey. It wasn't like that. Everything just kind of gave out. Ran out of steam. Except in some of the big cities. They've still got everything there. Everything that everybody used to have. Telephones. Telephones with pictures, which is why I want to get into the comm center. You can hook us up."

"I don't get it."

"My daughter. My wife. They've got a phone."

"In New York."

"Yes. In their room at the hospital."

"You're imagining things."

"I'm not. It's all true. A phone with a television screen, and I'll bet you can hook into it."

"If you're not crazy, that is. If they're actually out there."

"Oh, they're out there."

"If they are, then I've been lied to my whole life."

"You have."

"Which would make you the first person who's been straight with me in forever."

"I'm sorry. Somebody had to do it."

"It's a pretty big if, though. But I guess we'll find out."

*

Since no one ever got in to see Marlowe anyway, they figured they didn't need an appointment. They didn't even need to wait until morning. The town office was just on the other side of the street and they slipped across and tried the door. Nothing. There was a little white card faded to yellow in the window with the word HOURS printed on the top of it by what looked an old typewriter, but if there were any actual times written underneath that they weren't visible in this light. The light from the mercury vapor lamp down on the corner. Just houses beyond here under the lowering gradient of darkness and those all buttoned up. People inside them settled down in their beds.

Either there was no light upstairs where Marlowe lived or else the shades were drawn. They saw a dim light burning somewhere in the depths of the office, but it was so small and so faint that it probably signified nothing. Just a night light chasing off the darkness. Marlowe was an old man, at least Oates's age, and Weller pictured him creeping down here in the dark after something he'd left behind and relying on that little glow to find his way. They went around to the back and saw through sheer curtains the same dim light the same distance away. Apparently in some alcove or passageway near the center of the first floor. Its solitary glow was the grandest thing in the world to Weller. An electric light burning with nobody around to do anything by it. Nobody reading or working or whatever. Just a light. Turned on and waiting.

The rear door was locked just like the front. There was nothing back here in a residential way, just an alley leading someplace dark, and from this angle the houses on either side weren't really houses at all as much as bunkers without windows or any other kind of opening, so they just started knocking on the back door. Politely at first but then with more urgency. Making noise. Standing on the stoop and using their fists on an old wooden door with a window in it. There was a bicycle leaned up against the wall and Janey said that's Marlowe's bike right there. That's how he gets places.

Weller didn't care about any bicycle. He just kept hammering on the door.

Janey frowned through the glass and said, "The problem is he isn't always here. He goes out some."

"He won't go anywhere at night. He'll be here."

"No," she said. "I don't mean just out. I mean *out*. Like *outside*."

"Outside? I don't think so," said Weller. "You know the latest. Opening up is against Marlowe's own orders."

Holding up a hand to make him stop pounding on the door for a second. "Maybe for you," she said. "Not for him. He goes out for recon. Those reports we get."

Weller looked down at the bicycle with its fenders rusted out and the chain off and hanging down. Drooping down pooled in the dust. He started hammering on the door again.

Janey said this is no good. How about we go see Oates.

Weller said no. We're going straight to the top if we're going anywhere at all. Knowing there was no way Oates would let him into the comm center. Not after he'd burned that picture. But there was still a chance with Marlowe. He pressed her aside with one hand and elbowed the windowpane hard and the glass shattered. He reached in through the mess and turned the knob.

The downstairs was one big rambling kind of old-fashioned office with indoor-outdoor carpet and steel filing cabinets like anywhere municipal. Chairs on casters and stacks of paper on tabletops and a map on the wall like the map of a city. Drawn by hand and marked up in colors that all looked more or less gray. In one room was a big iron desk with nothing on it but a blotter and some pens in a cup. A big leather chair behind it. The carpets hadn't been vacuumed or swept or whatever they did to them in a long time and there was dust on the tabletops, kind of white behind the white curtains.

The little light they'd seen was in a narrow stairwell going up into blackness. That same gradient of light shading off and dark taking over. There was a rope across the opening with a wooden sign on it that Weller couldn't read because the night light was behind it. He guessed it said PRIVATE and he unhooked the rope and let it all fall. The hook clattering on the stairstep and the sign bumping the wall. He called Marlowe's name up the stairs and nothing came back. He found a switch that turned on the light on the landing and they went up.

*

He was just an old man.

Just an old man in a bed.

That was all.

His voice still had some power in it though, and when the bedroom door came open he said, "Major Oates?" The words not loud but abrupt. Clipped. He was not hoping for an answer but demanding one. "Major?" Growing impatient.

The low sound of a compressor in the room. Light leaking in around blackout shades lowered down past the sills, and a solitary red glow alongside the bed. One little red LED in the dark and an old man's wracking cough. Marlowe collecting himself and speaking again, wetly this time, "Major Oates, what time is it?"

Weller didn't approach the bed. He stayed close to the wall, feeling for a switch. "It's after midnight," he said. Then, finding a table lamp on a bureau and running his hand over it, "I'm not Oates."

The man in the bed was withdrawing into himself when Weller got the light on. Recoiling from the light and from whoever had switched it on. Wound up in his linens and receding deeper into them, he looked to Weller like nothing so much as an insect suffering under the influence of some poison. A delicate larval creature heartlessly exposed to sun or salt. Weller came near and Marlowe pulled away but a thin plastic tube held him. A tube stretched between him and the compressor. He was tangled up in it and Weller saw it pull away from his nose and catch around his ears and bend them downward. Pitiful flesh speckled and fishlike. Marlowe gasped for air and Weller kneeled and put the tube back into his nose and he gasped some more but with an end in sight. Slowing. Calming but still withdrawn into his linens. Janey watching from the door.

Marlowe opened his eyes wide and fixed them on Weller. Eyes pale as blue milk. Saying what more do you want. Pausing for a ragged breath. His eyes swimming. Saying I already gave it to you.

Janey cocked her head in the doorway.

Weller saying what did you give me. What did I take.

Janey stepped into the room. "He thinks you're somebody else," she said. Looking past Weller at Marlowe as at some truth revealed.

Weller spoke to her without turning. "I don't know who." Then to Marlowe. "What did you give me?"

No answer.

Abandoning that. Asking instead, "How long have you been here? How long have you been here like this?" One hand on sheets that were anything but clean.

Marlowe sucked air through his nose.

"In this bed, with the oxygen and all."

Marlowe looked up at him like a man with no use for time or its passage and no means for describing it. He opened his mouth and one word came out. *Oates.*

"I'm not Oates. Jesus." Throwing a look back over his shoulder at Janey, saying, "Oates told me this place runs itself, and I guess he wasn't kidding."

Marlowe lifted a hand and poked at the side of his neck. Fingering a scar just above the gray collar of his shirt. His long nail like a talon grazing it and a sly look growing in his eye, accumulating there. Weller reached over and touched the spot and although there was a hard ridge of scar tissue on the loose skin there wasn't anything else. There wasn't anything beneath it. Marlowe lifting his chin and Weller taking the flesh between his thumb and his finger and finding nothing. An empty socket. Marlowe with that sly look like he'd fooled him. Saying, "I gave it to you already."

"I didn't take your brand," said Weller, looking him in the eye, "but somebody sure did. How come is the question."

"The comm center," said Janey. "That Black Rose scout from before."

"Oates said he'd gotten smart. He told me not to do the same." Letting go of Marlowe and Marlowe's head drooping.

Janey reminded him. "He went there to sabotage us."

"Maybe not. Maybe he just wanted to call home. Maybe he wanted to make a point to somebody. It could be that he wasn't Black Rose any more than I am. Maybe all he wanted to do was prove to somebody that there's a whole different world out there."

Marlowe's head was on his chest. Sunken down into that sunken cage. The oxygen compressor humming away and the old man fast asleep once more.

"And you think Oates didn't want him to."

"It would be the worst kind of sabotage, as far as Oates is concerned. I get the impression that he likes things just the way they are."

"Who doesn't?"

"Me." Weller rose and went to the door and Janey got there before him. "You might not, if you'll give me a chance to prove it." He switched off the light and they went down the stairs and out the back door. Out the back door and into the night. But not to the comm center. There was no getting in there now, not with Marlowe's brand missing. They went to the car instead.

*

But they didn't go straight. They stopped at the workshop and picked up some portable equipment. A diagnostic scanner that ran off batteries and a handful of adapters for it and a long cable that Weller looped around himself. "There's some kind of hands-free phone setup in the dashboard," he said. "You think you can tap into that?"

She thought maybe she could if she could get the car going at all. Hurrying along under the weight of the scanner.

The fields weren't much out of their way and they stopped for provisions. Zucchinis and green beans and ripe melons heavy with water. Sweet corn and red potatoes and summer squash shaped like something a child would have drawn with a crayon. They filled burlap sacks they found between the rows and Weller took off his shirt and buttoned it up and used that too. Saying we'll need all we can carry and Janey saying what do you mean we.

Weller said, "I thought you'd want to go out and see the world."

She said she'd help him get the car running and she'd help him find a way out if he was so crazy about going, but that was it.

He said what if we get Penny and Liz on the phone.

She said we'll see. Like she was his mother or something. The kind of thing a person says to a child. *We'll see.*

186

The moon was high over the ballfield. It was the middle of the night or almost. Neither one of them had a watch, but they figured they had a few hours before people were up. Before Oates stopped by Marlowe's place and found the window smashed in. Before whatever fate had befallen that Black Rose scout befell them.

They found the car and opened the hood and connected the scanner. Booted it up and waited. She and Weller watching a round logo materialize on the screen and spin a few times like a propeller turning before it disappeared. Janey telling him you never knew. She'd never seen a car like this one before. If what she knew about working on other cars didn't pay off right away, this could take forever. It would be ten minutes if she was lucky or ten days if she wasn't, and no telling until it happened. Weller said they didn't have ten days and she said she knew that. Weller said if they ran into trouble she should get back to her apartment before dawn and go about her business. Let him take the heat since it was his to take.

At which point the scanner began talking to itself and to the car and then the car talking back. A pair of machines communing one to another without need for intervention. Janey said this was what she'd been hoping for, they'd shaken hands, and Weller liked that idea. Picturing them with hands to shake. The GPS booted too and it locked onto the satellites and a little likeness of the car began pulsing on its own dashboard against a map of the old South. Cities that were gone to ruin now and roads that weren't entirely navigable these days and other roads that didn't exist anymore period. Weller thinking that this car was a time machine. The trip to New York would be easy if only he could go back under its power to the world glowing on that bright and hopeful map. A world with smooth roads and cheap gas and fast food at every rest stop.

Once Janey had the car running, the phone circuitry booted itself. An interface coming together on the screen, but no signal to go with it. Apparently it wasn't a complete system after all. It was asking for a cell phone, and a cell phone was a nearly mythical thing down here. Just a rumor of something forsaken during Marlowe's Retreat. Never mind that whatever cell towers were nearby couldn't possibly be functioning anymore. Weller hadn't even thought of that. But he had an alternative. The dead Black Rose satellite phone that had set off alarms in Oates's mind. Let it set off some more alarms if it could. He dug in the back and found it in his rucksack and tossed it to Janey, saying the battery was dead but she could probably rig that too while she was at it.

Telecom had been deregulated under who, Reagan maybe, in a period as unknowable as some dark age. It had been a no-man's land of competing sources and signals back then, after the first phone company had exploded into a million pieces in that big deregulatory bang and before the slow cooling of it all into one great big corporation, the unironically named Ma Bell that ran what was left of the business anymore, its logo a stylized rendering of a grayheaded old woman at a switchboard or what some artist imagined as one. Not even Black Rose had been able to make Ma Bell share bandwidth, thus this crippled satellite phone right here that Janey made fast work of fixing. She wired it straight into the car and used the scanner to make them communicate. The car and the phone. Not just audio but video, at least incoming. Then the phone talking not just with the car but with the world, and not only on the military channels but on the civilian channels too.

Directory Assistance alone persuaded her that Weller had been right. Directory Assistance. Imagine that. A voice asking for the city and the state as if there were cities left and states too. Demonstrating the truth of it by the asking. The same voice asking for the name of the party once Janey had said New York New York, and then Janey giving up and handing the phone to Weller saying I don't know what hospital in case there's more than one. Saying maybe you'd better take it from here and giving him the phone and Weller's hands shaking.

A face bloomed up on the dashboard screen. Weller didn't think it was the receptionist he remembered from the hospital desk, but it could have been her twin. Another sophisticated old woman made young by science. Another strange miracle, this one working the night shift. The woman at the desk reached up a manicured hand and tapped on the screen in front of her as if it had gone dead. Leaning forward and squinting into the monitor without so much as a crow's foot materializing to mar her perfect skin.

Janey took Weller's arm and held on to it as if he might rescue her from something. Some sudden shifting of the universe.

"Hello?" the woman on the screen said. Her voice came through the car audio, eight or ten speakers' worth of it turned up louder than it needed to be. Weller finding the knob and turning it down. "Hello?'

Janey held on and studied the woman's face on the screen and whispered to Weller *is she real?* Thinking she might be a film of pixels wrapped over a wireframe. The look on her face was such a perfect approximation of genuine human curiosity. The mechanics of her face so strangely evocative of both great age and unblemished youth.

"She's real all right," he said low, and the woman quit tapping on the screen and sneezed into a lace handkerchief as if she intended to prove him correct.

Janey laughed out loud and the woman cocked an ear and leaned in again toward the monitor. Her eyebrows up in two perfect half-circles. "Hello?"

Weller asked for his daughter by name and room number and the woman said it was after visiting hours. No calls now. Weller said he was the girl's father and she said family included. He said it was an emergency and she said emergencies were an entirely different department, raising her hand and looking for a second as if she were going to transfer him, until he said he was working for Anderson Carmichael if she didn't mind, Anderson Carmichael who paid the bills that no doubt covered part of her salary and not just her salary but her benefits package which included that surgery she'd had and she'd keep having as long as she kept wanting to look young, and that changed everything. She patched him straight through.

*

"Henry?"

"It's me."

"I can't see you."

"That's all right. I can see you."

A dim light in the room and Liz hardly visible by it. Almost no light at all. Just the scattershot glow of a video screen with nothing to display but interference. On the table behind her, silhouetted by light rising up from the city below, he could still see the flowers. Those identical bouquets that came every day from *Mr. and Mrs. Anderson Carmichael* and *Your friends at PharmAgra*. Fresh and brand new, just as if he'd never left. As if nothing had changed.

"Oh, thank God, Henry. They told me you were dead." What looked like a tear in that weird light.

"Not yet. What do they know?" As if it were funny.

"Where are you?"

"Spartanburg."

"Jesus, Henry." Her look woeful and lonesome.

Weller wished he could comfort her somehow. Forcing a smile at her image on the screen as if that might do any good. "Never mind me," he said. "I understand Penny's had some setbacks."

"Penny's fine. Penny's perfect."

"But Bainbridge said—"

"Who's Bainbridge?"

"From Washington. The one who calls to check on you."

"Nobody calls, Henry."

"I told you he'd get word back to me."

"I'm sorry. Nobody calls. Nobody's ever called."

"He told me she'd had setbacks, Liz. This was couple of weeks ago."

She shrugged in the buzzing video light. "I don't know where he got that idea. Penny's fine. She's more than fine. You should see her."

"I will."

"I know." A little pause. "I hope so."

"Maybe he said it to light a fire underneath me. Like I needed that."

"We all want you back."

"Not Bainbridge. He just wants the car. Carmichael too."

"I don't care what they want. I want you. Just come home."

"I will."

"Hurry."

"I will."

"The thing is, Henry, they're getting ready to release her."

"Good. They'll take both of you home. Carmichael promised."

"Not without you. They're just going to turn us loose."

"I told Bainbridge that I wanted Carmichael to take you straight home."

"Carmichael doesn't care. He thinks you're dead."

"I'll bet he heard that from Bainbridge too. That guy's a fountain of good news, and not much of it's accurate." Looking at Liz on the dashboard screen, her face the only thing in the world. "I'm on my way now, honey. I'm keeping my promise. Don't you worry."

"We'll only be around until tomorrow or the next day. The doctor wants to run a few more tests and that's it. That's the end."

"I'll be there. You hang on. We'll all go home together."

*

Janey had already found the acetylene torch over by the sealed-up loading dock, as if she'd read his mind. She had everything set up by the time he got there, and she'd put on the helmet and snapped the visor down and was firing up the torch. He watched her adjust the yellow acetylene flame and watched her add oxygen through the regulator until it turned pure white. That little blue flame inside the stream of white fire. He squinted through his fingers as she knelt to the floor and began cutting a thin line straight up. Sparks like fireworks erupting into the air and falling to the concrete floor and bouncing. Janey moving the torch as slowly and steadily as a machine made for the job and stopping only when she'd gone as high as she could reach, and then Weller dragging the ladder over. She nodded thanks through the helmet.

He went back to the car and disconnected the scanner and tossed it into the back seat and closed the doors. Started the engine and let it rev for a minute until it smoothed out and settled down. The headlights came on all by themselves, which struck him as a nice touch. He had a little trouble navigating among the other parked cars and his initial impulse was to be careful so as not to dent anything but he thought of Bainbridge and Carmichael and he said to hell with it. A few badges of honor wouldn't hurt. It was going to be a rough ride anyhow. Inside of five minutes the steel door had fallen forward with a monstrous clang and Janey was in the passenger seat and they were on their way.

Through the opening and down the ramp and out into the world.

Twelve:

The Coming of the Fall

It was just dawn, and from the driver's seat Weller could see the footprints he'd made on the way in. The sun filling them up and the shadows overflowing them. He followed them like a trail of breadcrumbs and where he couldn't follow them he made his own path. It was easier after he got frustrated and took a chance and cut one of the tripwires and nothing happened. No explosion. No alarm. No landmine. The whole business a charade. He got back in the car and put it into gear.

Janey said she'd been told there'd be bodies out here, bodies among the fences and the trenches and the bombs. Corpses of everything that hadn't been able to get inside and wreak havoc. Everything that had made the attempt and gotten caught in the defenses and died trying. That's what Oates had said.

Weller shook his head and concentrated on the path in front of him. The barbed wire was real enough and they had only those two spares on the roof. Three or four solid days' driving ahead if they were lucky, and Penny undergoing those last few tests, and then what. There was no time for a blowout.

Janey said Oates had described the circle around Spartanburg as a battle zone and a graveyard. A hideous place filled with the bones of things that weren't human anymore. Poisonous things.

Weller said you never know.

Checking the rear view mirror and seeing the vacancy of the cut-open doorway gaping behind them like a missing tooth. A black spot in the rising sun. He imagined light filtering in through it and he wondered when someone would notice. They'd step away from that open doorway as if the very air and sunlight coming in would burn their skin. He thought how desperate Oates and his people would be to seal the gap before heaven knows what got in and ravaged them all. But the look backwards was just one rapid flick of his eyes, and an instant later he was concentrating on the path ahead once more. Just a few hundred yards and they'd be free. Free of Spartanburg and free of Oates. Free to locate the highway. Free to head north, all the way to Liz and Penny.

*

There were two of them now and they could take turns driving. Drive all day and all night if possible. If the headlights kept working and the roads didn't deteriorate much more. The car had four-wheel drive but the suspension wasn't built for anything much rougher than a tabletop. It rode hard and Weller fretted that something might give out if they pushed it, but he worried more about Penny and Liz so they pushed it anyhow.

They located Eighty-Five and got onto it where that exit sign for Spartanburg had been blown half to bits by machine gun fire. Weller realizing that that was meant as a warning too. SPARTA. Like in the history books. As if there were people here to be wary of. It was just a sign.

Up on the highway the world exploded in all directions. Janey hadn't known what to expect, but she hadn't expected this. These wide green expanses. These cornfields and beanfields, these vast undulating acres of kudzu. Everything mingled together and burgeoning. Weller said one thing they'd had correct in Spartanburg was that any plant you found growing out here might be poisonous. And the more familiar it was, the more likely it was to do you harm. He told her he'd run out of food on the way down and had had to eat kudzu. Nuts and berries. A two-headed turtle he'd come across in a ditch. Things that people didn't typically eat, which meant things that PharmAgra and NutraMax and the other chemical companies hadn't bothered modifying.

She reached into the back seat and rummaged around. Came back with a couple of knobby tomatoes all yellow and green and red. Splotchy things almost ready to explode with the power of their own ripeness. "Want one?"

"I don't think just yet," he said, looking down the long mossy road. "I believe I'll wait until I get good and hungry." Giving her a quick glance that sent both of the tomatoes back where they'd come from.

He planned to keep as much distance between himself and Greensboro as he could. South of town the highway was blocked just the way it had been from the north, barricaded with junked automobiles and shipping containers and railroad cars heaved up into a wall. They had to back away from it. Weller told Janey how on the way south he'd thought such a thing must be Marlowe's work, how he'd been led to understand that Marlowe ran a heavily-armed frontier fortress and it wasn't too big a leap to think that he'd have made it even more impregnable by setting up barricades as much as a day's ride distant. How he'd been wrong about all that. Wrong about everything. Wrong to have thought that Spartanburg was a big idea when it was really just a small one. Just a cramped little selfish idea huddling all by itself in a great big world.

"*Somebody* put all this junk here, though," she said. Looking away from the barricade as they backed up. Looking over the guardrail at Greensboro's tallest buildings.

Weller said she was correct about that. He said Greensboro was one tough town. He'd been held prisoner there for a week and more by people dressed in bearskins and rags. People who didn't speak English or any other language because one of them had been born without a tongue. Mutated.

"And he passed it on?" Being born without a tongue was bad, but it wasn't the worst thing in the world. It wasn't the worst fate she'd heard about by any means. She was having to adjust her perspective.

"Oh, he passed it on all right," Weller said. "But not the way you'd think. Not genetically. He was the big man, you see. He was the one with the power. And if you didn't want to go up against him, you had to pledge your allegiance."

"By—"

"That's right."

"Ow."

"The only one who escaped was his mother. Even his own little girl got caught up in it."

"No."

"People get caught up in things. I've learned that. People get caught up in things they shouldn't get caught up in."

"It must have broken your heart."

"It kind of did, but I was too busy trying to get out," Weller said. "Trying to get out and hoping they didn't eat me for dinner."

Janey was making herself small, sitting low in the passenger seat as they took the exit ramp. "So you don't think we could have gotten through that barricade?"

"Nope. And even if we did, there's another one just like it a few miles north. I'd hate to be trapped in between, wouldn't you?"

"I guess I would."

They stayed clear of the city and paralleled Eighty-Five as best they could, sticking to service roads and grassy embankments and only stopping when the way ahead grew utterly impassible. The two of them getting out together and cutting a path clear with the chainsaw and the hand axe. Weller volunteered to do the job himself each time, but she didn't want to be left alone in the car if something happened. If the roar of the chainsaw drew somebody. But it didn't. And by the time the sun was going down they were back on Eighty-Five.

*

He told Janey that Eighty-Five led to Ninety-Five below Richmond and Ninety-Five led to the Beltway around Washington and from the Beltway things would get easier. Somewhere on the Beltway National Motors took over, and the road would improve. It would actually be maintained. Smooth and fenced in and safe.

She wondered who National Motors was.

He explained everything as best he could. How National Motors ran the highways and the trucks that traveled them. How PharmAgra ran the food business and Family Health Partnership ran insurance and MobilGo ran energy. How AmeriBank handled the paperwork that tied everything together and kept it all going. He explained how he was working for Anderson Carmichael, the head of AmeriBank and one of the richest men in the world. Driving his car. A fortune in Carmichael's scrip in his back pocket and a chip loaded with credits in there too. More money than either one of them could imagine.

She asked what money was good for. Just like that. As innocent as that. She didn't know.

He said one thing it would be good for was getting them onto those nice smooth National Motors highways. He didn't guess there was any direct provision for that, any kind of a toll-taking mechanism set up, but money had a way of getting around things. He'd met Carmichael while the banker was driving his own private car on a National Motors road, hadn't he? It could happen again. It would happen again. No question.

*

The phone rang in the middle of the night. On Janey's watch, with Weller asleep beside her in the passenger seat. How a person could sleep in a car lurching over terrain this rough was a mystery to her but he did it all the same, with the moon shining down through the sunroof and a pair of high-output headlights turning the whole world blue. The image of a telephone appeared on the dashboard screen and Janey pressed it and the call connected.

"Weller?" A man's voice, all gravel.

"Hello?" Janey was amazed at her own reflex. At how easily you could talk on the telephone to people who lived in a place that you'd always thought was long gone.

"Weller?" said the voice. "Weller, is that you?"

"He's right here."

Weller stirred, coming awake in the glow of the screen. A man's face resolving.

"Put him on." A little squirt of audio interference on his end and nothing on the screen but a map. No video at all from Weller's end. "Put him on, for Christ's sake."

Weller sat up. "Bainbridge?" Mouthing *Black Rose* to Janey. Mouthing *Washington*.

"Where in hell have you been, buddy?"

"On my way," Weller said. Thinking if the phone was powered, its GPS was powered too. He'd forgotten that. "How's Penny?"

"Never mind Penny. Where've you been?"

"I told you. On my way."

"On your way my ass. Two weeks ago you were in Greensboro. Two whole weeks of travel time and you're not even in Richmond. What gives?"

"This car. It's a little touchy. Delicate."

"You're moving now, though. You're moving right along. I can see that."

"For now. We'll get there when we get there. Tell Carmichael it won't be long."

"He'll be happy to know that, son. I'd told him you'd gone silent. That's never a good sign. Tell you the truth, he didn't take it all that well. He offered to double our bonus if I could track you and that car down, but I told him he was out of luck. No way I'd send my own men down there. No offense."

"None taken."

"I sure am glad you're alive."

"Me too."

"It's a dream come true."

"It sure is."

"Who's the girl, anyhow?"

"What girl?"

"The girl who picked up the phone. Who is she?"

"She's one of Marlowe's. Off to see the world."

"No kidding. Leaving that paradise you told me about?"

"No kidding. But how's Penny?"

"Penny's fine. She's all better. They sent her home a week ago."

Janey looked at Weller. He looked back.

"Honest?"

"Honest."

"You'd said she was having setbacks."

"The miracles of modern medicine, my boy. She's recovered and she's gone home and your wife's gone home too. Safe and sound. Just waiting for Daddy."

Static burst through the speakers and Janey drove a little faster, thinking they might come to a place where the signal was clearer.

"Tell you what," Bainbridge said. "Since that car's so fussy, don't bother trying to drive all the way to New York."

"No?"

"Why mess with it? Just come right here to Washington. We'll airlift it up, and we'll fly you back home in the bargain. We'll use that big Chinook I showed you."

"That would sure be nice."

"I know you'd like to see that little girl as soon as you can."

"I sure would."

"Why wait?"

"Why wait."

"I figure you'll be here late tomorrow."

"Could be."

"We'll keep an eye out."

"I'd appreciate it."

"You can bunk at my place for old time's sake. One last night underneath the Angler. And I'll have you home the next day."

"It's a very kind offer."

"Think nothing of it."

Bainbridge clicked off and the dash went dark. Nothing but the moon through the sunroof and the blue light streaming ahead, two hard beams cutting the car a pathway north.

Janey didn't even turn her head. "I guess we're still going straight to New York," she said.

"No question about that," said Weller.

*

They'd have to go dark if they wanted to get back unseen. No GPS, no phone. No progress reports to Liz at the hospital, either, but she'd managed well enough on faith so far. She could endure. They'd have to make time, though. Not just to reach Liz and Penny, but to get on the Beltway and under the protection of National Motors before Bainbridge saw them coming. He'd said they could reach Washington late tomorrow, hadn't he? Weller figured that gave them until noon if they were lucky. Come dawn Bainbridge would start thinking about helicopter patrols. He had that double bonus money burning a hole in his pocket, but he still wouldn't start before the middle of the day. He wouldn't want helicopters out there wasting expensive fuel. Then again he might start early with a single unit. Send it south to intercept them on Ninety-Five and forget the Beltway. On the other hand he might even get started now. Especially if he saw how they'd cut the GPS and guessed that they were onto him. That they were trying to evade Black Rose altogether. He could go low-tech instead, throw up a couple of roadblocks, blow a couple of overpasses. That would be easy enough, and it would solve the problem of how to get his hands on the car without damaging it. Because even if Weller and Janey were worth less than nothing on the open market, the car had real value.

Janey asked if there wasn't another way around Washington. Weller said sure, there were a million roads and some of them might even be passable. A million ways to get lost down there too. Plus he didn't know where along the Beltway National Motors took over. They'd be better off making a run for it.

*

It cost them both of their spare tires before they were much past Richmond. And not the little self-inflating donut buried in the trunk, either—they still had that one, for all the use it would be on these impossible roads—but the two actual tires that Weller had roped to the roof. He cursed himself and wished he'd taken more, but it was too late for that now. Nothing to do but keep moving.

The sky went from black to gray and the blue headlights shut themselves off and for a little while they didn't feel so exposed. Weller drove and Janey kept an eye on the sky for surveillance, but there was nothing. Signs along the road ticked off the diminishing mileage to Washington. No roadblocks. All of the bridges and overpasses intact. Just the miles diminishing and the two of them thinking maybe they'd outsmarted Bainbridge by keeping up their speed overnight. Maybe those two flat tires had been worth it, provided they didn't have any more.

Janey asked Weller about all these towns. The exit ramps circling down. Were there people there? He said probably not. Without National Motors service there wasn't any way to get supplies. If anyone lived there at all, they were scavengers or hunters. Survivalists. Everybody had gone north in the Great Dying, north to the cities and then from the cities to the suburbs and then from the suburbs to the countryside where they could find manual work if there was any work to be found. Or else they died. Poisoned and whatever else. Just plain sick and nowhere to go. Eighty percent of the population of the country gone.

Janey said Spartanburg hadn't lost anybody under Marlowe.

Weller said people died. You couldn't say they hadn't lost anybody.

Janey said sure, but Marlowe had still had to put limits on population growth. Two children per couple. Just one child for a while, around the time her parents had had her, which was why she didn't have a brother or a sister. Her parents, God rest their souls.

Weller said he was sorry. He'd been wondering about her leaving. Who she might have left behind. He hadn't thought at the time.

She said don't be sorry. All this wreckage, though. She was beginning to wonder why she'd left home. It seemed to her like it was a bigger world all right, but it wasn't a better one. People in Spartanburg had to be told not to have extra children. People up here, well. She let that thought kind of drift away.

Weller didn't look at her. He didn't acknowledge that she'd said anything in particular. Thinking that in his case people back home watched their children get sick and die. He moved his hands on the wheel and watched another sign go past with miles marked on it. They were almost there.

The Beltway was just as bad as Ninety-Five had been. Indistinguishable from it, really. They had to get out of the car and cut through a dense patch of greenery halfway around a low spot in an access ramp, where the road ran through water. Brush and reeds and a great weeping willow right in the middle of the lane. It took forever. Weller taking down the willow and worrying that its movement against the skyline might be a flag to someone watching for them. Janey cutting brush with the hand axe and looking like a person who wondered what she'd gotten herself into.

"There are people working to make things better out here," Weller said once they were back in the car and moving. "People disengineering crops. The idea is to bring back the old days, when you could grow something for yourself and eat it for supper without having to sell it to PharmAgra first and buy it back. Feed it right to your family."

"You mean the old days like in Spartanburg right now," she said. Fishing in the back seat for breakfast. Rummaging in one of the burlap sacks and pulling out a summer squash and rejecting it and pulling out a muskmelon instead. Little Jack Horner himself. "Remember Spartanburg?" she said. "That place we just left?"

"Point taken." He reached in his pocket and pulled out a jackknife. "Anyhow," he said, opening it up and locking it back and handing it over, "now that I think about it, you'll want to save those seeds. I know somebody who could use them."

He told her all about the tobacco farm in Connecticut. How Dr. Patel had disengineered one of the oldest agricultural products in the world, stealing untainted tobacco back from PharmAgra. A regular Prometheus. He told her how she sold it on the black market to fund more research, and how the next thing on her agenda was wheat. *Wheat.* The staff of life. Once people got their hands on wheat, he said, there'd be no stopping them.

Janey turned and looked at what they had in the back seat and said maybe they should have brought more.

He said maybe. "Then again," he said, "I understand there are places all over where folks are doing the same kind of thing. Places close to the highways where people can travel in and out, but not too close. Like that old underground railroad during the Civil War. Maybe somebody already has muskmelons going. She'd know. We'll stop in Connecticut after we get Penny and Liz, and we'll drop off everything we've got. Seeds included. Especially seeds."

She was already scraping them from the muskmelon and transferring them wetly into one of the cup holders for safekeeping. A fortune in seeds and a future too. Either way, he said, it was contraband of the highest order.

*

The road ahead was closed off, but not by a Black Rose roadblock. This was a permanent thing. It meant they'd gotten the jump on Bainbridge, which was good news. The bad news was that it was National Motors security. Just the thought of those hard men in their black serge and black leather sent Weller's mind back to the trip south. His last minutes on Ninety-Five with the driver who'd smuggled him through one checkpoint and turned on him at the next on account of the tobacco he'd been carrying. How security had pulled the driver clean out of his cab and gotten him down on the ground with that taser they had, gotten him down on the ground twitching. How they'd cut his brand out and sent him off to live in the world however he might be able to live if he lived at all. How one of them had taken Penny's chin in his hand in the middle of it and told her not to worry about a thing. The cruel audacity of it. A little child.

They'd never treat Anderson Carmichael that way. No sir. And there was nothing special about Anderson Carmichael except his money, a good bit of which Weller himself was still sitting on since nobody in Spartanburg had had any use for it.

They drew near the place where the road was closed off, chained hurricane fence and soggy sandbags and barbed wire, and he slowed the car to a stop. This sleek maroon car straight out of some old dream of the future. Caked with dust and splashed with mud and scraped here and there by passing branches but fantastic nonetheless. Fantastic in the old true sense.

He blew the horn and flashed the headlights. Got the flashers going and climbed out. Approached the barricade and climbed on the sandbags and put out one finger to touch the fence in case it was electrified but it wasn't. Back in the car, Janey blew the horn again and again. Weller climbing a few feet up the fence to holler through it at a little guard shack standing all alone about fifty yards distant but deciding that climbing on a chain link fence wasn't something that a man with Carmichael's money would do. It was undignified. So he climbed down and just stood. Stopped hollering and signaled over at Janey to quit blowing the horn and just waited there beyond the fence with the car's emergency flashers going. Patient as any other man with money in his pocket.

Someone came out of the guard shack by and by. A kid or not much more than a kid. His uniform didn't even fit him. It was loose and kind of cockeyed and bunched up around the waist. The belt buckle was off-center, yanked tight. It all looked as if it belonged to someone else. He came out of the guard shack and looked around and drew his pistol from its holster. Came walking toward Weller unhurried. Little clouds of gray dust coming up around his shoes as he walked across the empty pavement. Even his shoes looking new in spite of the dust, smooth and deeply waxed and the color of oxblood. With the dust accumulating they were beginning to resemble the dark maroon car behind Weller. Everything got dirty no matter what.

Weller raised his hand in greeting. Didn't look away. Didn't look over his shoulder to have Janey kill the flashers but she killed them anyhow. Their red glow on the wires of the hurricane fence blinking out.

The kid's uniform looked brand new, perfectly clean out here in the middle of nowhere and pressed sharp. He had the barrel of the pistol pointed right between Weller's eyes and he kept it there as he approached. Calling out as he drew nearer. "What you want?" He stumbled over a rough spot where the pavement had heaved up. The gun unmoving. Like it was the only steady thing in the universe, the thing holding him up. Like he was following it.

"I want to pay to use your road."

As the distance closed, the kid's face began to resolve. He had a pinched and sour look, dull and irritable and mean. He didn't wear a helmet the way the National Motors security men on Ninety-Five had, and his yellow hair jutted up in the front like he'd been caught napping. Weller didn't like him and he didn't like the way he was studying him from behind that gun. He didn't like the way he wasn't wearing whatever headgear was required or the way his uniform didn't fit or the way his belt buckle was off-center. Like he was just an ignorant and ill-tempered kid out here un-supervised at the end of the line. Only the gun in charge of things.

"I want to pay to use your road," Weller said again. Not louder. Not different in any way. Just stating a fact that the kid might not know.

"No can do," said the kid.

"I've got plenty of money," said Weller.

The kid came near the fence with the gun steady. Indicating the car by tilting his head a few degrees in that direction, but not moving the gun. "What kind is that."

"BMW X9. From the plant in Spartanburg." Saying it flatly, like it was an ordinary thing not worth remarking on other than to inform ignorant people like this kid here.

"Never seen one," said the kid. "I guess they ain't making them no more."

"They're not. But they had this one. They had a few. You could go down and get one for yourself if you wanted."

The kid looked at Weller through the chain link as if he were looking at a gorilla in a zoo. A talking gorilla that said words that didn't make any more sense than a gorilla would make. Just words. "I guess I could," he said, "but I'm happy right here. I don't need no car to make me happy."

"I'll bet you don't. You look like a very contented individual."

The kid narrowed his eyes and held his breath. Holding that pistol even steadier than before. Daring Weller to press his luck.

Weller said, "I'm going to reach into my pocket now, if you don't mind."

"I don't mind," said the kid. Not moving the gun. Still daring him.

Weller dug around in his pocket and began to pull something out and the kid smiled. It wasn't a smile that made a person comfortable. "You're sure it's all right?" Weller asked. His hand still in his pocket.

"It's all right with me," said the kid.

Weller drew out the chip loaded with Carmichael's credits. "I don't know how much you folks might be charging these days—"

"I don't know either."

"You could look it up. You could find out."

The kid didn't say anything back. He pointed the gun at the car. At Janey in the car. "Who's the gal?"

"She's with me." Which he figured was all that needed saying. A rich man keeping his private life as close as he kept everything else.

"*I know she's with you, shit-head. I got eyes.*"

"Whoa." Hands up in front of him, that little silver chip gleaming between the index finger and thumb of his right hand and the sun glinting on it.

"Just don't try me," the kid said.

"I won't. We're hoping to use your road is all. We'll pay our own way. How much do you suppose it would be, from here to New York?"

"Like I said, I don't know."

"I figured you might charge by the mile. Or it could be just a flat amount."

"Like I said, mister, I don't know." The gun wobbling a little now. The kid looking back at Janey.

"All right. All right." Weller put his hands down slow. "I'll bet you've got some kind of manual back there that we could look at. Something we could consult. A price list or something in the shack."

The kid looked hurt. "That's where I live."

"Nice place."

"That's where the guard always lives."

"It's very nice."

"Ever since I can remember."

"I understand."

"It ain't no shack."

"I didn't mean anything. It's a common term. A guard shack."

"All right."

"Let's go see if we can find some kind of an operations manual. Maybe call somebody."

"The phone don't work."

"There still might be a manual." Moving slowly toward a hinged gate in the fence, held shut by chains and a padlock. A man-sized gate inside a bigger gate. Giving the kid the idea.

The kid went toward the gate too. The pistol still in his hand and a keyring in the other. Sorting through the keys. Without looking up he said, "If she wants to get out of that car and come on in too, it'd be all right." Talking about Janey.

Weller said no, he thought she ought to stay. But if they could leave that chain unlocked just in case, well that would be great.

The kid said no, he thought she'd better come.

Weller said but he'd hate to leave the car all alone. Out here unprotected.

The kid said all right then, he'd come back for her later on if he had to.

*

The guard shack was a steel shipping container repurposed. One door cut into the front with a muddy shovel standing beside it, and a window cut into each wall. Inside were two rooms with a plywood door between them. An office out front where the guard worked, and what was probably a bedroom behind it. Solar panels on the corrugated roof to power the lights and the refrigerator and the water pump, and behind a curtain something that smelled like a chemical toilet.

"Nice place," said Weller. "Are you here all alone?"

"Most times."

"How far are we from the nearest checkpoint?"

"Fifty miles I guess. They say everything's fifty miles." The kid was ill at ease in here. He holstered the pistol and pointed to a little stack of books on a table and said Weller could check those if he wanted to find that manual and figure out how much money to give him. He'd try the phone again in case it had come back on.

The books were old. Paperbacks read and reread dozens of times. A couple of mysteries with the mysteries all gone out of them by now, and three or four thrillers emptied out the same. The book on the top of the stack had a picture on its cover of a woman lying on her back looking toward you with her lips red and wet and Weller thought it was probably dirty and it was. This last one was the one most ruined by use if it was possible to tell such a thing.

The kid slammed the phone down and said, "You find it?"

Weller said yes, he believed he had.

"And?"

"How about you show me around the rest of the facilities first," he said. "I'd like the grand tour."

"I don't think I'm supposed to do that."

"It says right here you can." Opening one of the books and pointing. "Visitor policies are pretty liberal, according to this."

"I don't know," said the kid. But he showed him into the bedroom anyhow. More dirty books and a lamp on a nightstand and sticky twists of flypaper hanging here and there. A chifforobe in one corner standing open, full of freshly laundered uniforms in plastic. The bed unmade and a pair of filthy boots kicked off under the edge of it. Muddy footprints leading toward them across the tile.

"A person could be very comfortable here," said Weller.

"That's what I always thought growing up," said the kid. "I always wanted this job."

"How often do you get supplies?"

"First of the month like clockwork. All you can eat." The kid grinning. Like a person who'd achieved something.

Weller nodded. Coming out of the bedroom and going to the front door and stepping outside into the air. Standing there alongside the shovel that had the same mud on it the boots did. More mud coming this way from a little cut in the wire fence. Weller knowing what the kid had buried out there. "It said a dollar a mile," he said, "which makes fifty to the next checkpoint."

The kid brightened.

"Can you read credits or is your scanner down too?"

"I don't think they give me one."

"That's fine," said Weller. "I've got AmeriBank scrip. And a little something extra for you, if management doesn't mind too much."

"I guess that'd be all right," said the kid. "You're the one's got the book." It was almost as if he were onto something. Smiling and coming toward the door and beginning to draw the pistol again. But Weller already had the shovel raised.

*

The National Motors road was pure silk compared with what they'd gotten used to, and the kid had been right about one thing. It was fifty miles to the first checkpoint. Money talked there. Weller was surprised at how easily a rough squad of hardcore ex-Black Rose mercenaries could be persuaded that he and Janey and that fancy car had every right to be driving on their road. He didn't care where the money went in the end. It was just lubrication.

Toward Baltimore they powered the phone back up because why worry about Bainbridge and his Black Rose helicopters now that they were on good National Motors roads and only a few hours from New York. They'd be there by nightfall. The satellite signal was good and Janey raised the hospital. The receptionist couldn't find Penny and Liz at first, and it just about gave Weller heart failure. The system said they'd been checked out, but he persuaded her to try their old room and they hadn't. They were on their way, though. Any minute now.

They were sitting at the table in the front room. Penny's backpack with the white cat on the back of it all loaded up and a couple of plastic bags stuffed full of Liz's things. Apparently they couldn't even supply her with a backpack of her own or a suitcase or anything substantial. Just a couple of plastic bags. *Here's your hat, what's your hurry. And don't let the screen door hit you on the way out.*

Penny was studying the screen on the wall, squinting at it with a kind of intensity that she had once used all the time, only instead of trying to coax a clear picture from the fog of her failing vision she was trying now to resolve a picture of her father from a stream of pure and persistent video noise. Weller saw that little face of hers and the earnest expression it wore and it was all he could do to keep driving. He pulled over and the words tumbled out and he said Penny, I'm coming and Liz, I'm coming. Tell them. Tell them I'm almost there and don't let them put you out on the street. Not yet. I'll be in New York today.

Penny jumped up and down in her chair. "Today?"

"Today, honey. Hang on."

"I can't wait," said Penny.

"Neither can I," said Liz. "It's been too long."

"It's almost over." He could hardly believe it himself. "So the tests went fine, I guess? That's good news."

"The tests went fine. More than fine."

Penny blinked at the noisy screen. Looked over at her mother. "Are you sure he can see us?" Liz nodded. The little girl turned and reached behind her to get the backpack from the table, drew it around and struggled to get it onto her lap, and unzipped it.

"She's one hundred percent," said Liz. "Complete recovery. One for the medical books, they said."

"Thank God," said Weller.

"And thank you," said Liz.

"Thanks to you too, Mom," he said. "It took teamwork."

She smiled into the camera and he smiled right back. Just from the happy reflex of it. As if she were right there and as if she could see him. He watched Penny searching for something, his heart running over. The mere presence of the little girl on the screen was almost enough for him, and the notion that he would see her very soon was more than enough for him, and the quick way that she sorted through the contents of her backpack—taking papers out and glancing at them and rejecting them one after another with an acuity of vision that she'd never had before—was in the end almost more than he could bear.

"You haven't seen all of my pictures," she said.

"I've seen some," her father said.

"You can show him when he gets here," said her mother. Words she had just about given up on saying.

"Just a couple. Please?"

"All right."

She found her latest, her best, and she began putting them in some kind of order. Starting with one of her mother that made Weller's heart leap. There was truth in it and love too. Truth and love that turned out to be the same thing, from the hand of one so small and one whose vision had only just now cleared. Next there was a drawing of him, less sharp and less precise, with something generic about it. She had his hair color right. The nose was about five sizes smaller than his but finely rendered as if she'd been particularly careful about it, and he wondered if the picture were based more on some doctor than on him. That one doctor who looked like a whippet. There would be time now to get those things right, though. Time to fill in all of the blank spots.

"They're fantastic," he said, and he meant it.

She had others. A sunset over the tall wire canopy of the park just outside her window. A still life of the flower arrangements that had been on the table every single day. A drawing of her own hand at many times life size. Last of all was one she said she'd done just yesterday as a part of those final tests. A kind of fanciful landscape, a map of some storybook setting, with a maze of black roads and undulant green fields and a little white building off in one corner that looked like somebody's idea of home. He thought maybe she and Liz had been reading a storybook with a map in the front of it, a map showing places like Pooh's House or Injun Joe's Cave or the location of Long John Silver's treasure, and she'd been inspired to invent something of her own. He asked if that's what it was. Some imaginary place.

"No," she said. "It's Connecticut." Looking into the camera as if she could see him through it and as if he were crazy. Or half-blind himself.

"Ahh," he said. "Home sweet home." The little white building that looked nothing like home whatsoever. A sad reminder, in its way, of how far she'd come.

"Not *home*, silly. Just Connecticut." She ducked out of the frame and put the drawing up closer to the camera. One little hand coming in from one side to point out the white building in the corner. "The schoolhouse? Remember?"

But he wasn't looking at the schoolhouse. He was looking at the places she'd labeled on the map in careful letters—she'd learned something about that, too—and in spite of the misspellings and the backwards bits and the perilous slant of everything he could see exactly what part of Connecticut she had rendered after all. *Tunnell. Tobaco feelds. Ninetyfive.* It wasn't accurate but it was accurate enough.

Weller could hardly breathe. Between the hole that he'd cut in the fence a few weeks ago and the direction they'd been traveling back then and this map, it wouldn't be any problem to locate Patel's station. "I'm so proud of you," he said.

"Thanks, Daddy."

"Did someone ask you to draw these things? These particular things?"

"Mostly" she said. Putting a finger to her head and thinking. "The flowers and Mommy and the map, I guess."

"Has anybody else seen them?"

"Everybody's seen them," Liz put in. "They were part of her therapy."

"Did anybody keep copies?"

"Why?"

"Just asking. I'll bet they kept copies is all. They're really first-rate." Looking beyond his wife and daughter, at the flower arrangements standing side by side on the table behind them. The little card that he couldn't make out but that he knew was there all the same. *Your friends at PharmAgra.*

It had cost them so little to get this information. A month's worth of cut flowers. Some technician paid off or maybe the therapist or even the person who delivered the arrangements. Either way, they knew where to find Patel. They were probably on their way right now.

He told Liz and Penny that he had to go. He'd try to raise Carmichael and get them a reprieve since he was just hours away, but as a precaution they ought to tell everybody they could that he was almost there. Anybody and everybody. He was coming with the car and he'd be in New York soon. He was keeping his promise.

In the meantime, though, it was time get back on the road. Time to get moving again. Because he just couldn't wait to see them.

*

"She's adorable," said Janey.

"Both of them," he said. "I know." He hadn't thought about it in exactly those terms before, but he thought about it now.

"That last drawing," Janey said. "That map." Giving him an opening.

"It's Dr. Patel's station."

"I thought maybe."

He glanced at the melon seeds drying in the cup holder. "If those are worth a fortune, imagine what her entire tobacco operation is worth. Plus the engineering she does for other folks." He goosed the engine and the car hunkered down and flew. "People would kill for it," he said. "They'd kill to get rid of it."

"Honest?"

"Penny and I met a fellow on our way down, this truck driver who gave us a lift. PharmAgra security took him for a smuggler. Not even a smuggler. Somebody who gave a little help to a smuggler. I don't know that he lived through it. I don't know that he wanted to, by the time they were done."

"So we're heading to Connecticut first?"

"Unless one of us comes up with a better idea."

*

The better idea turned out to be the PharmAgra checkpoint on the George Washington Bridge. Call it a hostage swap, the car for Penny and Liz. Except Weller didn't exactly plan on giving up the car.

Janey tried raising Carmichael on the satellite phone but he was out of the office and nobody knew where. Nobody who'd say. His cell number wasn't listed and they wouldn't give it to her no matter how she pleaded.

Weller got on and said he was somewhere south of Philadelphia with that car that the boss had been so eager to get his hands on, and the woman on the other end played it cool. Said if he was who he said he was then why didn't he turn on his video. A person with nothing to hide didn't go around switching off his video. Weller getting the idea that she thought he was dead too. He said give me Carmichael's assistant if you won't give me Carmichael. He said she knows me. She knows who I am. But that didn't help either.

So he hung up and tried Bainbridge in Washington. They had a signal for a minute but it died as they drew near the smoking wreckage of the Marcus Hook refineries. Some kind of work still going on there. MobilGo insignia on smokestacks and gray towers with blue gas flames. They ran onward for a while, the car eating up the miles, until they reached the Delaware and veered northward. Janey trying the phone again and again and Weller's hands going white on the leather steering wheel. They passed the sunken ruin of the Benjamin Franklin bridge, with nowhere to connect to anymore since the fall of Camden. The deck broken to pieces and slanting down into the deep green of the Delaware, the tops of the first towers still just visible above the waterline, the long iron cables snapped and coiled back on themselves in great looping filigrees of rust.

A few miles later Janey raised Black Rose headquarters and got patched through. Bainbridge zapped onto the screen with that little knife-cut mustache of his that couldn't hide his grin, looking bright-eyed. "I must say you've become a regular goldmine for us, sonny boy. You're a fighting man's new best friend."

"How's that?"

"First we get paid for your training, then there's bonus money to be had, and now there seem to be new missions popping up everywhere. Our profile's never been higher. Between AmeriBank and PharmAgra, I might owe you a commission."

"That'd be nice."

"The military kind, I mean."

"I'll let you know," said Weller. "How does PharmAgra come into it?"

Bainbridge didn't even look abashed. He didn't miss a beat. "Jesus, buddy," he said. "They've got a finger in everything."

Weller didn't pursue it. Now that Bainbridge was working for PharmAgra, it wouldn't be just a team of corporate security thugs on their way to Patel's station. It would be Black Rose. The real deal. He kicked the accelerator to the floor, glad that the satellite phone had no video and Bainbridge couldn't see the distress on his face. "Look," he said. "What I was really calling about was I seem to have mislaid Anderson Carmichael's private number."

Bainbridge was happy to turn it over. Why not.

*

A checkpoint every fifty miles. Sometimes purpose-built and sometimes born from the ruins of whatever had come before. A service station or a shopping center or whatever. Truck traffic was heavier north of Philadelphia and the checkpoints were congested, but just the look of the car got them waved right to the front of every line. The air was thick with diesel fumes and loud with the sounds of engines idling and radio static and men calling out. The shriek and shudder of air brakes. Weller and Janey felt like insects in that low silent car among these fuming diesel-powered monsters, but they were treated like a king and a queen. Especially once money started changing hands. Tough National Motors security men climbing down from their glass-walled perches to greet them face to face. To look in the driver's side window and marvel. Their sunglasses coming off and their habituated grimaces softening. They took the money and sent them on their way.

They may have seen the sacks of vegetables in the back seat or even the melon seeds drying to muck inside the cup holder, but they were interested only in the red white and blue AmeriBank scrip. There was plenty of it to go around. That other kind of green.

*

Carmichael was off having a good time in the great outdoors, but he looked angry when he picked up the phone. Either he turned angry fast, or else he'd been on the verge of it already. Judging by the video he was on a boat. A power boat in New York Harbor. Gunning the engine and leaping over some other boat's wake and the Statue of Liberty behind him leaping the same way. Green Liberty jumping up and down against a blue sky. Her torch arm missing and the spikes sawn away from her crown for the copper until nobody needed all that much copper anymore and they started leaving her alone.

"Who is it." Glaring at the black screen.

"Weller."

Nothing. The roar of the power boat and the hammering sound of wind gusting. Carmichael turned his head away, his attention drawn elsewhere.

"Henry Weller. Remember me?"

"Huh?" Barking it toward the phone but not as if he cared.

"I've got your car."

Which seemed to catch Carmichael's attention. "Weller! Bainbridge said—"

"I guess he was wrong."

"I guess he was." Laughing and shouting into the cell phone over the engines and the wind noise, his face coming too near the camera and blowing up big. Cutting the engine back and saying something to somebody else beside him and the whole world spinning. Someone else at the wheel and fishing poles and antennas pointing up everywhere and then pointing sideways and the Statue of Liberty visible again for a fraction of a second before she disappeared for good. Everything getting dim. Carmichael gone into someplace quieter but not entirely quiet. Down below.

"How soon can you get my wife and daughter to the George Washington Bridge?" Weller asked. "The National Motors checkpoint on the George Washington Bridge?"

Carmichael checked his watch. His image still bouncing as the room bounced. "Three hours," he said.

"Make it two."

"No way. I'm in the middle of New York Harbor."

"I know that. Make it two."

"I'm on a boat, for Christ's sake."

"I know that. Nobody expects you to deliver them personally. Make a call."

"I'd like to see them off myself."

"Bullshit. You'd like to see the car. You can see it in two hours. No more."

Carmichael glared into the camera. "After the weeks I've given you to get this thing done, you're going to start pushing me now."

"That's right."

"You're going to start pushing me over an hour's time."

"I am."

"What's your hurry?"

"None of your business."

"Then you'll accommodate my schedule, Henry."

"Try me." He waited a second. Listening to the muffled churning of the engines and the crying-out of gulls. "You wouldn't believe how much abuse this car might have taken along the way."

A pause on Carmichael's end. "Nobody ever said anything about abuse."

Janey sat in the passenger seat, shaking her head, looking out the window at the fenced farmland and the empty suburbs as they flickered past in turn.

"Things happen," said Weller.

"All right. I'll be there as soon as I can."

"Two hours," said Weller. He pressed the screen to shut off the phone. "Carmichael's a person who knows just what he wants," he told Janey. "That means you can count on him."

*

They blew a tire at high speed somewhere in the swamps of Jersey. Left it alongside the highway leaned up against a hurricane fence that had the National Motors logo rusting away on it and rolled onward with that little inflatable donut instead, the car tilting forward and to the passenger side as a reminder to take it easy. The manual said don't go over forty-five miles an hour but they did. They went twice that. What was Weller going to do, call Carmichael and say never mind? Say you can have three hours if you need it, because I've run into a little difficulty? Let the rich man think he was weakening? No way. No way he'd lose that psychological advantage now that he'd earned it, and no way he'd let the people on the tobacco station go a minute longer than they had to.

They ran into a convoy of Black Rose vehicles just south of New Brunswick. Troop transports and big armored Humvees headed north in a line that looked from the rear as if it stretched for the better part of a mile. Old-fashioned Jeeps with their canvas tops up in spite of the heat and their lights on and their whip antennas lashed down back to front in long quivering arcs. The convoy went slow, and Weller and Janey came up on it from behind as if it weren't moving at all. Weller saying, "I see those boys aren't in any hurry."

Because they were unstoppable after all, and there was nobody even to try. Nobody who knew where they were headed. Nobody who saw them coming. It was just a routine movement of troops and hardware as far as anyone who might see them would know, probably some kind of a drill, an event that would mean almost nothing to the truckers on Ninety-Five and less than that to somebody passing them in a low-slung four by four going eighty or ninety miles an hour toward a destination beyond their imagining.

One or two of them might notice such a car, though. One or two of them who'd registered Weller's visit to Washington and recalled the mission he'd been on and were able to put two and two together. It was possible. And even if they couldn't speed up to catch a car like that, they could still make a call. Report in to headquarters.

Weller touched the brakes and slowed down behind them. Pulled over onto the shoulder and braked the car to a stop and waited for them to disappear over a low rise. It took forever at the speed they were crawling. Weller sitting there tapping his foot. Thinking of Penny and Liz. Thinking of everybody on the tobacco farm and the progress they'd made in restoring something that had been taken from them.

Thinking of the world that lay ahead if only.

Janey unbuckled her seat belt and asked if he thought it was her turn to drive, and he said she'd been reading his mind. She got out and went around and got behind the wheel, while he crawled into the back.

A minute later they went sailing past the convoy, with the front windows open and Janey's hair blowing like she was on some kind of pleasure trip. Weller crouching in the rear under burlap sacks. Janey honked the horn and waved out the sunroof to the men in every single vehicle she passed. And a hundred-fifty Black Rose mercenaries waved back, blowing little kisses, revved up and gleeful as schoolboys.

*

Janey told the man in the booth that they were here to meet Anderson Carmichael and he made a call and they sat for a while with the engine running and the air on until somebody came and showed them into a little parking area behind a low building. No one was back there. Not even any cars. There weren't even any markings for cars painted on the old sun-blasted pavement. Everyone who worked here came and went in big black

National Motors vans. Like riding the bus, but how would riding the bus have looked. These career toughs riding a city bus like any other day laborers. Only out in the country, on those long desolate stretches where the sole inhabited structure every fifty miles was a National Motors checkpoint, did they commute in cars anymore. Only out in the country where the cost of living was low and they could save enough to drive themselves.

Weller got out and walked around a little, scoping out the route to the northbound exit. There was a garden hose alongside the building and he squirted the car for a while. He didn't know why. It was just something to do. A way to distract himself from the fact that Carmichael was late and the fact that he was dying to see his wife and daughter and the fact that the Black Rose convoy got closer with every minute that passed. He couldn't get much pressure out of the hose and it didn't do much to clean off the mud but he kept at it for a while. Carmichael's big ugly yellow Hummer arrived just as he was coiling up the hose. The rich man behind the wheel and his assistant in the passenger seat and Liz and Penny in the rear, blacked out by dark glass. Weller glanced at Janey and she goosed the engine just to reassure him that it was running. It ran so quietly you couldn't tell. Just a shimmer of heat from the tailpipes mingling with other shimmers of heat from the pavement. All of it indistinguishable. Everything steaming and everything wet.

Weller dropped the hose and went to the yellow car and opened the back door while Carmichael opened the front. Filthy as he was, and underweight from his weeks away, he looked like a ravenous animal—but they didn't care. How could they. They all just threw themselves on one another in an embrace that wouldn't end because none of them wanted to be the first to quit. The assistant in the front seat turned and looked back at them as if to say how could they. As if to ask had they no decency. It was the look of a person who had never been as bereft as they had been, a person who had never recovered what they had just now recovered. After a minute she pulled herself away and moved over to take the driver's seat, ready to get shut of these individuals and head back into the city.

"Safe travels," she said.

Not one of them acknowledged her.

Carmichael was at the window of the X9, trying to talk Janey out from behind the wheel but not having any luck. She'd unbuckled her seat belt, but that was it. She wouldn't even unlock the door. He couldn't blame her and he said so and she smiled back at him. He said he could hardly imagine driving a car like this all the way up the coast knowing the whole time that when it was over you'd have to turn it over to somebody else. You could get accustomed to this kind of luxury and this kind of performance. Letting her know that he wanted to start getting used to it himself right about now, after all the trouble he'd gone through to get his hands on it, but being generous and letting her enjoy it for a few more minutes since he'd have to wait anyhow. They'd want to empty out their things. There was no way he'd drive this beauty home loaded up with the crap they had in it. They'd been living in there like a couple of animals. What kind of relationship was going on between Weller and this girl wasn't any of his business and he didn't care what they'd been doing all the way from Spartanburg in his car but he figured Weller's wife might have something to say about it. Good luck to the two of them. It was going to be a fun walk back to wherever. They'd certainly have plenty to talk about, and in front of the kid, too. It might be good for the kid. He'd seen to it that she'd gotten her sight back, and it was time she saw what the world was like. All of this going through his mind while the girl sat in the car with the engine running and cool air blasting out the vents and a screen in front of her with pictograms of some kind he couldn't quite make out.

She ran her hands over the leather steering wheel and shot a quick look at that antique Hummer and told Carmichael it might take him a while to figure out the technology of a car this advanced. He just laughed. He said is that a phone there on the screen blinking and she said yes sir it is. We hardwired the Black Rose satellite phone into it but you can probably hook your cell up over the air without too much trouble. Won't that be something. Bluetooth or whatever. He looked past her knees and saw the wires dangling down and the greasy Black Rose satellite phone on the carpet and he said you'd better get busy disconnecting that, I don't have all day. She shrugged and said she didn't know how. Said that end was Weller's business and he'd take care of it just as soon as he got back.

So Carmichael stepped to the rear of the maroon car and shouted at them. Weller and Liz and Penny separated now by at least a few inches and talking but with the wife and child still sitting in the back seat. He got Weller's attention, though, and Weller took the other two by the hands and brought them over. He opened the rear door on the other side and got his wife busy emptying stuff out of the back seat. Just piling it on up the ground. Trash or what looked to him like trash. Then he came around to Carmichael's side and did the same himself. Lifting the little girl up once he'd cleared an empty spot for her to sit in and letting her enjoy herself for a minute up there. The little girl looking all around inside the car like this was the only time she'd ever see anything quite like this in her whole life because it was. Memorizing the interior for safekeeping. Weller tossing a couple of things over into the trunk behind the seats and Carmichael not thinking anything of it. The girl behind the wheel leaning out the window and handing him an owner's manual a couple of inches thick. Saying we found this and brought it along in case you could use it. Saying there's a maintenance schedule that's separate but it's in the glove box. Carmichael paging through for the part about how to hook up that cell phone because he just couldn't get over it. Amazing. A car like this was worth the trouble.

He said to Weller don't forget to take out that satellite phone you wired in and Weller said yes sir just as soon as I'm finished here. Clicking the seatbelt around his little girl probably just for the fun of it. Shoulder harness and all. Wasting time, putting off the inevitable, and Carmichael saying again that he ought to get on with taking that satellite phone out and he'd appreciate it if he'd be careful not to do any more damage than he'd already done putting it in. Looking at dents and scratches in the paint job that he was just now beginning to notice. Scars that would never go away entirely, no matter how much he paid the best body shop in New York. Not in his mind, anyhow. Carmichael getting a little steamed and watching Weller go around to the passenger side and open the front door and begin messing with the phone. The little girl in the back closing her door and folding her hands in her lap like she was ready to go. A kid going on a trip with her mom and dad. Let her have that. What was the harm.

Weller said something to the girl behind the wheel and she slid over his way. Bent to help him with the phone. Apparently it took two but that was all right with Carmichael. Just as long as they got it done.

God, it was a beautiful car.

He stepped around to the back and admired it from that angle. Ran his hand over the sheetmetal and squinted hard and said didn't they have any black ones and Weller said this was as close as they had. This dark maroon. He was sorry, but they'd been out of black and what could you do. They sure weren't making any more. He said you could have it repainted if you wanted to. He said Carmichael could probably afford that couldn't he and Carmichael laughed. Beginning to enjoy himself for a change.

They were still horsing around with the phone and Weller's wife was still sorting stuff from the back seat so he went around the front and admired it from there. Down on one knee looking up. That feline car glowering down at the man who owned it now. The headlights were different from the headlights on any other car he'd seen and he studied them thinking he should have asked Weller to get spares. He realized that the whole car was tilting down toward the passenger side and he edged that way to discover the little spare tire they'd put on. Said to Weller of course you saved the tire you blew and the rim that went with it and Weller said sure, sure. Not even paying him any attention. Not wanting to deal with him.

Weller said that about does it and stood up. Dusting off his pantlegs. A sound from inside the car of the doors unlocking and then Weller going around the back and opening the driver's door and getting in and Liz getting in too and the both of them slamming the doors shut while Carmichael was still down on one knee lamenting that pathetic little spare tire he was stuck with. The transmission slamming into reverse and the engine screaming and the car, the car for which he'd gone to so much trouble, slipping through his fingers just like that.

*

The yellow Hummer was no match for the X9 and Carmichael didn't know the exits the way Weller did. The yellow car ended up southbound back into New Jersey while Weller and Janey and Liz and Penny roared out over the bridge toward Manhattan and beyond. Penny in the back seat looking out the window and saying she hoped this was the last time she'd ever see that city and her father agreeing with her. Once was enough. But at least she'd seen it.

Janey looked too, southward, awed by the approaching glory of Manhattan itself and by the contrasting unplugged ruin of Jersey City. All of the life drained out of it. The Hudson held more water than she had ever seen in her life and she said so. She asked was this a part of the ocean and Weller said he guessed you could say that since it drained into it. He wasn't much on the geography around here. Liz told her just wait until Long Island Sound if she wanted to see water. If she wanted to see the ocean more or less.

Weller adjusted the rearview mirror to look in Liz's eyes and tell her he was sorry she'd had to make that trip all by herself. Her first and only time out of Farmington and under such circumstances. Liz said at least she'd ridden in a car instead of having to go the way he and Penny had gone. On

foot and hitchhiking and everything else. Everything else Penny had told
her about. The man with the knife and the truck driver who'd gotten in
trouble. At least she'd had a safe trip down, although that was more than
she was going to be able to say about the trip back. The way he was driving. The way they'd run off with Carmichael's car here. Saying he'd told her
it was an emergency and he'd told her what to do about getting in the car,
but he hadn't told her why.

Janey put down her window and stuck her arm out. Pointing south.
Saying, "That's why, right there."

Helicopters. Tearing up the Hudson toward the bridge. Two of them
one after the other, little black ones that looked venomous with the sun
from the western sky glinting hard off their glossy surfaces and gleaming
against the bright globes of their windows. Their rotors just a couple of
blurs. No sooner had Janey seen them than the telephone came alive all on
its own. The Black Rose satellite phone they hadn't disconnected. A series
of lights flashed in sequence on the phone down by her feet and the picto-
gram throbbed to life on the dashboard screen and she pushed it.

Weller gritted his teeth and shook his head and said, "You think we
can listen in? Maybe we can find out where they're headed." As if they
didn't already know. Pressing his foot to the floor and the car bounding
past a line of National Motors trucks and the helicopters drawing nearer.
Truckers gawking southward from their open windows at the murderous
pair of them as they approached over the water. The helicopters low and
the green surface of the river bucking and shimmering beneath their
blades. The truckers waving at them like idiots. Blasting their air horns and
gaily greeting death itself.

Voices snarled over the air. Numbers mostly. This vector and that heading. None of it meant much. Weller said Penny, we're headed for that tobacco farm. Remember the tobacco farm?

She said she did and Liz said she'd told her all about it.

"The bad news is that these fellows in the helicopters are headed there
too. They mean to hurt our friends, I'm sad to say. And they're an awful lot
faster than we are."

Janey said, "Maybe we can slow them down." Pushing on a corner of
the touchscreen and sending it into some other mode. Asking Liz to hand
her that black box with the screen on it from behind the seat and hooking
the scanner up to something under the dash with a pair of alligator clips.
Switching it on. One black helicopter beginning to rise up from the water

now to arc over the bridge and the other one not far behind it. Its path the upward movement of a cobra.

Numbers streamed across the screens on both the dashboard and the scanner. Numbers too fast for anyone to read. The high rasping bark of men's voices came from the car speakers and straight from the little grainy speaker in the satellite phone too, but none of it was intelligible. Janey typed something into the scanner and cursed and looked back at Penny and said she was sorry and typed something else into the scanner and cursed again. Oops, she said.

They were halfway across the bridge. The traffic had slowed to let a hundred National Motors drivers gawk like little children, and Weller used the brakes. Softly at first and then harder. Stuck in the middle of a hundred oversized imbeciles and no way out. The first Black Rose helicopter disappearing from sight as it neared the bridge and then surging up and back into view with its engine roaring and its rotors beating the world into submission. The noise too much to bear. It was pretty much straight overhead, Penny and Liz looking up at it through the sunroof.

A beeping came from the scanner and the same beeping with the same urgent steadiness came from the satellite phone and Janey said she had it. She was in. Weller said in what. Hollering over the roar. She said in the system. The helicopter's navigation system. She could bring it down, she was pretty sure. Take it out of the air just like that. Janey hollering too. Weller said not now and she said I know not now. With any luck she could bring it down, though, just like they did back home in Spartanburg. Black Rose would never know what had hit them.

The trucks were still crawling but they picked up a little speed now and small gaps began to open up between them and Weller threaded the car through. The first helicopter barreling on north and the second one disappearing now in its approach to the bridge. Dropping out of sight. Liz and Penny turned around to look for it between the trucks. Janey studying the screens and saying I think I can do it. I actually think I can.

"It'd be one way to stop that convoy," Weller said, "if you could time it right."

The traffic continued to ease up and Weller found more spaces between trucks and longer ones too and the car gained speed. The first helicopter upriver now, hanging from the blur of its rotors and getting smaller and smaller and the roar of the second one already deafening even though they couldn't quite see it yet. Then a great blaring of air horns from behind and the helicopter itself bursting into view over the lip of the bridge and just clearing the tops of the trucks like the pilot was already getting a thrill out of terrorizing people. Like he usually didn't get chance enough.

They were a quarter of a mile from the New York side and Janey was flicking between two different displays on the scanner and the helicopter was almost dead-centered over the eastbound lanes, rising and moving fast. Tilted nose-down. Janey saying how much faster can you drive and Weller saying no faster. Exactly no faster than this is how much faster I can drive and you can't bring that thing down with us still on the bridge. We'll go into the water and what then. What good will that do anybody. Janey saying no, it can't be that heavy. You saw one hanging from a tree for Christ's sake it's not that heavy it won't bring down the bridge and Weller saying don't you dare. Looking in the rear view at Liz and Penny and yanking the wheel left to veer around a truck and saying don't you dare do it or we'll all drown and if we don't all drown I'll drown you myself. Just for trying.

She didn't put the scanner down but she didn't push anything on it either. She waited two seconds until the helicopter was clear of the bridge altogether and then she keyed in a command and pressed a sequence of keys to execute it and nothing happened. Almost nothing. Maybe a little kind of a stagger from the helicopter. As if it had forgotten which way was up or its forward motion had been arrested for an instant by a cable strung across the sky or the engines driving its rotors had skipped a beat. Just a little hiccup as if the pilot had lost control for a minute and then gotten it back.

Weller watched it pass from his rear view mirror into the sky to his left and said, "So much for that."

"I almost had it."

"Do you think?"

"Yes. I do. I almost had it."

"Better luck next time, then."

"I don't know that there'll be a next time." Sitting there looking like it was all over already.

"It's only two helicopters," Weller said. "Four men. They'll just be scoping things out for the convoy, don't you think? It's the convoy that they're counting on to do the serious work."

"I hope so."

*

222

They didn't even slow down for the next checkpoint. The one in Stamford where they'd gotten through clean on the way south. They didn't have time to talk and they didn't care to find out if anyone had thought to set National Motors security after them. Probably not. That would require contracts and the exchange of money, and nothing involving large sums of money happened fast. Thank God for the fracturing of law enforcement into a million little pieces, each one working for itself and as greedy as it could be. Once that happened, things got easier down at this level. Weller just flashed the lights and gunned the engine and swerved around the trucks, throwing a handful of red white and blue AmeriBank scrip out the window as they tore past.

That was about the last of it, but then again they were just about at the end of the line.

*

Finding the spot where they'd come through the fence wasn't going to be easy. Everything looked the same along this stretch of Ninety-Five. The same gray concrete buildings falling to ruin. The same little bunches of underbrush and trees sprouting up among them as if life went on anyhow. The road was one long elevated arc, a single steady stretch punctuated by fenced off-ramps that led to nowhere every quarter-mile or so. The population had been dense here and the commerce had been rampant and together they had generated a tangle of roads that National Motors had spared no expense in blocking off. Nothing left now but a straight line and a million broken promises. Penny unbuckled and stuck her head between the front seats and said, "It wasn't here, Dad. It was someplace greener. There was grass along the side of the road."

She was right. He remembered clambering up a steep berm into tall grass. He remembered kneeling and getting shocked when he touched the fence and using the plastic tarp folded over on itself for insulation. Bending the chain link back to let her squeak through. It was so long ago now. A different life. Leave it to Penny to remember the color of things and by remembering to bring it back. He told her to buckle herself in now, and he drove on.

The grass was a little paler and a little yellower with the passing of the high summer and the coming of the fall but they found the spot all the same. A half-mile or so of grass running alongside the westbound lanes opposite them, and a sign on this side announcing a checkpoint in one mile, and Weller saying, "This is it. I remember now. It's here." And sure enough there it was, over on the southbound side. Not the hole he'd cut in the fence but a new length of fence replacing what he'd damaged. One panel of ordinary National Motors chain link replaced with a brand new panel gleaming silver and stretched tight.

They stopped at the first off-ramp, not caring where it led. Weller and Janey bailing out and going at the fencing with wirecutters, starting near ground level on each side. Weller could reach higher than Janey could, and when he was done he went over to her side and made more cuts. About to work his way across the top when he heard a car door and looked back to see Liz climb behind the wheel and guessed what she was up to. She blew the horn and he and Janey stepped back and she dropped the transmission into gear, the car plowing through the fencing and losing paint in long parallel slashes about three inches apart because why wait for them to cut the top of the hole when they were in a hurry.

"Did you see that?" he said to Janey. "That's my girl right there." And then they were on the road again.

*

Northward through nothing. The car had a compass built into it but it didn't work. All those electronics and you couldn't tell one direction from another. Weller still had a pocket compass with a Black Rose logo on it. He hated looking at it but it worked and the electronic one didn't so they followed it through the maze of ruined roads. Angling north by northeast and trying to approximate their old steps even if they couldn't quite recreate them.

They thought they remembered a few landmarks, but it was impossible to be certain. They wove through intersections jammed with abandoned cars where people had lived for a little while until the coyotes and the bears had moved in and where the coyotes and the bears had lived for a little while until they were supplanted by foxes and crows and rabbits and mice and so on down the food chain all the way to bugs and then not even bugs anymore. Weeds and lichen and mold. The world of living things winding down all the way. They passed squat buildings that could have been shopping centers or offices or hotels, and tall buildings that looked more or less like the squat ones stood on end. There was no particularizing mark on anything beyond stains where electrical signage had been taken down long ago for scrap, and the sameness of it all merged into one compounded uncertain thing that disoriented them and made them desperate. Weller said he wished he'd taken notes or blazed a trail or something. He'd never thought. Penny on the other hand said she was pretty sure she would remember every inch of this on her next time through if there should be a next time, since she could see perfectly now and every single object looked just like itself, and even though her father wasn't so certain about that he didn't say.

They passed through the commercial districts and into the moonlike landscape of the drained-out suburbs. House after emptied house. Cars left where their gas tanks had run dry. A school bus the same, yellow and black and rust-red, squatting on bare wheels stripped of rubber. Penny had never seen a school bus and her father didn't tell her what it was. It was just another wreck.

Weller looked at the road. Penny looked at everything but. And Liz and Janey watched the sky for helicopters.

They pressed forward. Along blacktop roads gone back to gravel and gravel roads gone back to dirt and dirt roads gone back to plain earth. The fencing on either side was PharmAgra now, not National Motors, for there were crops to fence in but not highways. Strange as it seemed it felt like home. In the distance a handful of people walking slow down a dirt lane, their day finished and their tools shouldered, men and women and children all alike. Their people, in their world.

They knew they were heading in the right direction when they saw the smoke.

*

Just a thin gray column going straight up into the air. Creeping upward into a heavy atmosphere as still as the grave, and dissipating as it went.

Weller spun the wheel and took the car down into a gully and across an unfenced field toward a fenced one. The car bounding over ruts and Weller not slowing it in the least. Never lifting his foot from the gas. Hoping that that fragile little spare held out but not actually caring if it blew because he'd just keep going on the rim. Everybody hanging on.

The fence wasn't new and it wasn't in good or even fair condition. It was rusted through everywhere and painted over. Salvage of a sort that Weller recognized. A battered PharmAgra badge stolen from someplace else and held on by string. Whatever was behind it hadn't been fenced in by PharmAgra but by Patel and her people, which meant they were close now. The gray column of smoke maybe a half-mile away as the crow flies but farther than that by the way they had to go. Along the fence until they found what looked like the weakest spot and straight through without so much as slowing down and along the culvert he remembered to where it vanished under the earth and then straight.

Keeping an eye on the column of smoke and navigating toward it as it began to move. The draft from a rising helicopter buffeting it and dissipating it in places and in other places making it whip snakelike. It was an earthbound tornado and it made Weller think of those pictures on the movie film he'd found in Greensboro. The little girl and her dog and the danger she was in. Watching the smoke waver and watching the helicopter rise before him.

He looked at Janey. "There's your second chance," he said.

"There were two," she said.

"Get them one at a time."

"But there's just the one signal. This one, I guess. Where do you suppose the other one is?"

"Down, maybe," he said. "Maybe it hit a different bridge or something. They were cutting it close. Playing around. Bunch of yahoos."

"Maybe they stayed behind to meet the convoy."

"Either way, there's just the one right here to worry about now." Pressing forward. The car bouncing along the margin of the field, toward the place where Patel's people lived underground. Whatever it was that was burning, it wasn't tobacco. The fire was too small, too confined.

A burst of gunfire came from up ahead, preceded by a flash of light from the helicopter. Janey stood up and pushed her head and shoulders out through the sunroof and said it's one of the houses. The underground houses. Smoke's coming from the roof and somebody just tried to climb out and they shot him. They shot him coming out.

Weller wanted to look over his shoulder at Penny but the car was going too fast. He could count on Liz and he had to. The helicopter swooping this way.

Janey said they hadn't even let him come out, and Weller grabbed her hand and pulled her back down. She sat and breathed hard and wiped dirt from her eyes and said they were laughing up there. She'd made out two men in the helicopter and they were laughing at what they'd done. Up there in the sky enjoying this.

*

Somebody closed the sunroof as if that would help. Janey back in her seat working the scanner and Weller looking out the top of the windshield over the tops of his glasses and that synchronized beeping starting up between the scanner and the satellite phone. The beeping and the lights that meant she was in.

Janey said, "All right." She said, "Let's see how much they enjoy this."

Penny pointed out her window and said, "Oh no."

"Oh no what?" asked her mother. Reaching to pull her close but Penny holding onto the windowsill.

"The schoolhouse," she said. One hand on the sill and one hand pointing toward the helicopter as it veered eastward and away. Its black body the body of an insect and the men within it insects too in bulletproof vests and curved helmets and glinting goggles that witnessed more than men should.

Weller kept on toward the clearing and the smoke, which was growing thicker now, asking Janey if she could take the helicopter down now before it went any farther. Wondering in his heart if the men in the helicopter had seen the little white building and thought they'd have some fun, or if they knew from Penny's map that it was a real schoolhouse. Where there would be children. The children of these people they'd come here to harm for pay. But not saying that. Just asking if she could bring the helicopter down, which was a ridiculous question because she was trying. Paging back and forth between two screens of crawling data and blinking schematics and zeroing in on something he couldn't make out for the movement of the car and keying in some command sequence. Looking out the window and back at the scanner and saying come back here, you. Deleting the command sequence and paging between screens again and cursing as the signal from the helicopter faded out. Hitting the scanner with her fist and saying go after him Weller we don't have enough signal but Weller couldn't go after him any more than he could fly.

*

The men in the helicopter must have had grenades.

The schoolhouse went up almost directly behind the car, back where nobody but Weller could see what had happened because he had the bene-fit of the mirrors. The sound was a muffled boom that blended in with eve-rything else and shook the earth they were bouncing over and then flames leapt up and more smoke. The helicopter disappearing behind the ragged black plume of it and not coming back.

Between the seatbelt and her mother's arms Penny wasn't protected but felt that way. Sobbing into her mother's breast. Not even saying what she thought. None of them saying.

They reached the clearing and Weller stopped the car. He told the rest of them to wait. Wait and don't look at what he had to do, there was no need to look, and he got out and sprinted to the underground house where the smoke was coming up. The humped-up roof of it gaping open in the middle and the tobacco plants on top smoking and the steel beams under-neath exposed and scorched. Another grenade. On the far side of the humped-up roof he found the door and it was half open and there was a man or the body of a man crumpled just inside it. His clothes burned and his hair burned and his back full of bullets. Bullets hammered into the dirt all around him like things planted. Like things planted that would never grow.

Weller dropped to his knees when he recognized the body. The tall young man who taught the children at the schoolhouse. If he were here, they must be here too. This late in the afternoon they'd be done. He turned back toward the car and waved his hand knowing that despite his having told them not to look they'd be looking anyhow, and when he saw that they were looking he gave them a thumbs-up. Signaling that all was well. Thinking they could draw from it what they might. The three of them started moving within the car and he shook his head and showed them the same hand palm out, warning them off. All might be well but they'd better stay put.

He pulled the man free and laid him down among the tobacco plants and went down the ramp himself. Two or three families down there cower-ing. Hidden beneath the dining table and beneath the benches along the walls and beneath the beds. Light shone down from the hole in the roof but it didn't illuminate anything for illumination wasn't the order of the day. The air was clogged with cinders and dirt and smoke that choked off the light and swirled in it. Settling the way death settles. Children crying and the low murmur of parents comforting them and comforting themselves for it was all they had. Each other.

Weller called out to them. He didn't identify himself because what difference would it make. A couple of faces poking out from the shadows and a couple of gleams of recognition. He said the helicopters were gone but they weren't gone forever and when they came back they'd bring worse. These were just spotters, and they'd be back with a whole army. Black Rose soldiers here to wipe out their crops for money and kill any one of them that got in their way. Maybe just for fun. Like this right here. This grenade they'd tossed just because they could. Waving his arm in the thick dustlight and stirring it up and coughing. Saying grab anything you can't live without and let's go.

He took the linens from a bed by the ramp and went back up to the door and out into the sun. Drew a sheet over the schoolteacher. Told him he was sorry he hadn't gotten here sooner.

*

Regardless of what her mother said, Penny burst from the car the instant she caught sight of the children. Leaving the door open behind her and flying across the tobacco field to meet three of them who'd come up the ramp from the bombed house and then flying to meet two more just emerging from the next house over. A brother and sister coming up into the sun and blinking, as astonished to see her as they were astonished to be alive at all. Figures from a dream spying a figure from a dream. Not one of them looked at the sheet or what was under it. Her father was at some remove, sending other men off to other doorways and ducking down himself into the last one. Getting halfway down and then coming up again and signaling to Liz and Janey in the car. Come.

Patel looked up from her desk as if she had last seen him just a moment ago. As if she'd known he would appear at the very moment of their greatest extremity, and as if she didn't entirely need him to find a way through it. "I can't say how they found us," she said, "but we can hold out. We have to hold out." Not even looking at the stores and samples and equipment spread beneath the light of a gas lamp that someone had piped from the main in Weller's absence. Inspired by what he'd done and extending it. The way people will, given a chance.

"It's worse than you think," he said. He had a pillowcase and a folded-over patchwork quilt from the bed in the other house and he started filling them. Samples in glassine envelopes. Damp bagged vegetable matter that smelled like death and life at the same time. Telling her as he worked the same thing he'd told the others, how the helicopters would come back and they'd bring an army with them and they'd destroy everything. Janey and Liz bursting down the stairs and Weller saying this is Dr. Patel. Strip the beds. Pack up what she tells you and don't take no for an answer.

Patel stood up. "Where would you have us go?"

"Anywhere. North." Opening the freezer and glad to see that it was still working even though it wouldn't stay working for long. "Someplace other than here." Thinking if you could do this once you could do it again. Start over. Build everything up from nothing.

"Not north," Patel said, going to Liz and beginning the process of take this, don't take that, take this. "The climate is better to the south, if anything."

"South, then. Fine. South it is."

"Where?"

"You said there were others. Other people doing this."

"I don't know where they are."

"The runners will still be out there. They'll know."

"And if you're wrong?"

"I'm not wrong. There's a whole army coming and we want to get out of their way."

"But if you're wrong?"

"If I'm wrong we'll come back. No harm done."

"We." A statement and a question. Patel was the one who said it, but she was speaking for everyone.

Weller was leaning over into the freezer, chipping away at ice. "I thought the chances of saving this stuff would be better if all of us pitched in. We'll all go south if we're going south and we'll all see a little bit of the world we haven't seen. Janey knows some people down there, don't you, Janey? In Spartanburg. They've got tomatoes down there like you wouldn't believe."

But Janey didn't hear. Janey was gone.

*

She'd heard the sound of rotors, and she'd be damned if that helicopter would get away from her again. Coming up the ramp into the sun with the air smelling of smoke and a high hammering everywhere. The unnerving and unplaceable sound of a helicopter you can't see yet. She ran to the car. If she couldn't see the helicopter she probably couldn't raise it on the scanner but you never knew.

There were people out. Adults and children both, with sacks and backpacks and bed linens tied up into bundles. Some of them sitting patiently on their belongings and some of them pacing along the tobacco rows or ducking down into their underground houses for something they'd missed and some of them just standing still, watching the sky. Watching Janey watch the sky. She hollered at them to go down. Go down below where it was safe. She'd stay with the car. She had something she had to do. She watched them go and she thought how they'd never get away from here if those helicopters were still circling. Thinking they could gather up what they needed while she rode shotgun. She started the engine and the scanner fired up and she opened the sunroof again to look at the sky. It wasn't enough. She couldn't see enough. She unspooled the cables from the scanner and got out of the car and stood alongside it. Seeing everything now. Seeing that she was all alone up here, and glad of it.

The hammering kept up and it didn't seem to be coming from anywhere in particular because it was coming from everywhere. Janey looking from the scanner to the sky and back again. The hammering growing louder and more oppressive and one or two faces appearing in doorways as people came to look. Other doorways closing up. People withdrawing and lowering the doors after them. Weller sticking his head out, though, and Penny squeezing up in front of him.

Janey looked over toward them and he said, "You be careful."

She said, "I will."

Penny piped up. "You be careful." Like father like daughter.

Janey said, "Don't worry." But the words didn't make it back to Penny because they were drowned out. Drowned out not by one of those little bumblebee helicopters she'd been expecting, but by the real thing. That one last Black Rose Chinook. It came in low over the trees and the fences, as slow and stately in its forward movement as a battleship or an undersized planet or death itself. Ungainly and unappeasable.

Weller saw the flamethrowers on the belly of it and he knew. An array of black tubes spitting fire. Warmed up in hell and staying hot now for the real event to come.

Napalm.

He hollered at Janey to get clear, but she didn't hear him. She was working the scanner and dust was flying everywhere and clods of dirt and metal and loose fencing mingled with it because the pressure of the Chinook's passage was enough to uproot a swath of tobacco twenty yards wide. Just tearing a slice in the earth without even touching it. She had been able to see the pilot in the other helicopter, the little helicopter that was nothing compared to this, but she couldn't see whoever was controlling this one. He was faceless, a machine inside a machine. She shielded her eyes against the dust and looked into the car to see the lights on the satellite phone blinking in time with the display on the scanner. Meaning she was in. The Chinook almost overhead but at least she had enough signal. It was close enough and she wasn't going to lose it this time. Not this one and not this time. She didn't hear Weller shouting at her. Shouting at her to get clear, not to risk it. Not to risk bringing that thing down right here with the load it was carrying.

He knew he couldn't reach her. He knew because he couldn't hear his own voice. He couldn't hear anything as he watched her work the keys on the scanner and as he doubled himself over Penny's small body in the hole and said close your eyes, honey. Wrapping himself around her entirely. Offering himself up to withstand the worst that the world might have in store for this his only child.

The helicopter went down in slow motion, the same way it had come. A ponderous black blot moving through the air and battering it. The sound of it growing unsteady and beginning to wobble and smoke coming from someplace it shouldn't have been coming from. The two great rotors going out of synch and the whole machine staggering as if it had struck some invisible obstacle. The ground itself seeming almost to draw up to it. As if the big black Chinook and the earth itself possessed equal gravity, but only one of them could endure.

Only Janey saw it go. The arc of its passing overshot her by a hundred yards or more, and when the helicopter finally struck ground the drums of jellied gasoline in its belly burst and caught fire. The scorched earth that Black Rose had had in mind from the beginning but not quite. Janey dropping the scanner and covering her face with her arms and then falling to her knees. Doubling over and feeling the heat of the burning Chinook on the back of her neck. Breathing slow and deep to collect herself and then deciding she was ready to go on. Standing up.

Down in the hole, Weller began to unfold himself as well. The ruin of the helicopter a good distance off to the north. The world silent, and the way ahead clear.

He loosened his hold on Penny. "Open your eyes," he said.

About the Author

Sam Winston is the pen name of Jon Clinch, prizewinning author of *Finn,*
Kings of the Earth, and *The Thief of Auschwitz.*

Web site: jonclinch.com
Twitter: @jonclinch
Facebook: facebook.com/JonClinchBooks

Made in the USA
Monee, IL
28 December 2019